NO GOOD TIME

NO GOOD TIME

A Nick Donahue Adventure

CATHI STOLER

First published by Level Best Books 2025

Copyright © 2025 by Cathi Stoler

All rights reserved. No part of this publication may be reproduced, stored or transmitted in any form or by any means, electronic, mechanical, photocopying, recording, scanning, or otherwise without written permission from the publisher. It is illegal to copy this book, post it to a website, or distribute it by any other means without permission.

This novel is entirely a work of fiction. The names, characters and incidents portrayed in it are the work of the author's imagination. Any resemblance to actual persons, living or dead, events or localities is entirely coincidental.

Cathi Stoler asserts the moral right to be identified as the author of this work.

Author Photo Credit: Oskar Martinez

First edition

ISBN: 978-1-68512-997-2

Cover art by Level Best Designs

This book was professionally typeset on Reedsy.
Find out more at reedsy.com

To Paul
My best friend always

Praise for No Good Time

"Cathi Stoler's latest Nick Donahue adventure, *No Good Time*, threads together high finance and high art in a thriller as stylish and suave as its hero. A professional gambler, Nick can spot a bluff from the most experienced blackjack player, but even he is stumped by an elaborate art heist that threatens to hit painfully close to home. With precise and vivid details, Stoler brings to life a story of greed, deception, and murder that takes place in a rarified world where winner-takes-all is a matter of life and death. Readers in search of a suspenseful page-turner should go all in on *No Good Time*. It's a sure bet."—Lori Robbins, award-winning author of The En Pointe Mysteries and the Master Class Mysteries

"*No Good Time* is a gripping mystery that again pulls readers into the high-end world of professional gambler Nick Donahue, and his partner, private investigator, Martina DiPietro. As Nick unravels a web of art forgery and hunts for the ruthless ring of thieves behind the theft of a priceless painting, the stakes escalate to murder—and he narrowly escapes becoming the next victim. With its fast-paced twists and vivid settings, the story immerses readers in London's most exclusive haunts and the hidden corners of its prestigious museums. Sharp, suspenseful, and full of surprises, *No Good Time* will keep you guessing who can be trusted until the very last page."—Mally Becker, three-time Agatha Award-nominated author of the Revolutionary War mysteries

"What a tangled web Cathi Stoler weaves in her latest Nick Donahue thriller about deception, misdirection, and stolen art. This fast-paced, twisty, well-researched adventure kept me guessing and left me wanting more when it was over."—Gerri Lewis, author of *The Last Word*, a Deadly Deadlines Mystery

"No Good Time is unputdownable! Professional Blackjack player, Nick Donahue, is a wisecracking, tuxedo-wearing, standup guy. Stoler writes him in a manner that makes him fresh and familiar at the same time. Brava! This American in London must save the day (the professional reputation) of friend and tenant Gabi, in the third installment of this stylish and smart series."—Lane Stone, author of the Big Picture art thriller trilogy

"An unearthed painting worth millions may just be a forgery. And there's that murder. Once again, professional blackjack player and sleuth Nick Donahue is up to his neck. But, just now, there isn't much he can do. Nick's tied up, bloodied, in a warehouse, surrounded by hungry rats. So begins Cathi Stoler's newest, *No Good Time.* It's set in London, full of rain and fog and mystery. And quite the page-turner. Clever plot, clever dialogue, great story-telling…characters we care about. And a blistering pace. Donahue is an expert at reading the smallest signs around a blackjack table, which helps when so many have a motive to go after those millions. He and partner Marina DiPietro, a beautiful red-headed private investigator, have a dual mission. Solve the crime…and stay alive."—Mike Ludden, author of the Tate Drawdry Mysteries

"Art forgery, a long con, a London museum, a professional blackjack player with a gift for wiseass imagery and his PI partner with a network of contacts from her MI6 days—anyone who doesn't get a charge out of this book might want to check their pulse. Me, I ate it up."—SJ Rozan, bestselling author of *The Railway Conspiracy*

"Mystery fans and art lovers alike will love Cathi Stoler's *No Good Time,* a delightful and dangerous tour of the posh but perilous world of art crime."—Tim Maleeny, bestselling author of the award-winning Cape Weathers Mysteries

Chapter One

The rats, sniffing at my bloody face, brought me around. Their squeals of pleasure inviting the group to join them for their next meal—me—gave me shivers that ran up my spine. I growled low in my throat, and they dispersed. For now. Their red eyes the only light in the blackness that surrounded me. I tried to lift my hand to scare them further away, but it wouldn't move. It and the other one were tied behind me, as were my legs with rope wrapped around my body like a package ready for delivery. The bindings so unyielding, I could hardly feel my limbs. I struggled against them, only succeeding in making them tighter.

My head wasn't doing great, either. Bloodied from being tossed around and pounding from whatever drug they'd given me, like a heavy metal drummer going all out on a ten-minute solo.

I was woozy and semi-conscious enough to know I was alive. Well, at least not dead. *Concentrate*, I told myself. *Remember it all, like the cards at a Blackjack table.*

Slowly, the evening began to meander back through my drugged and damaged brain, and with it, the pain that racked my body.

Dad and I had been at the Hamilton Capital Gala at his London office. We were the last to leave. We'd shrugged into our coats and were waiting for the Uber we'd called when two people stepped out of the shadows and came flying at us.

Before I could react or protest, I was in the back of a waiting black SUV. "What's…who are…?"

"Just get in. Now." The anxiety and stress-filled voice punctuated the words with a powerful shove. I attempted to twist away and find Dad. Too late. I felt a prick on my neck. I tried to speak, stumbling over my words, slurring them. Then I started to slip away.

Dad, I thought, *where...are...?* That's as far as I got before I was out.

* * *

I hurt like hell, felt bruised all over, and every joint was screaming in agony. It was cold and damp wherever we were, the rough, rotting wood floor giving off the rank, mildewed smell of a long-unused space near the water. It wormed its way into my nose and made my stomach turn over.

Shake it off, I told myself. It didn't take much to see this was a losing hand, figuratively if not literally. No more Blackjack for me. Instead, I'd be tossed into the river as fish food.

I shuddered and then thought I heard a noise. There were voices nearby, arguing loudly. My head was pounding so hard, it was difficult for me to make out all the words.

"You said... be here..."

"Where...it?

"Moved...

"Where?"

"Not now...Later. After...get rid...Kill them..."

I focused on the words that did penetrate my brain: "kill them."

Kill? Dad. Me.

I moved my eyes to the right and left and still saw...nothing but those beady red eyes staring at me. Were they inching closer? Was this karmic payback for unleashing those rats in New York?

I lay like that for a while and realized this might be it. I'd be as dead as the floor of a low-end casino at four a.m. I felt myself slipping in and out of consciousness. The drug was still flowing through my body.

The next time I came around, Marina was there, a shimmering vision in front of me, laughingly pouring out stacks of black hundred-dollar chips that floated in the air surrounding me. *"All for you, Nick, my love."* Underneath the laughter and the chips was a whispery noise that sounded like a moan. Was that a casino bigwig angry at losing all his money? I forced my brain to focus and doubled down on my efforts to shake off my bonds. All I did was pull them even tighter and cause myself more agony.

The angry voices had gone silent. Were they still here? Waiting for…what?

Another groan reached my ears, softer and plaintive. "Dad? Is that you?" My voice was a hoarse whisper, I hoped he could hear.

"I'm here, Dad," I finally croaked out through the fear coiling up from deep inside. When there was no response, I knew he could neither see nor hear me. I tried to put it all together: that person showing up, this place, the voices. Some of it was still just out of reach. A few bits came back slowly. They'd drugged us. Then dragged us into an enormous warehouse. Through my dazed state, I saw broken crates, boxes, and mismatched pieces of furniture, which appeared to be floating and swirling around me. The detritus of abandonment. Then everything went dark until the rats.

"Don't worry, Dad. I'll get you out of here. I'll fix this." I don't know if I said this aloud or if it was just in my head.

A familiar voice answered me. *"You'd better, Nick,"* it whispered into my ear. *"You know this is all your fault,"* it continued.

Could it be possible? Was my mother lurking in a dark corner somewhere, blaming me as usual? I must be hallucinating from the drugs flowing through my system like a poisonous stream.

"Go away," I muttered.

"Not until you do something to save your father." Mother was nothing if not relentless.

Had she conveniently forgotten that she'd asked me to investigate the problem at Dad's firm, Hamilton Capital? *"This was all your idea,"* I replied.

Silence greeted me. My mother had spoken, and, like Elvis, she had left the building.

* * *

I thought I knew who'd done this to us and why. They couldn't get away with it. I'd make sure of that. We'd get out of here. Then I'd get even.

Mom and Marina, my partner in life and business, were at the theater and dinner. Dad and I made an appearance at the firm's London office gala to unveil the latest art acquisition for the Hamilton Capital collection. Then we were kidnapped.

No one would miss us until the wee hours of the morning; by then, it could be too late.

The voices were back, now accompanied by footsteps getting closer. I heard the unmistakable sound of someone pulling back the slide of a gun.

This was no good time to be out of luck. One man was already dead. I could be next. And so could my dad.

Chapter Two

Marina and I were practically dead on our feet. We had been globetrotting from New York to Dubai to Kentucky and were finally back in our home in London. Kensington seemed a little tame after the excitement of the Kentucky Derby and galloping like a racehorse chasing a deranged former ISIS member with a bomb. Not that I'd ever want to go through all that again, but I was missing the adrenaline rush of the chase, not to mention the glory of the win.

However, being at home gave me time to return to my favorite pastime: Blackjack. It wasn't just a hobby. It was how I earned my living, and being away from the tables for too long was a lousy idea professionally. I couldn't afford to have the casino's brass treat me with less than the respect I deserved as I gleefully gave them a wave and a wink and pocketed their money.

After we returned to London, I'd taken a few days to settle in. Marina and I had made a pilgrimage to Harrods' Food Halls on Brompton Road to restock our cupboards. Of course, I wanted everything I saw.

"Let's find you a new tuxedo instead," Marina said, guiding me away from the chocolate and toward the men's department. "You'll need it for your dad's event at the bank next week."

A generous payday from our last client meant I could go all in on the Tom Ford number that fit perfectly and seemed to have my name on it.

"And for this evening, as well," I added. I'd be ready to face the green baize and stacks of chips at The St. James, my favorite casino in the city, where I'd planned to go right after dinner.

Carrying my new purchase in the famous Harrods green garment bag, I smiled all the way home, hoping the passersby would notice and ignoring the exasperated looks Marina was shooting my way.

* * *

After we devoured our foodie favorites, I dressed to kill...at the tables, that is.

"How do I look?" I asked Marina as I exited the bedroom and adjusted my red bowtie.

"Gorgeous," she replied. "Shouldn't you get going?" she added, looking at her watch and opening our front door.

Standing outside it were our upstairs neighbors, Lady Gabriella Peake Jones and The Honorable Sydney Parker Glynne, aka Syd, just about knock. The young women looked upset, and I lifted an eyebrow toward Marina.

She tilted her head toward the door. I got it—she wanted me out of the flat. There was something going on with our usually affable neighbors, and I wasn't included.

Marina stood at the door and waited while I walked through. It felt like I was getting the boot from the casino's security staff at closing time, with a pat on the shoulder and an "Off you go now, sir." And it smarted.

Syd gave me a shaky smile. "Nicky, luv, don't you look dashing. Off to do some damage in the casino?" she asked.

Ignoring Nicky, which I hated, and trying not to preen at her compliment, I said, "Why, thank you, Syd." Happy that at least someone appreciated my sartorial splendor.

She added a half-hearted swat on my arm. "Break a leg," she said, while Gabi remained unusually quiet.

I gulped. Gamblers didn't like to hear about any body parts being assaulted. Except when it came to breaking the bank. "Thanks, I said to Syd.

Marina walked me out our front door and whispered. "Syd and Gabi need my help, Nick. Our help. There's a problem at The New London Arts Museum—a big problem—and Gabi doesn't know how to handle it."

"What kind of problem?" I asked in a low voice.

Marina's face grew serious as it always did when she discussed business, her mouth tightening into a straight line and her forehead furrowed. "Gabi believes the latest painting she's borrowing for the special European Masters Event at the New London Arts Museum is a forgery."

The New London was the city's hottest new museum. How could it be a forgery, I wondered as I made my way to the casino. At Gabi's museum? Marina would find out more, and we'd discuss it when I arrived back home.

"And, why would Gabi think that? Wouldn't the museum have twigged to this before now?" My questions were tumbling around my head like a pair of dice rolling down the craps table. New London had been touted as one of the most prestigious new museums in the country, and I thought they must have other curators and evaluators who vet the canvases. Why put this all on Gabi?

* * *

Soon, the sound of people having a good time in the casino distracted me from my musings. The slot machine bells were going off, cheering, and some sighs were coming from the craps, roulette, and poker tables.

It was good to be back at the Blackjack table, which was more subdued. The dealer, a man I'd known for a while, greeted me effusively. "Mr. Donahue, welcome back! We've missed you. Good luck," he added as he began to deal the cards.

"Thank you, Peter," I said, sliding my new tux-clad bottom onto the corner seat to his right. It was the anchorman position, my seat of choice. It allowed me to go last, as well as to assess the other players' hands and, most importantly, to help me decide my move before the dealer had to reveal his cards.

The player to my right, who'd listened to our brief conversation, turned to me and smiled. "Nick Donahue...from New York?" he asked in an 'it must be you' tone as he held out his hand.

After what happened in Dubai and at the Kentucky Derby, fending off ISIS and their threats, I was a little leery of strangers. Instead of taking his hand, I lifted mine toward him and asked, "And you are?"

"Clive Hastings Cargill," he replied, sitting up straighter. *Conjuring King Charles 111?* "I'm an associate of your father," he added. "He mentioned you were back living in London."

I played my hand while I thought about Clive Hastings Cargill. Back living here wouldn't be how I, or Dad, described my residency in London. I'd lived here for many years.

Who was this guy, and what had Dad told him? *Not much,* I thought. He didn't like to spill the family beans to almost strangers.

I'd spoken to Dad when Marina and I arrived home, and he hadn't mentioned a new associate, or anyone named Cargill. He said that the trip he and Mom were planning to London next week was still ongoing. They'd be here for an event at the Hamilton Capital branch office on Lombard Street within what Londoners called "The City." Dad was no slouch in the financial arena and, as CEO of the main office, knew how to play well with others, even those like Clive Hastings Cargill.

After I raked in the chips I'd just won and placed my next bet, I turned to my neighbor while the dealer used the automatic shuffler to mix the cards and confuse any would-be card counters. "How is it you know my father?" I asked, taking him in and looking for his tell. Nothing jumped out at me. I'd have to watch him play and see what I could find out.

He smiled, showing a lot of white teeth. Not as large as Devil Wind's, the horse Marina and I had recently protected for his wealthy Arab owner, but just as off-putting.

He looked around nervously, as though a thief might jump up and steal his chips. "Ahh," he stammered and gulped. "My firm, Oxford Alliance Ltd, is working on a deal with the Hamilton Capital branch here."

He cleared his throat and somehow found his rhythm.

"I'm looking forward to meeting your parents next week. I want to show them our offices and the firm's art collection. I believe they have quite the collection in their New York space." He paused, giving me a quizzical look. "You did know they were coming, didn't you?"

What a twit, I thought. "Of course," I said, dismissing allegations of filial non-interest. "We didn't discuss your project," I added with some snark and a shrug." I paused. "You know how my father is." *Did he?* "Likes to keep the details close until he finalizes a deal." I hoped that would give him something to chew on.

And what was all this about an art collection? The firm had a sizeable investment in primo masterpieces as part of its portfolio, but Dad was not that involved in the acquisitions. Hamilton Capital had a well-known art dealer on retainer who found appropriate works for the firm. Dad and the board just signed the checks. Was Cargill hatching a plan to sell Hamilton Capital a piece of art and make a quick buck? Coming on top of learning about the forgery at the New London, it made me leery of Cargill.

He continued as if something of great importance had occurred to him. "You and Ms. DiPietro must join us one evening when your family is here," he said. So, he knew about Marina, as well. "Perhaps we can all have an evening at the casino."

Mom would love that, I thought. She didn't understand that Blackjack was a profession. Ten years ago, I realized it was what I wanted to do. It was exciting and adventurous, sometimes too much so. But it was my chosen career, and I earned a living from it. If not, I'd have to find another line of work. Helping Marina with her cases didn't count. She basically let me hang out and do some of the heavy lifting when she needed assistance.

As Peter dealt the next few hands, I secretly watched Clive Cargill as he handled his chips and his cards. I figured out his tell right away. When he thought he had the dealer beat, the right side of his mouth ticked up just a little. After he lost most of his stake, he rose to leave the table.

"A pleasure to meet you, Nick," he said. "I do hope to see you again with your parents."

Not if I could help it, I thought. Something was off about the guy. Way off. Alternating between extreme nervousness and too much English upper crust? Maybe I was wrong, but I'd have to speak with Dad and learn more about this supposed deal with an English firm during his upcoming visit to London.

When I was ready to cash in, I asked Peter if Clive Hastings Cargill was a regular.

"Never seen him before," answered the dark-haired older dealer with a shake of his head as he accepted my large tip.

* * *

I'd had a good run at the casino, joking with the other players and glaring at the managers who patrolled the area like soldiers on a search-and-destroy mission.

My evening had been very successful. My spirits were high, and careful betting and good luck bolstered my bank account.

I'd beat the odds. Again. I wasn't so sure that would be the outcome at the Kentucky Derby. I'd been lucky, or as my mom would say, *"God watches over babies and fools."* I know which one she thought I was. My only saving grace, to keep the religious metaphor going, was that I was with Marina, who my family thought was a saint and way too good for me.

I headed home to the woman I loved, wondering how her meeting with Gabi and Syd had gone.

Unfortunately, not very well.

Chapter Three

I returned to our flat and I heard voices muted in what sounded like a serious discussion.

The voices grew silent as I entered the room. "Nick," Marina said, "Gabi and Syd—"

Syd interrupted. "—We were just leaving, Nick." She jumped up too quickly from her chair in front of the fireplace, looking at her watch. "Early meeting with my editor tomorrow.

"And I need to be at the museum at the crack." Gabi looked down at her clenched hands and scooted for the door.

When I heard the women trooping up the stairs, I turned toward Marina. "What was that about a forgery?" I asked in bewilderment. Both women looked distressed. And Gabi's tear-stained face was a mask of misery.

Marina was seated on our velvet couch that faced the low-burning fire that cast soft, glowing shadows in the room. She patted the spot next to her, inviting me to join her. I poured a tumbler of Scotch and sat.

"Did you have fun at the casino?" she asked, stalling.

What was going on here? "It was fine. I won. I met a jerk from The City, Clive Hastings Cargill, whose firm is doing a deal with Dad's. Or so he said." Then I shut up, tilted my head toward her, and waited.

It didn't take long. "The forgery at the museum I mentioned earlier?" Marina paused. "Gabi's afraid her boss will put the blame squarely on her, and the museum will dismiss her."

The European Masters Event was part of a year-long National Exhibition at various arts centers across Britain. The New London Arts Museum was honored to be chosen to participate.

"That can't be possible." Gabi was the Assistant Director and Chief Curator of later Italian, Spanish, and French paintings for the exhibit. She was incredibly knowledgeable about art, extremely intelligent, and took her job seriously.

Since we'd met Gabi, Marina and I visited 'her' museum several times. She'd explained the process of creating an exhibit and selecting the art included, as well as the criteria for authenticating a selected piece. It was more demanding than ever because of all the looted artifacts that art institutions around the world were returning, not to mention the forgeries floating around. Although, it wasn't foolproof.

I recalled what we'd spoken about. "What about the provenance?" The ultimate proof that a painting was vetted by professionals. "Don't their experts examine everything, from the brushwork and pigments to the composition and signature, to the age of the canvas and frame of a work? Did they X-ray it to confirm the canvas was the right age and check for damage?"

Marina smiled at me for remembering what Gabi had told us. "I believe they did all those things, Nick, including receiving an AI report on the work certifying it as an original.

"Only, it wasn't a purchased acquisition. Gabi worked out a loan arrangement with a gallery in New York to have it included in the blockbuster European Masters Event." She paused, and her eyes met mine. "There's a lot riding on this—Gabi's reputation, for one, not to mention the museum's.

"What painting did Gabi borrow?" I asked. Even I knew that institutions like New London borrowed and loaned paintings to each other for special exhibits.

"It's a recently rediscovered painting by Artemisia Gentileschi, a self-portrait of her as a 'Weeping Mary Magdalene.'

"What does recently rediscovered mean? Was it hidden away in a wall like all those looted Nazi paintings they found in the apartment of that hermit in Munich?"

Marina nodded. "Umm. I remember that case," she said. "I think there were over a thousand artworks worth over a billion dollars."

Marina consulted her laptop, which contained the notes she'd taken when she'd talked with Gabi.

"I have no idea if the Gentileschi has a similar story or how it was rediscovered." She sat forward in the chair. "It came to Gabi's attention about a year ago through a recommendation of a friend of a friend from New York at the Meade and Medina Gallery." Marina waited for a beat. "Gabi's friend, George Colabello, knew all about the exhibit New London was planning. She'd discussed the exhibition with him the last time he was in London. When the Gentileschi came onto the scene, he mentioned it to her. Gentileschi painted several other versions of Mary Magdalene, one of them the 'Penitent Mary Magdalene,' also recently rediscovered and authenticated as an original. Of course, Gabi was thrilled at the prospect of including her find in the show."

Marina was aware I didn't know very much about art, and continued. "A new Artemisia Gentileschi is a huge find, and, of course, if it's authentic, it's worth millions, which I'm sure the buyer paid.

"That AI report I mentioned? It's one of the new programs that can certify a work of art as genuine. The company uploads hundreds of images of the artist's work. In this case, Artemisia Gentileschi and matches them to the new work, everything from the brushstrokes to the palette, to the signature. The same things the experts evaluate only in more precise detail. The 'Weeping Mary Magdalene' passed.

"The New London Arts Museum knew it would be a coup to display the painting as part of the exhibit."

"How well does Gabi know this George Colabello?" I asked.

"She met him when she took her Master's in Arts program at Ca' Foscari University in Venice. They've been friends ever since and kept in touch."

"So, he lives in New York City now?"

Marina nodded. "Gabi visited him last year and was anxious to see the painting. It was all very hush-hush, and they Ubered to the Free Port at the JFK Airport to view it, where the owner was storing it."

She noticed my puzzled expression and said, "I'll explain about Free Ports later. Gabi was overwhelmed by the painting. She was sure it was an original. A magnificent piece by an extraordinary artist. When she returned to London, she discussed it with her superiors, and the plan was for her to go back to New York with one of the Trustees." She paused and ran her fingers through her red hair as her sparkling green eyes focused inward, another sign that her brain was firing on several levels at once. "By now, the painting had been shipped to Meade and Medina and placed in the gallery's vault, where they viewed it again. They both believed it was a genuine Artemisia."

"So, who's George Colabello's friend at the Meade and Medina Gallery representing the painting for the collector?"

"His name is Maxime Meade, the son of the gallery owner. Gabi met with him and George when she returned to view the painting in New York for the second time."

"What about the collector? Who is he?"

"He prefers to remain anonymous, according to George."

I didn't like the sound of that. "Is that usual?

"It may be. I know there've been anonymous buyers at some big auctions, so it might be more usual than I think." She lifted her hand skyward. "Gabi didn't mention that the anonymous collector was a problem. She said everything was in order, and all the paperwork was complete."

"Did she do this all on her own? Her superiors must have trusted her."

"They did trust her, but she wasn't alone." Marina shook her head. "There was a third visit to New York. Since it was from such a famous artist, it would be such a magnificent addition to the show. This time, Gabi was accompanied by the same trustee and two members of her staff. They brought in their own well-known New York art forensics expert, Jerome Benedict, to examine the painting, and he concurred that it was an original."

I'd have to ask Dad who the expert was that Hamilton Capital used for their collection. It was private and extensive, an asset the bank could bank on.

Probably only a few big-name experts assessed artwork of this caliber. Dad might have worked with Jerome Benedict on the bank's behalf.

Marina took a sip of the scotch she'd been drinking. "You can imagine how excited Gabi was. This was a triumph for her and for The New London Arts Museum. A perfect addition to the line-up of the old masters."

"So, all of this," I searched for the right word, "authenticating, took about a year?" That seemed like plenty of time for something to go wrong. One other thing I'd have to ask Dad. "Who else is in the show?"

"Watteau, Fragonard, La Tour, Boucher, Velasquez, Caravaggio, Canaletto, and Tiepolo." Marina reeled off the names like a like an art connoisseur with lots of empty wall space. "The addition of a newly rediscovered Artemisia Gentileschi would be incredible."

There it was again, that 'rediscovered.' I needed to find out more about what that meant.

Marina plunked down her drink, concern playing over her face. "You can see the problem, though, can't you?" she asked.

I could. If the painting was a forgery, the original buyer who preferred to 'remain anonymous' would blame it on The New London Arts Museum, insisting that they'd sent them the original work, authenticated not only by the most well-regarded outside expert in New York, but also by the institution's professionals who had traveled there several times. And, then authenticated again by the top-rated London expert, Tamara Capitani, once it arrived at the gallery. A triple-threat New London would have trouble denying. They would, in turn, place the blame on them for not assuring its provenance. This was not good. Not good at all.

Chapter Four

The next day, I found Marina sitting on our deck sipping a Cappuccino, the sun streaming down over the treetops, turning the top of her hair a fiery golden red as she stared at her laptop.

"Good morning," I said, bent down, and kissed her. I noticed an article about Artemisia Gentileschi open on her screen.

"Find out anything else about her painting?" I nodded my head toward the laptop.

"Not much. I searched, and it's not the only rediscovered painting by her. Besides the 'Penitent Magdalene,' which was rediscovered not long ago, there's also "Susanna and the Elders," which had been at Hampton Court in England for over a hundred years hidden away before they unearthed it." She clicked over to an image of another painting titled 'Lucretia.' "It sold for major money at auction a few years ago, making finding a new, authentic Artemisia Gentileschi even more valuable."

If it's genuine, I thought.

Then she switched to an image of Gabi's 'Weeping Magdalene.' It was dark and stained in several places, with some nicks on the frame. It, too, looked as though it had been hidden away and now needed quite a bit of repair work, which raised even more doubts in my mind. *Where had this painting been all this time?*

Marina continued. "The composition has some similarities with 'Lucretia,' who has become known as an old master poster girl of the #MeToo movement. The subject committed suicide after being raped.

"Artemisia is the most celebrated female painter of the Seventeenth

Century. It's no wonder she painted this 'Weeping Magdalene.' A strong woman like herself, shedding tears for justice." She paused.

"When she was young, a painter in her father's studio, Agostino Tassi raped her. The trial made her famous, even though Tassi went free. Afterwards, she began to paint brave and heroic women, which were well-received by everyone.

"Like the 'Lucretia,' the 'Weeping Magdalene' is 39" x 30" and done in the same rich, saturated colors."

"I'll take your word for it," I replied, looking at the image on Marina's screen.

"When did the New London begin to think it was a forgery?" I asked.

"Just a few days ago, when one of the restorers was preparing it for the exhibit. The restorer had already cleaned it."

"And he noticed something that could mark it as a fake?" I asked.

Marina nodded. "It appears so." She checked her notes again. "His name is Jonathan Hudson. As I understand it, a restorer's job is to make sure the work is either in its original condition or takes measures to repair it. He wasn't finished yet and was examining the painting inch by inch. It's something they do right before they install the work."

"Jonathan was reexamining the signature, comparing it to other Gentileschi signatures on the works the museum owns. It was in the right place on the canvas, at the right angle, but something about it had bothered him right from when he began the inspection."

"Was he one of the people who accompanied Gabi to New York?" I asked.

"No. His job was to examine the painting in situ before he would install it."

She picked up the pages of notes she'd been jotting down in her scrawling handwriting and continued. "Gabi said Jonathan laid down a small flashlight he was using next to the painting, and while he was picking up a magnifying glass, the flashlight rolled sideways and revealed a slight glow over the signature, which he hadn't noticed before. He thought it was odd. and decided to get a closer look.

"She told me one technique to check a signature is to turn the work upside down to look for differences. When Jonathan did this, he noticed the signature had perfectly filled in smooth lines, a sign that it might have been created with an Autopen and not by Gentileschi's brush. It was enough to question the authenticity of the work.

"After he reported it, they decided they would have to perform additional tests on the pigments and the canvas to see if they were original to the period. When they notified the anonymous owner and the New York gallery, they started complaining."

"Who else was with Gabi in New York on her last trip?

"The Assistant Curator, Mia Fondsworth, Jose Bidenstock, who is an art handler, and one of the Cultural Trustees, Dame Rosemary Harris, who had accompanied Gabi previously."

It seemed like New London had as many layers of staff as the government. Easier to pass the buck and assign blame.

"And none of them suspected something was wrong? Or noticed the odd signature?"

"Evidently not."

"Do you think Meade and Medina will say the museum switched the painting?

Marina showed me her 'What do you think?' face. "I'm positive they will. Their client, the anonymous original owner, will certainly blame them, but I'm sure Meade and Medina will put the responsibility on Gabi and The New London Arts Museum. Maxime Meade has insisted that he, George Colabello, and the gallery's attorney come to London to view the painting. They're determined to know how this happened."

"They already know how it happened," I replied. Maybe it was my gambler's intuition, but I was positive they were aware it would be discovered as a fake when they shipped it to London, or at least one of them was. *Trying to cover their asses,* I thought, but kept all that to myself, an idea taking hold in my brain that I needed to think on.

"The financial consequences will likely be astronomical. It's certain Gabi will be the ultimate victim. Her reputation and career will be in tatters." Marina's beautiful face was taut with worry.

I thought about the young woman we'd come to embrace as a friend and a neighbor. This was a bad situation. "What else did Gabi tell you?" I asked.

"She said the staff who accompanied her from London, and the art expert they'd retained in New York, all signed off on its provenance as an original Gentileschi. A priceless painting and a rare find for the exhibit."

"What do you think?" I asked Marina.

"I'm sure someone switched it somewhere along the way. We need to find out where, when, and by whom, then get the real painting back to clear Gabi's name."

She finished the rest of her coffee and plunked the mug down on the patio table with the finality of a steel door clanging shut.

That's all? I thought. Another easy assignment. And people thought gambling was a hard way to make a living.

Chapter Five

We'd met Gabi and Syd when they moved in after the pandemic. Marina and I occupied two floors of our white stucco row house. The lower ground floor held two bedrooms and baths, and the upper floor contained our kitchen and lounge—a beautiful tree-lined spot located on Vicarage Gate in Kensington. The flat, which had recently been remodeled, even offered a deck outside our bedroom.

"Our Royals," as we called them, had the two floors above us and shared the main entrance.

We'd received a few of their deliveries by mistake and left them on the staircase with a note. They responded with an invitation to join them for Champagne and caviar. We accepted and hit the jackpot. The two women were great company, and Marina immediately adopted them as friends and cohorts.

Lady Gabriella, a dark-eyed beauty with black hair that tumbled around her usually smiling heart-shaped face, hadn't been embroiled in her tumultuous workplace mess when we'd met.

The Honorable Sydney, a tall, willowy blonde given to wearing vintage clothing and piles of jewelry, like a young version of Agatha Christie's Ariadne Oliver, was a mystery crime writer. Her main character was a six-foot-two, good-looking private investigator, Jake Apton, who solved high-profile crimes in London while dining and clubbing with the city's elite.

It was no wonder I liked him before I even read a word of her stories. He kind of reminded me of me. Even though Marina was the investigator, and I was just the sidekick. After all, I was tall and good-looking, at least I thought so. Something Marina would roll her eyes at if I said it out loud. I made it my business to ask about any plots Syd had that might involve a suave gambler taking on crime at a casino.

"Oh, Nick." She laughed. "You're thinking of you, aren't you? That's hilarious!"

Not really, I wanted to say.

The women had known each other since they were 'toddling around', as they put it. They'd attended boarding school together and then went on to Oxford. They'd spent as much time together as possible while Gabi studied art in Venice with Syd visiting on most weekends. They'd always been best friends, and somewhere along the way, had fallen in love and were getting married.

"We're planning a massive party in fancy dress for our big day," Gabi told us. "You two must promise to come along!"

"Absolutely, added Syd. It's going to be at the Duke's estate." She lifted her nose into the air and put on an upper-crust accent as she continued. "A huge guest list of notables," she said snidely, spreading her arms wide. "Perhaps one or two from the Royal Family might attend," she added and burst out laughing. Her family wasn't as noble as Gabi's, but they were in Burke's Peerage, the quintessential guide to the aristocracy. I'd looked them up.

Gabi shook her head in mock anger at her partner's words. "She means to say all of our weird and socially awkward friends will be there, and my parents and their friends will have a cow." She paused and looked from Marina to me. "Please say you'll attend. You will, won't you? You'll fit in perfectly."

She didn't have to ask twice. Of course, we'd go to a wedding at a manor house, or anywhere these two were getting married. But the invite seemed double-edged to me. Well, the weird part anyway.

Now, here we were trying to determine the best way to help Gabi. Besides losing her reputation and position, her father, The Umpteenth Duke of Warwick, would not take the news well.

Marina and Gabi had drifted out to the deck to continue discussing the problem at the museum.

Syd looked over her shoulder to make sure Gabi was out of earshot before she continued. "He's a bit bossy, and Gabi is a touch afraid of him." She thought over what she'd said. "Actually, he's a bully, and Gabi needs to stand up to him.

"Duke Harrington Peake Jones owns a vast vineyard, The Falcon Vintage Winery, with acres and acres of vines and a giant warehouse, which is probably filled with hundreds of unsold bottles. Somehow, he considers himself an exceptional wine producer, top of the pyramid." Syd lifted her chin into the air and gave a snarky laugh. "The output is pretty awful, and I can't imagine who's purchasing it, let alone drinking it." She paused. "I've been toying with the idea of creating a character like the Duke who Jake would kill off. Harrington would never recognize himself, but Gabi might, and I wouldn't want to hurt her."

Gabi had never mentioned the Duke's winery to either Marina or me.

Syd continued. "It's all a façade. Gabi doesn't like to speak about it, but the family is having tremendous financial trouble, which the Duke won't admit." Her face scrunched into a scowl, and thunderclouds flashed across her eyes. "That big old pile they own is taxed to the limit. He's always convincing old friends to 'invest' in his business, such as it is. I can't imagine why they would."

Political clout, most likely, or hoping for royal influence. "What about the wedding?" I asked.

"Harrington told Gabi it wouldn't be a problem, that he'd be coming into a large sum of money rather soon. But he hasn't said where he's getting the funds to pay for it." She looked down at her hands. "I find it quite troubling. We don't need all this fuss." Her eyes flew up to meet mine. "The registry office would be fine. I just don't want to disappoint Gabi."

I wondered where those funds would come from. Maybe he hadn't tapped out all his friends yet. Or maybe he had something more nefarious in mind.

Then she realized that she'd told me more than she meant to. "Nick, give me your word you won't 'rat me out' to Gabi, as you Americans would say. Please, can you do that?"

I agreed and hugged her before she left. Sometimes, bucking a parent was easier said than done. My Dad was as easygoing as they came, my mom not so much. To be fair, she didn't bully or become insistent; she just turned those ice blue eyes in your direction and reminded you of what she wanted until you gave in.

While I'd been thinking about the two women, Marina had devised a plan. "Your parents, and Alex and Simone, are arriving tomorrow morning, you know."

Why did everyone think they had to remind me that my family was coming to London?

"When they arrive, we'll ask Gabi to arrange a special tour for later in the week. We can float the idea that your Dad is very interested in art and might be considering having Hamilton Capital create an endowment for the museum.

"You don't think he'll mind a bit of pretending, do you?" she asked.

"Not if you're the one asking," I replied. Both my parents adored Marina.

She nodded. "It will be a good way to meet some of Gabi's colleagues and see what they're all about."

See if they act suspicious, I thought. I could use my spidey skills to ferret out a suspect or two. I must have smiled excitedly, because Marina said, "Don't get any ideas about investigating. You can just be charming and observe."

Put off to the side again like a used deck of cards with worn-out edges. Well, we'd see about that.

"In the meantime," she continued, "I'll ask Ana to compile information on all the people who went to New York with Gabi. We can start by looking into them."

Our prime suspects, I thought.

Marina continued. "As soon as possible, I think we should have our own unannounced visit to The New London Arts Museum and look at the paintings and galleries that Gabi oversees. Maybe we can even get a look at the Gentileschi."

That sounded like spying to me. An idea I could get on board with. When I'd met Marina, she'd been with MI6. And, as the saying goes, you can take the girl out of the agency, but not the agency out of the girl.

Chapter Six

Delta flight DL5992 from JFK was scheduled to land at Heathrow at 6:45 a.m. tomorrow. Way too early for a gambler like me, who generally stays up until one or two. I decided to forgo the casino and hit the sack early. Even so, Marina's 5:00 a.m. wake-up call left me groggy and out of sorts. The Donahues were flying premium first-class and would deplane first. Of course, we were meeting all four of them, and Dad, being Dad, had hired a large Cadillac Escalade SUV and driver to transport us all. Good thing the London Streets were wide enough.

"It should only take us forty minutes to get to the airport," I said, snuggling back into our soft, down comforter.

"Not if we hit traffic," Marina countered, snatching it off my sleepy body. "We wouldn't want to keep your parents waiting, would we?"

Well, not Dad, I thought, as she handed me a mug of coffee and headed for the shower.

* * *

We'd made ourselves comfortable in the plush leather of the three-row, 'Slade SUV, tinted windows up, air conditioning softly humming, when Marina's phone beeped with a text. She frowned as she read it.

"What's wrong?" I asked, immediately thinking of my family up in the air, my stomach doing flips, and my gambler's mind calculating the odds that something terrible might have happened on the flight.

Marina must have read my mind and shook her head. "It's from Gabi."

She handed me her cell. "Take a look."

> Marina, I know Nick's parents are arriving this morning, but I just
> got word that someone broke into the museum last night, and one
> of the restorers was severely injured. He may not live. I'm leaving
> for the hospital now. After you settle Nick's family, can you come
> to my office? I'll be back by then, and I'll need your help.

Marina's thumbs flew over the keys, tapping out a quick reply, assuring Gabi she would be there as soon as possible.

"Nick, let's get your mom and Dad to the hotel, and Simone and Alex to our place, then we'll head to Gabi. She should have more information by the time we arrive. Let's not mention this to your parents just yet. They're probably tired from flying all night, and they'll be concerned about what's happening."

Marina was right. No need to get Mom and Dad's worry meter ticking the minute they set down in London. I was sure I'd give Mom something to fuss over while they were here.

Mom and Dad were staying in the Grosvenor Suite at the Connaught. Dad was going all in for this visit, spending mucho big bucks for a forty-fifth-anniversary celebration, to which he'd tacked on a business meeting. Canny banker that he was, he'd at least be able to write off some of it.

The recently wed Alex and Simone would be our guests at the apartment. They'd both been to London before and were excited at the prospect of being back in Europe, although thankful England was an island and not remotely near Switzerland, and Herr Emminger, formerly of the SuisseDeutsche bank, from which they'd barely escaped with their lives. It was not on their agenda. Now or ever. Parliament, Big Ben, and Churchill's War Rooms would offer excitement enough.

Marina and I reached the airport with a few minutes to spare and stationed ourselves at the arrivals gate. The plane was on time, and soon after it landed, my family was among the first to exit.

As soon as I saw the piles of luggage, I was relieved that Dad had rented that huge Cadillac SUV. "I thought the visit was only going to be for a few days," I whined to Marina, wondering how we'd fit everything in the 'Slade. She kicked me in the shin in response.

"Behave, Nick," she added, as my mom would have. "Your mom and dad will be here for over a week."

After hugs and kisses all around, we moved off toward Jules, our driver, who was waiting by the car. His smile dimmed just a bit when he saw all the suitcases and backpacks he'd have to tuck into the cargo area.

I noticed Dad giving me an appraising look. He took my arm as we exited the terminal, holding me back a little. "Everything okay, Nick?" he asked, taking me in. And here I thought my poker face was firmly in place.

"All good, Dad. We'll speak a little later," I said, and he nodded, letting it go for now.

* * *

The Grosvenor Suite at the Connaught was perfect. I hadn't heard my mom oh an ah like this since I told her I was moving to London, and she could use my childhood room as a den.

Two huge rooms and a large marble bath made it feel more than roomy. It was bigger than most Manhattan apartments, with a fireplace, an antique mantelpiece, and a gilded plaster ceiling in the sitting room. The women checked out the bedroom and bath, and Dad headed straight for the vintage cocktail cabinet. Alex and I weren't far behind. He opened the door and noticed it was filled with high-end bottles of his favorite liquor.

"That's nice," I said, gesturing at the gleaming bottles lined up like the King's Guard.

"It should be for what I'm paying for this," he added.

"You did good," I whispered in his ear as I looked over at my beaming mother as he handed Alex and me a mid-morning drink and a sly wink.

We made sure they were comfortable and told them to get some rest before we picked them up for a late afternoon tea at Fortnum and Mason.

"Sounds like a good idea," Dad said while tossing me another searching look. It was interesting to me that parents never lost the ability to sense when something was going on with one of their kids. Dad was as astute as ever.

Fortunately, Simone and Alex didn't have a clue. They pointed out the sights to each other as we drove toward Vicarage Gate and were delighted to enter our home, a restored Victorian with all the bells and whistles. Simone headed straight for the bay window that looked out on a bright and cheery garden, then turned, and walked into the open plan kitchen with its gleaming appliances.

"It's so beautiful, Marina," Simone said as she took in the velvet curved couch in front of the restored, working marble fireplace, the two leather armchairs, the contemporary artwork, and the bright modern rug on the lounge floor. All Marina's updates to the classic London Victorian.

"Thank you. Let me show you to your room so you guys can unpack and settle in."

When the women were downstairs in the bedroom, I gave Alex a big brother man hug. "It is so good to see you," I smiled at him. "You look happy."

"You were right, Nick. Simone is great. Getting married was the best idea I ever had."

Had he forgotten I had to practically talk him into it the morning of the wedding?

"Listen," I replied. "Why don't you and Simone check out the neighborhood while Marina and I do an errand?" I tossed him an extra set of keys. "We'll be back in time to head out for tea."

"Everything okay, Nick?" he asked, with the same perceptiveness Dad had. Alex had seemed more mature since his marriage. Like father like son? In this case, I thought so.

"All good," I said for the second time that day. I only wished it were true.

Chapter Seven

Dad had hired the car and driver for the length of their stay. We hopped in and didn't waste any time getting to The New London Arts Museum.

We stopped at the front desk and asked how to get to Gabi's office. She'd let them know we would be coming, and a host in a well-tailored navy-blue suit arrived to guide us to her. We followed him to the private elevator at the back of the main floor, and he inserted the key needed to access the third floor, where the employee offices were located. A few minutes later, we were at her door, which was slightly ajar. "Lady Peake Jones is expecting you," he said, then left us.

Her office was a serene pale blue. A perfect color for setting off the art she'd chosen to display. Sunlight filtered in through gauzy shades on the large window, making the space appear bright and welcoming. Gabi was seated, talking quietly with a young woman when we entered. She made the introductions to Mia Fondsworth, her assistant, a petite brunette with a shaggy brown haircut and bright blue eyes that darted around like a firefly on a dark night. Was it just jitters? Or did she have something to hide?

As soon as Mia left, our friend immediately burst into tears. She'd been trying to control her emotions, but seeing Marina, she let it all out.

"Was it Jonathan who was attacked?" Marina asked, remembering the name of the restorer working on the painting. "How is he doing?" Her voice was gentle.

Gabi dabbed at her eyes, which were still spilling over with tears. "Yes," she replied, and I don't think he's going to survive." She sobbed even harder.

"Even if he does, the surgeons say he will most likely have permanent brain damage." Pulling herself together, she continued. "He was coshed on the head from behind multiple times. The police think he might have known his attacker, who, according to the crime scene techs, would have had to have been standing close to him when they bludgeoned him. He and whoever it was had moved away from the painting. The security staff found him on the floor behind one of the worktables. They almost didn't see him. If they hadn't…" her voice trailed off.

"Was the Gentileschi in the room?" Marina asked.

Gabi nodded and looked at us as her eyes started brimming again. "I don't understand why anyone would do this. We already knew the painting had…a problem…the signature Jonathan was examining…so why…?" Her words trailed off.

"Who else was working last night?" Marina asked.

"No one that I know of. My team had all gone home except for Jonathan. Since we were going to do further tests, he wanted to take one more look at the painting to be unequivocally positive about the signature being false. He must have let in someone he knew. And now…"

Marina changed tacks. "Is there any video of the restoration room where Jonathan was working?"

She shook her head. "There should be, but the cameras were off last evening."

I looked at Marina, and she sensed what I was thinking: someone had manipulated the system.

"The security staff knew Jonathan was still here and didn't go into the workroom to check." She paused. "They'd normally inspect the work areas after all the staff are gone to ensure everything was secure."

"What about the rest of the galleries?" Marina prodded.

"There have been some complaints from the directors that security had become a little lax, and the video feeds were spotty and needed to be updated." She lifted an eyebrow. "The Exhibits Director, Lloyd Bennings, knows the wiring is old and faulty. It's from when the building was constructed and wasn't updated in the renovation. They don't want to spend the money to modernize it. They've been doing patchwork fixes as needed. Some of us have appealed to Stella Manning, the Managing Director." She paused. "Stella was more positive about agreeing to the repairs, but they'd have to ask the Crown for the cash, and it's a bit political."

At a prestigious museum like this? What were they thinking, I wondered. It reminded me of The Museum of Natural History and the Isabella Stewart Gardner Museum, whose gems and art worth millions and millions were stolen because of poor security coverage. They weren't the only places who'd had robberies. Security seemed subpar at many of the world's most famous art institutions, and the thieves knew this.

Marina looked directly at Gabi before asking her next question. "I want you to think about who here might have benefited from the Gentileschi deal. Once the exhibit is over and the painting is returned to its owner or to the Meade and Medina Gallery, its price will undoubtedly increase." She paused. "Someone could stand to make a great deal of money."

The young woman looked stricken. "It's unthinkable. No one here would do such a thing." She shook her head adamantly.

"I know you trust your colleagues. But think about it. Please."

I thought she was wrong: it felt like an inside job to me, and I'd bet we could prove it. Marina took Gabi's hand in hers. "Nick and I will be looking into the situation, and I promise you, we'll get some answers."

Marina was hedging her bet to spare the young woman's feelings. Gabi didn't know her like I did. She'd do more than 'look into it.' She'd find out who did this, and I'd help.

Chapter Eight

A thought occurred to me as we were on our way home to pick up Alex and Simone. After a few minutes, I voiced it to Marina. "What if the painting that arrived was never an original?" I queried. Marina turned to me. "What do you mean?"

"What if it's all a scam, an enormous setup scrupulously planned by a gang of con artists? What if there never was a genuine 'rediscovered' Gentileschi? You know, present a perfect forgery to Gabi and company. Make certain it's certified as real, then send it on its way to London?

"And, once it's here for the exhibit, make sure someone discovers it's a fake." I sat back in the soft leather seat of the SUV and crossed my arms in front of me. "What if that was always the plan?"

Marina was shaking her head before I'd even finished. "That's impossible. Are you saying there never was an original self-portrait of Artemisia as a Weeping Mary Magdalene? All those experts from The New London Arts Museum and New York were sure it was authentic."

"I think they were wrong." I ran this around my brain for a moment, then continued. "People have been forging paintings for years and selling them as the real deal." I had some examples to relate to her, but I'd save them for later when she came around to my way of thinking. The 'Weeping Magdalene' photograph online could have been placed there by anyone after its 'rediscovery' with a big fanfare and a story that made it sound solid.

As a kid, I was always interested in tales involving these kinds of cons, and I could think of a couple that had worked. Marina had conned me when we first met, and I fell for it. But it wouldn't be wise to mention that to her now.

"Grifters have been setting up cons since the beginning of time. I'd bet a crafty caveman swindled his neighbor out of making fire and claimed it for himself. All he'd need was a pretty cavewoman as a distraction. And, poof, he was the inventor of fire."

Marina was looking at me like I'd lost my mind. "We'd need to prove this, Nick," she replied. "I don't think you're right. And, if we start an investigation into a con, it could turn the museum and the London art world upside down." She bit her lower lip, a sign that she was considering what to do next.

I hoped she was at least thinking that my theory might be a possibility.

First, I wanted to do some research into the painting, to see if it could be the real thing and not a copy. Given what I learned, I was pretty sure it wasn't. I'd noticed the dirty surface and a few smeared spots that anyone could have added to give the painting an air of age and credibility, the assurance that it had been around since 1625, when Artemisia had painted a Magdalene.

Maybe Marina's theory that somebody switched the painting was correct. But I wanted to explore my theory, and I knew just the person to help.

* * *

Gamblers acquire many skills. Among them is the ability to read people, as well as cards. The casinos where I gambled were host to every kind of person you could imagine. Some were degenerate gamblers, addicts ready to bet away the family home on a sure thing. Others were what the casinos called 'whales', super-rich dudes who expected comped rooms, meals, and more as they lost a fortune at the tables. Losers who thought the high-end treatment they received meant they were valued customers, while the casino owners laughed all the way to the basement vault.

Then there were the regular people, some like me who made their living playing Blackjack, and others who were not professionals but enjoyed playing cards for the thrill of it.

Over the course of my travels, I'd met and become friends with several of these players. Most of them were men with a few women scattered among them. One of these men and I had become gambling buddies and friends and met up three or four times a year in London, Prague, or Venice, wherever was convenient, to sit at the Blackjack table together.

Marcus Aurelius Rivera—what can I say, his mom loved Roman history—hailed from West Harlem in New York City. Marc Rivers, as he now went by, owned a chain of automotive repair shops and a great deal of the City's real estate.

We'd grown up on opposite sides of the town but had one other thing in common besides cards: we were native New Yorkers and always would be. It was a bond that would be hard to break.

Our lives had taken very different paths to where we found ourselves now. Before he left the life of a Grifter, Marc had been one of the best con artists that ever plied his trade. He gave it up fifteen years ago when a con he was running almost took the life of a young woman who worked for him.

Marc's specialty had been the long con, and I'd thought of him the moment the idea of a 'not really rediscovered Gentileschi' took hold in my brain. He kept his affluence low-key, and I'd always wondered how he obtained that first automotive repair shop but never asked. We gamblers often like to keep things close to the vest. Besides, it was none of my business.

He answered his cell on the first beep. "Nick! How are you? Where are you? Want to play some Blackjack?" He laughed, thinking cards were why I'd called.

I told him I was home in London and needed his advice and expertise from his former life. I could almost hear the wheels turning, trying to figure out what I was up to before he replied. "Okay. Whatever you need. I'll meet you at Maxim's in two days at 4:00 pm I'm closing a big deal on a new building and can't leave the city yet. That work for you?" he asked.

"Absolutely," I replied. Maxim's was a very private casino in South Kensington, London, and another one of my favorites. I was looking forward to going there despite the circumstances. Marc had a small flat nearby that he used whenever he was in town, and it would no doubt be ready for his stay.

My gambling buddy was tall with swept-back black hair and a caramel complexion with just the right amount of stubble to be attractive. But it was his light brown eyes that could mesmerize every pair he gazed into, which was an asset for a gambler and gave people the impression that he was paying attention to their every word. It was a good look. One that women, including Marina, appreciated. Not that I was jealous, exactly.

After I clicked off, I realized I'd have to tell Marina, who'd met Marc before, what I had planned for the day after tomorrow.

That was the easy part. Explaining that while Dad was in his meeting at the London office, and Simone and Alex were sightseeing, she'd have to occupy Mom for a few hours was more difficult.

I should have known better. Marina enjoyed spending time with my mom, and I knew she'd agree, especially when I told her I was meeting Marc and what I had in mind.

"I think you're wrong about this," she said again, shrugging her shoulders. "But Elizabeth and I will have fun." She pinched my cheek, which she knew I hated. "We'll just have to go shopping with your credit card until we meet for dinner.

"Now, let's gather the family and go have our tea," she added. "Everyone is probably starving."

Chapter Nine

Fortnum and Mason never disappointed. "Meet Me At Fortnum's." was a tradition among Londoners who wanted what they considered the best tea in the city with unmatched sandwiches, scones, and pastries. Given that its reputation had preceded it, my family was no exception. Everyone was looking forward to this unique London experience, me included. I hadn't eaten all day, and I was starving. And we also dressed for it in our best casual chic clothes. Marina wore a gray and white silk blouse and dark gray wide-leg pants, and I'd traded in my jeans and Henley for khakis and a long-sleeve shirt. Mom even added a Deco-inspired 'diamond and ruby' brooch to her pink suit jacket in honor of the late Queen Elizabeth.

The minute we entered the store, Mom's eyes widened, and she stopped dead, causing other shoppers to divert around her like she was a monument in the middle of Trafalgar Square.

She held up her hand for us to stop. Throwing her shoulders back, she looked straight ahead. Then she commanded the small troop of Americans behind her: "Let's go."

This was Mom at her most focused. She loved shopping and had spent time and money in upscale, fancy stores most of her life, but being in London seemed to make it more extraordinary. All those colorful blue and gold shiny boxes that decorated the shelves had a special appeal that Mom was obviously attuned to. Her blue eyes glittered, and her petite nose lifted as if on the scent of a rare treasure. I could see Dad's face turn pale, more from thinking of the packages to carry home rather than the expense.

* * *

I stepped in, took her arm, propelled her through the ground floor with its teas and housewares, and marched her to the elevator, trying to shield her eyes from the treats that threatened to stop her forward motion. I thought of General Douglas MacArthur, who supposedly said, 'I shall return,' upon leaving the Philippines. He had nothing on Mom.

Marina, who was a few steps behind, was laughing quietly, surprised that my usually self-contained mom was so determined about shopping.

"We'll have time for you to look at every floor," I added as the elevator doors closed and whisked us to the Diamond Jubilee Tea Salon at the top of Fortnum's. I didn't look at Dad while explaining everything Fortnum had to offer. He knew when he was defeated.

* * *

Fortnum's was a magnificent Neo-Georgian building in the heart of Piccadilly. A landmark of the city with a four-foot-high mechanical clock on its façade. A stone's throw from Buckingham Palace. Their high tea was famous for freshly baked cakes, mini sandwiches, mouth-watering scones, and pots and pots of tea. The choice was yours, and you could always have more of everything.

We were seated at a roomy table for six next to a sun-filled window overlooking Piccadilly Street. I made sure Mom and Dad had a view of the busy thoroughfare and the buildings across the way.

Perched on the edge of her gilt chair, Mom's head was swiveling, taking in the salon. Was she hoping one of the royals would appear? I'd bet the bank Fortnum's delivered to them daily—no need to cross the park and dine in.

I lifted an eyebrow toward Marina, who seemed to know what I was thinking. She began chatting with Mom, who finally settled back in her chair and smiled. It made her look ten years younger. She was in London. With her whole family. What else could make her happier? Nothing I could think of except finding myself a new profession.

The waitstaff had set our table with classic Fortnum linen topped by China cups and saucers, pastry plates, and sparkling silverware and glasses. We took our server's suggestion and started with a glass of Fortnum's Blanc de Blanc, Grand Cru. Then we got down to business, perusing the selection of teas and delicious treats.

"I'm starving," I said, rubbing my hands together in anticipation. I didn't dare look at Marina, who I was sure would be shooting me 'fat face' glances, which I'd ignore.

By the time we ordered, we'd covered the menu and would have enough food for our small army of Americans.

As I lifted my cup of Royal Blend to my lips, I looked around the room and almost spit it out. Staring at me from two tables away was Clive Hastings Cargill. He looked away the moment he realized I'd noticed him. What the hell was he doing here?

I tried to catch Marina's eye, but she was busy listening to a story Mom was telling her, probably about something awful I'd done when I was a kid.

Dad was a little quicker on the uptake. He'd caught my surprised expression. He put his napkin down and stood up. "Nick, why don't you show me where the men's room is?"

Once we were inside the fancy men's lounge, I told him about Cargill introducing himself at the casino and talking about an upcoming meeting with Dad and his firm, Oxford Alliance Ltd.

"Do you know this guy, or his company?"

"Not him, but the Director, John Windsor Smythe." I rolled my eyes at yet another three-part name. Did everyone in this country have one?

Dad shrugged. "Cargill's name hasn't come up in any of our discussions with his firm. Maybe he's trying to score some insider information to make points with his boss."

I know I didn't look convinced. "Don't worry. I'm sure he was just trying to gain some leverage. Our meeting is the day after tomorrow. It will be fine."

Famous last words, I thought, but I nodded at Dad as if I agreed.

* * *

By the time the last sips of tea and the last crumbs of pastries were gone, the six of us were as full as a Botero statue gracing the floral divider on New York's Park Avenue. We sat for a little while; then I fought Dad for the check. He finally acquiesced, and I paid the bill.

We'd promised Mom a tour of the store, and she held us to it. She showed some restraint but ordered enough merchandise to fill her kitchen cupboards and her friends. "That was wonderful," she said as we exited Fortnum's, and Dad rang the driver to bring the car around.

The parental units and Simone and Alex were going to see "The Mouse-trap," the classic Agatha Christie mystery play that had been running for over 60 years. It was a real who-done-it with lots of clues, set in a remote, snowed-in guesthouse.

We knew they would enjoy it and sent them to the theater, with a suggestion to stop at The Ivy, a famous restaurant right across the street, after the performance.

"See you tomorrow," I said to the gang as Marina, and I hailed a taxi and headed for home.

It had been an eventful day, and I was ashamed to say I snoozed on the way to our apartment in Vicarage Gate and crawled into bed with a mumbled "good night."

Marina patted my stomach and kissed me on the cheek before heading to the lounge, where I knew she'd be up for a while working on her computer.

The bad guys didn't stand a chance.

Chapter Ten

I woke up around ten and found a note that Marina was meeting Nikki and Ana at her office. Simone and Alex were in the kitchen tucking into the remaining scones and pastries we'd taken home from Fortnum's. They'd insisted the leftovers were ours. Who were we to refuse?

"You were right about The Ivy," Alex said. 'It used to be a real celebrity hangout. It has pictures of all the famous old-time actors, and Princess Margaret had her own table.

"Mom and Dad loved it and the show. It was a great day and evening," he added as he popped a petit four into his mouth.

"What are your plans for today?" I asked Simone.

"First stop the London Eye, then Parliament." She paused. "Your dad was able to get us tickets to both."

I bet he was, I thought. He knew how to pull strings when he had to.

Even though I was meeting Marc tomorrow, I wanted to understand the basics of what went into a long con. I planned to spend the rest of the morning doing research.

* * *

There were plenty of examples. One of the first long cons was set up by Charles Ponzi, whose pyramid scheme paid off old investors with money from new ones. It worked for over twenty years until it didn't, and it collapsed with Ponzi facing a trial and prison.

Years later, Bernie Madoff came along and raised the bar to celestial heights. His investors lost millions and were out for blood. I remember seeing a news clip with one man shouting up to his penthouse Park Avenue apartment, "There's still time to do the right thing, Bernie. Jump!" He didn't; instead, he died in jail, and most of the people he swindled lost everything.

I knew there was way more to a long con than that. When I googled it, I got a list of the characters involved that was as long as a craps player on a roll. Everyone on the team had to be one hundred percent committed to the con for it to work. My head was spinning like a roulette wheel from trying to figure it out. I decided to wait until Marc arrived tomorrow and let him explain it all.

In the meantime, I needed something to occupy me. Checking out Clive Hastings Cargill at his firm in The City seemed like a good idea. Until it wasn't.

Chapter Eleven

I t wasn't hard to find Oxford Alliance Ltd. They occupied a new, flash building on Canary Wharf, all odd-shaped panes of glass with pieces of steel jutting out at weird angles. If it was supposed to project power and wealth, it did a piss-poor job. When I looked them up, I discovered they were a Hedge Fund, a partnership of private investors managed by professional fund managers. Talk about hedging your bets; these types of funds were designed to beat average investments, which meant boatloads of money and wealthy investors. It would be interesting to find out just whose money they managed.

I was sure Dad would have the same reaction. He didn't do flash. Hamilton Capital on Seventy-sixth Street and Madison Avenue looked like a private townhouse among the high-end boutiques surrounding it. A discreet brass plaque on the front door was the only thing that marked it as a financial institution. You might walk right past it without noticing a thing. Dad and his partners liked it that way. I'd have to see what he thought of Oxford Alliance Ltd and its associates.

I opened my laptop and cracked my knuckles like a dealer getting ready to shuffle four decks of cards by hand. I logged on to Google. My target was the only firm member I'd met, Clive Hastings Cargill. I needed to know everything there was to know about him, from where he went to grammar school to where he earned his financial chops.

Several links opened when I entered his name into the search engine. All the usual social media and private club affiliations, but most of the listings were professional. My screen lit up with information on his current job and title as a Manager at Oxford Alliance Ltd, and a list of the clients he worked with. I wondered how they'd feel about him spending his free time gambling at a casino. Not to mention pondering whose money he was playing with.

Several links offered his previous employment history along with his education. The schools listed, from St. Paul's primary school to the City of London secondary school and The London School of Economics, indicated old Clive had had it pretty good. The ace in the deck was his MSc in Finance from Oxford University.

Privilege didn't begin to explain it. Cargill's family evidently had money, and with an education like his, he should be smart. So why was he acting like a dumb wanna be spy?

I had to know more, so I used a trick I recycled from our job in Dubai to find out about Adnan's employees. It worked then, and I hoped it would work now. I clicked onto Cargill's Facebook page and looked at a list of his friends. I found a likely prospect in one James Cumberbatch, a co-worker at Oxford Alliance Ltd, who had black hair falling into his eyes and an open, amiable face. Someone I hoped would buy what I was selling. I used a fake name and profile and said I was moving to London, looking for a position in finance. I'd heard his firm had an excellent reputation, and could he fill me in before I applied? I sent him a friend request with this message and crossed my fingers for luck.

About twenty minutes later, James accepted my request. I was in. Well, at least on his Facebook page. There were hundreds of photos. Evidently, hedge fund guys and gals liked to party as well as gamble. I'd probably enjoy hanging out with them if I wasn't otherwise engaged. Several posts tagged Cargill, and Caroline Wickham Cargill, his wife, I presumed, and snaps of their tony high-rise flat on the south bank of the Thames.

A few posts referred to 'Hasty' at several events that seemed to include imbibing lots of beer. I wondered how he'd gotten his nickname.

He hadn't looked like an impulsive type when he approached me at the casino. He'd kept the come-on low-key, but he may have been on his best behavior for my benefit.

James said to let him know when I was arriving, and perhaps we could meet for a beer. I wasn't going to take it any further. I found out what I needed to know. There was no reason to put myself in the spotlight by meeting up.

I felt terrible tricking James. But only just a little. Then I remembered why I was scoping out Clive Hastings Cargill. I wanted to make sure he wasn't up to something shady with Dad as his target.

Marina was going to be occupied with her research into Gabi's workmates while the rest of my family was out and about in London. Mom had wanted to visit Buckingham Palace, and once again, Dad pulled some strings. An afternoon tour was on the schedule. Everyone would be busy until we met up for dinner at our place, so I had the rest of the day to myself.

* * *

It was nearly noon, and I decided to do some sleuthing on my own at Oxford Alliance Ltd. It was a long trip from our home. It would be a twenty-minute walk to the tube and then an hour on the Jubilee line to Canary Wharf, where the building was located. Instead, I opted for a taxi. Once I got there, it would be boots on the ground, well, my Gucci loafers, as I practiced my tailing skills, which were almost non-existent, as I'd proven in Kentucky.

This time, I would do better. I found the Oxford Alliance Ltd building. With its distinctive shape, it would be hard to miss. It was located just across from the north dock. I ducked into a small café across the street and settled in to wait as I sipped an espresso and watched the revolving doors of the building, looking for my intended target. I had a hunch these guys stepped out for lunch every day. I wasn't wrong. After my second espresso, Cargill emerged with a few other banker types. All were dressed in bespoke black suits and looked like they'd just attended a fashion show. Or a funeral. I suppose appearance counted when you were hedging other people's millions. The group spoke for a minute, shared a laugh, and then he moved off in a different direction from his pals.

Now was my opportunity to tail him. He pushed his slightly long light brown hair away from his face, *another tell, or just* nerves? I wondered as he walked toward Jubilee Park, which was a few minutes from his office. He entered, strolled deeper into the park, and sat on a bench in a secluded spot next to the lake. I kept well behind, thankful for the large trees and bright green foliage that hid me. It would be humiliating for him to catch me out. Not to mention, I'd be hard-pressed to explain what I was doing there.

After about ten minutes, a young woman arrived and sat on the other end of the bench, her back toward me. Even from where I stood, I could see the nervous tension radiating off her. At first, I wasn't sure if they were together, but there weren't many people in the park, and plenty of empty benches she could have chosen. When she turned her body to face Cargill, who'd spoken to her, I immediately recognized her. It was Mia Fondsworth, Gabi's friend, and Assistant Curator at The New London Arts Museum.

Cargill reached his hand toward her. She slapped it away, and her face morphed into a mask of anger.

Whoa, what was going on here? This was no coincidence. It was a planned meeting, and I wondered what they were up to.

Chapter Twelve

I watched the pair for a while, my brain shooting off sparks as bright as the lights in a casino with thoughts of what they were doing together. Neither one looked particularly happy to be there. Was this a love affair about to end? Or does it have something to do with New London and the forged Gentileschi? Cargill had spoken about artworks and talking to Dad. What was this all about?

The couple spoke for about ten more minutes, with Cargill doing most of the talking and gesturing wildly with his hands. Then Mia surprised me, stood up quickly, and gave Cargill a passionate kiss goodbye. And him a married man. Well, that was an unexpected turnabout.

After she left, he just sat there, elbows on knees and head in his hands. Despite the kiss, I could see he was not a happy camper.

It felt like their business was personal, not professional. But I could be wrong. Either way, I could understand them meeting secretly. I might be totally off the mark about all of this. There was no way around it. I'd have to tell Marina where I'd been and what I'd seen. She was looking into Mia and the rest of the staff that had accompanied Gabi to New York, which, on the surface, had nothing to do with Cargill.

As a gambler, I didn't believe in coincidences. I'd take another crack at Clive 'Hasty' Cargill and his personal life. After all, this could have been an innocent meeting. The kiss may not have meant anything. *Right,* I thought, nodding to myself. And I'd pull an ace just when I needed it.

I decided to take the long way home, first the Jubilee line from Canary Wharf station and then a walk to Vicarage Gate. Maybe by the time I arrived,

I have some insight into what I'd just seen.

* * *

Marina was home when I got there, out on the deck, sipping a glass of wine and scrolling on her laptop.

"Hello, you," she said, smiling up at me as I bent to kiss her. "What have you been up to today?"

Now was as good a time as any to tell her about my jaunt to Canary Wharf. I was pretty sure she wouldn't be overjoyed about my sleuthing. I'd most likely get a lecture about it.

Just as I was about to speak, the front door opened, and Simone and Alex walked in, talking and laughing like two school kids.

All bets were off. I'd live to tell my story another day.

"Hi, you guys," Simone said. "We had the most perfect day,' she added as she plopped down next to Marina.

"Your dad was so incredibly nice in getting us tickets to everything we wanted to see." Her blond hair flew as she gestured, and her blue eyes gleamed with happiness.

"We started with the London Eye and had an amazing view of the city. I wish we had one in New York," she added.

I bit my tongue. *That would be a disaster,* I thought, but didn't say anything. New York had more than enough attractions as it was. The residents would rebel and make their displeasure known, as they were doing regarding the proposal for a casino in Times Square. Even though I didn't live there anymore, I learned many people opposed the idea. Especially Mom. I could see her shaking her head and sighing at the idea of it. Knowing her, she'd probably force Dad to start an anti-Times Square Casino committee and make the developers' lives miserable.

Simone didn't notice my dour look. She was excited to tell us about the rest of her and Alex's day. "We were able to attend a Parliament session, and it was incredible to watch. The MPs of the Government all sit on benches to the Speaker's right, and the Opposition MPs are to the left."

Alex interrupted. "There's a red line in front of each set of benches, which members aren't allowed to cross while debating. The lines are two sword lengths apart, a holdover from the days when members wore swords and tried to impale each other.

"I can see why. There was a lot of booing and rattling of papers at those who were speaking," he continued.

"We had no idea what proposal they were discussing, but it got very heated," Simone added. "It was great fun."

I caught Marina's eye and shook my head slightly. I was happy that these two were having such a wonderful time in London. Happier than I'd be when I told Marina about my recent exploits, which would have to wait until after family dinner.

Chapter Thirteen

Dinner was delicious. Marina made her famous pasta con vongole, spaghetti with clam sauce, and Mom put together a caprese salad with fresh mozzarella, ripe juicy tomatoes, olive oil, and fresh basil—all ingredients from Harrods Food Halls. For dessert, we had several flavors of gelato from La Gelateria in Covent Garden. It was a good thing all I'd had for lunch was coffee, or Marina would have had to roll me away from the table.

Talk turned to sightseeing for tomorrow. Simone was armed with a list of places not to be missed: the British Museum, the Tower of London, a walk across Abbey Road, and, if there was time, a stroll through Hyde Park. Alex, standing slightly behind her as she filled us in, looked like he might fall over at the thought of all that running around.

I ignored him and spoke to Simone. "Perfect. You'll have a fabulous day. But make sure you take lots of breaks." I didn't need to look to know that Alex was shooting me daggers.

Mom piped in with some sightseeing ideas of her own. "Marina and I are going to Churchill's War Rooms, then a pub lunch at The Red Lion before we move on to Oxford Street for some shopping." She gave Dad one of her signature looks. The disappointed one. "It's a shame you have that meeting and can't join us."

Dad just shrugged. "It's only one meeting, Elizabeth." He kissed her on the cheek, and she smiled. "We'll have the rest of the week together."

Although, I'm sure he'd arranged the tickets and reservations. I knew Marina would never disappoint my mom and that she'd be up most of the night going over what she and the team had uncovered about Gabi's coworkers.

"What about you, Nick? What have you got on for tomorrow?" Dad asked.

"I'm going to meet an old friend from New York, Marc Rivers. He's in town for a couple of days, and it will be nice to get together."

"Is he…still…in Real Estate?" Dad asked. I thought he might ask if Mark was still running a confidence ring. Thankfully, he didn't. He'd known enough about him from our younger days to be somewhat skeptical of his current career.

I nodded, avoiding his eyes. "Yeah, he has been doing very well for a while now."

"Good to hear, Nick. Give him my best." I didn't miss the slight hint of suspicion coloring his voice or the uptick at the corner of his mouth.

* * *

Soon after, Mom and Dad left for their luxury suite at the Connaught, and Alex and Simone retired to their room, exhausted from their busy day. We hadn't told them about Gabi's predicament with the 'maybe fake' Artemisia Gentileschi. Both my parents would worry about the danger Marina might face when dealing with art forgers and thieves, even though that was her business, and she was more than up to the task. They'd both tell me I should stay out of the way and leave the sleuthing to the professionals.

Marina and I went out to the deck with a nightcap. Like in New York, it was hard to see the stars because of all the lights, but a few twinkled through as I filled her in on my snooping expedition.

To her credit, she didn't take me to task. Instead, she asked, "What do you think it means?"

I tilted my head back and raised my hands to the sky. "I have no idea. It seemed like it might have been a conversation about a love affair gone wrong or a business deal that was breaking bad." I paused. "That might be because I know about Mia working with Gabi on the Gentileschi project and connected the two in my mind. I just can't figure out where Cargill fits in."

"We'll have to find out, won't we?"

Was Marina offering me a bone? I sat up and turned toward her. "I could do more digging into Cargill, if you like."

She nodded. "As long as it's online and not in person. If he's involved in some way, we don't want to spook him." She paused. "Let's see what your dad's impression of Oxford Alliance Ltd and their employees is when we meet tomorrow evening. After your mom and I finish our shopping, I'll drop her off at the hotel." Marina chuckled. "I think she might want a rest before their trip to the theater for "Witness for the Prosecution." Your dad got tickets for the jury seats, and it's up to the audience to decide whether the defendant is guilty or innocent. It was another well-known Christie story, and I was sure my folks would enjoy it.

"Maybe I should leave Cargill until after Dad's meeting," I said.

"Might be a good idea," Marina replied. "At least until we know if he's involved in what's happening at New London. That's more important."

"So, what did you uncover about Mia Fondsworth and the rest of the bunch, so far?" I asked.

She handed me her laptop, which was open to a folder with documents for each of Gabi's associates and the New York Meade and Medina art people.

"Take a look, and we can discuss it in the morning before I leave to meet your mom."

Oh, I thought. So, I was the one who was going to be up all night, delving into the dangerous world of art forgery. It figured.

Chapter Fourteen

I didn't get very far with Marina's reports before I fell asleep despite her snoring softly beside me. I promised I'd read them while she was out with Mom, since I had most of the day before I planned to meet Marc. I knew having my family here was a distraction for Marina and the case. I appreciated that it was taking time away from her investigation and was determined to help however I could. Marina was just leaving when I opened the laptop and got ready to do a deep dive into Mia Fondsworth's file. "Okay, here I go," I said to her like a bettor going all in, trying to impress his date.

"Hmm," was all she said as she left.

The young marrieds departed soon after, ready for another whirlwind day of sightseeing.

London was experiencing an unexpected stretch of mild, sunny weather. So, I decided to read Marina's notes out on the deck. Armed with a large cappuccino and a tasty croissant, I clicked on and began.

Mia Fondsworth had a Bachelor's degree from University College London in Italian, History of Art, and Museum Studies, as well as a Master of Fine Arts from Cambridge, which she attended on a scholarship. Gabi had told Marina that Mia had a disadvantaged upbringing. She implied there'd been some neglect, or worse, and it appeared Mia had had to work while she attended school and had relied heavily on the scholarships she'd received along the way. She was twenty-seven and had worked at the museum for two years, adding to her expertise and experience. When I looked at what was expected of an assistant curator, Mia seemed to click all the boxes. She was knowledgeable, accurate, and motivated to do well.

Marina hadn't found any damaging information on her personal life. She lived alone in a small flat in Shoreditch. It had a reputation as a fun neighborhood close to the city's center.

Although it was an expensive area, which might be a stretch on her salary. Could that offer the motivation to make ends meet by doing a deal with an art forger?

No one single man stood out as a boyfriend. She had a close group of three other young women who went to bars, restaurants, and the shops together. I was still wondering where Cargill fit in. Was he her sugar Daddy? Or was her interest in finding out more about his company's art holdings to advance her career? Was a relationship with Cargill her way into a more lucrative position in the art sector at Oxford Alliance?

He was like a crumpled bill poking out of a stack of fresh, new hundreds. A counterfeit, or just a little worse for wear?

On paper, Mia Fondsworth seemed genuine, not to mention that Gabi liked her and trusted her. Tonight, Marina and I would need to speak to Gabi again to see if we were on track.

The other two 'prime suspects', Jose Bidenstock and Dame Rosemary Harris, would have to wait.

It was almost time for me to meet Marc Rivers. While Blackjack was on the table, so was a lesson in running a long con. I was prepared to get schooled.

Chapter Fifteen

Maxim's gave new meaning to the term understated elegance. The very private, members-only casino was all burnished wood and polished brass. There were no slot machines with screeching bells, whistles, or bright lights marring the cultured atmosphere. Just subdued pools of soft lighting shining down on the Blackjack, Poker, Roulette, Craps, and Baccarat tables. There were no ten-pound or fifty-pound tables either. The buy-in for each game started at one hundred pounds and up. Subdued whooping and screaming when winning was an implied rule, and few players broke it.

The Maxim's players were serious or wouldn't be gambling here. Of course, a few unsavory characters slipped in. But since they were the very, very rich of the richest, the management overlooked their bad behavior. The pit bosses even managed to smile every so often. Lots of money can have that effect on a person.

No tuxedos today for our afternoon of gambling. We were both in dark slacks, white linen shirts open at the neck, and tweedy sports jackets. Casual but elegant, as befitting of two skilled Blackjack players. We both noticed our wardrobe similarities and laughed as we said our hellos.

Once inside the casino, Marc and I retired to a small lounge for our chat, with tumblers of The Macallan 15-year-old Scotch in hand. We spent a few minutes catching up. Then, I explained my theory about the rediscovered Gentileschi being a fake and part of a long con.

He listened carefully, those mesmerizing eyes staring off into the distance as I spoke. When I finished, he nodded. "I think you may be right about the con," he said. "But I think the painting may have started as the original, then been switched."

"What makes you believe that?"

"You mentioned there have been other 'rediscovered' Gentileschi's authenticated as original. It's possible this one is also and the people running the scam saw a way to a very big payday.

"A long con like this can take a year or more to set up, and everyone involved needs to be in place at the exact right time.

I remembered that Gabi said George Collabello had told her about the painting sometime last year.

Marc continued. "It involves a lot of planning and prep work. And the right crew is critical to pull it off. The con ends when the Mark, or the intended victim, gives up the goods. In this case, the money from the sale, or the insurance, of a valuable painting, or both."

I was taking notes on my phone as he spoke. "What if the painting is not real? Who benefits then?" I asked.

"The person who set up the whole con, the Grifter." He shrugged before continuing. "He'll still get the money, but he'll have to share it with a person called a Roper, who has no obvious connection to the con. You can be sure the Roper would get some of whatever money is to be made. It doesn't matter if the painting is a forgery." He shook his head. "The Mark thinks it's real and believes they can profit from it.

"There are other people involved, but let's start with them. It seems to me that George Colabello was both the Grifter and the Roper."

I'm sure I looked confused, but Marc clarified.

"It's not unusual for a con artist to have multiple roles. But it most likely began with a compatriot, let's call him the Shill, who the Grifter worked with. I have no doubt they have done this before and know how to operate.

"Now, they've been on the lookout for someone interested in valuable, original paintings. They troll the museums and galleries until they find a likely Mark, in this case, our 'anonymous collector.' Maybe the Shill strikes up a conversation at a supposedly chance meeting at a gallery or art show, and over their mutual appreciation of art they become fast friends. The collector appears intent on acquiring more art." Marc paused.

"The Shill strings him along for a few months, until one day over coffee, they have an 'ah ha' moment and tell the collector they just thought of someone who can help him, in this case, George Colabello, who they claim is an old friend involved in the art world and who has come upon a recently rediscovered Artemisia Gentileschi.

"Although they mention, they haven't seen George for years and don't know much about art, just like looking at it. But if the collector has his heart set on it, they could introduce him to Colabello. They let it go for a while and don't mention it again, but when the collector keeps bringing it up, they make the introduction to Colabello, who guides him to the Meade and Medina Gallery, who've been holding the Gentileschi.

"As I said, this all takes time, half a year at least, maybe a year, to build up the relationship and trust until the collector is hooked."

Marc sat forward in his chair and shook his head. "Nick, you need to find the Shill. They are the person who plays it, so the collector would never suspect they have any overt connection to the con. They'd keep the relationship going for a while so it wouldn't look suspicious. The Shill might still be in the picture because the con isn't over yet."

My head was spinning faster than a casino's wheel of fortune. "And then, I asked?

"Well, there's always an Inside Man," he said like I should know this.

The only Inside Man I was familiar with was from a movie.

"In this case, I'd say it was Maxime Meade in New York who sold the rediscovered Gentileschi to the collector and encouraged them to loan the painting to The New London Arts Museum, knowing at some point someone would substitute it for a fake and it would be discovered as such. I'm sure the Meade and Medina Gallery had their 'experts' involved in the con. I'm also positive they'll convince the collector to reinvest the insurance money they receive, so the collector loses out twice."

Not to mention Gabi and New London. "Would someone from New London be involved, as well?

Marc nodded. "That would be a Second Inside Man, in position to steer things in the direction they wanted the con to take." He paused and took a sip of his Scotch. "They'd be in place, ready to make sure the con moved forward. In this case, support the idea that the painting is a forgery. I'm certain this person will receive some of the insurance money and may even help convince the collector to use it to invest in another piece of art. Maybe another original this time. But who knows?"

I thought of that adage: 'Fool me once, shame on you. Fool me twice, shame on me.'

"Thank God, you don't do this anymore. No one would be safe." I gulped down the rest of my Scotch. No filter, I know.

Marc just started laughing. "I thank her every day I got out when I did." He plunked his empty tumbler on the table between us. "Now, let's get down to the real business at hand and play some Blackjack."

We spent the next few hours playing our favorite game and both of us walked away as winners. Marc was flying back to New York early tomorrow morning. He'd come to London to help me out, and I appreciated it.

I was still unsure if I understood how a long con worked, but I knew more now than I did a few days ago. Many millions of dollars were at stake in a fake painting. Only the bad guys would profit. Unless we could catch them out. I'd need more skill than luck to figure that out.

Chapter Sixteen

When I returned home, Marina was snuggled in an armchair, engrossed in a podcast. "What are you listening to?" I asked.

She removed the headphones nestled in her red hair. "A true crime story about a serial killer who made jewelry from the bones of his victims and was finally caught selling it at a country fair," she replied and turned off the podcast.

How cheery. Didn't she get enough of real-life crime in her day-to-day business?

"How was your meeting with Marc?" I could see the dreamy look in her eyes at the mention of my friend's name.

"He sends his love." Now, her face broke into a smile. I wasn't jealous. Okay, maybe just a little.

"I learned quite a bit about running a long con. I'm not sure I understand it entirely, but let me fill you in."

I pulled out my phone and began to paraphrase from the notes I'd taken. "So, we need to find the Shill, the person who introduced the Mark to George Colabello, and the Second Inside man," I said as if that were as easy as pulling four of a kind in a five-card stud poker game.

"*Oh, Marone,*" Marina exclaimed. "It sounds very elaborate, don't you think? Are you still sure it's a con?" she asked.

"More than ever. Everything Marc told me fits about how the events have played out. It's important to speak with Gabi and see where things stand now."

Marina's face turned into a grimace of despair. "Gabi called me earlier. The restorer who was attacked, Jonathan Hudson, passed away this afternoon."

The case had just gotten darker. It was more than forgery. Now, it was murder.

Marina continued. "I've arranged for us to see her tomorrow." She tapped a finger on her chin, thinking things through. "I'd like your mom and dad to come with us. We promised them a visit to the museum, and this would be a perfect opportunity.

"We can float the idea of an endowment from Hamilton Capital and get your dad talking with the Cultural Trustee, Dame Rosemary Harris. I think his impression of her will be valuable. He deals with people like her daily." She paused. "Wealthy, upper-class investors, and I'm sure he'll know how to read her. It's time to fill him in on what's going on."

"What about Mia Fondsworth?" I asked.

She patted me on the knee. "Oh, let's leave her to you, why don't we?"

How'd I get so lucky? I wondered.

* * *

Marina and I had a quiet dinner. Simone and Alex were running all over London and would probably get home just in time to do it all over again tomorrow.

At around eleven, I called Dad's cell, figuring they'd be back at the hotel by then, and asked how they'd enjoyed the play.

"We had a difference of opinion on the defendant's guilt. I'll let your mom explain it to you in person."

Something to look forward to. I put that thought aside and told Dad about the probably fake Gentileschi and the murdered restorer. I kept the idea of a long con to myself. It was a complicated concept, and I needed more time to think it through.

I told him Marina would explain our plan for tomorrow and handed her the cell phone. They spoke for a few minutes, and then she offered the phone back to me.

"Nick, is there anything you can tell me about Dame Harris before I grill her?" he asked with a hint of a tough cop in his voice.

"Marina will send you what she's learned so far." I paused. "I haven't had a chance to review the info yet."

Then I remembered his meeting at Oxford Alliance Ltd. "Hey, how was your meeting today?" I asked.

There was such a long pause that I thought we'd been disconnected. Finally, Dad spoke. "It was interesting and weird."

I wasn't sure I liked the sound of that.

"I'll tell you all about it tomorrow. See you at The New London Arts Museum at ten."

Chapter Seventeen

A bell in a nearby church chimed ten just as we arrived on the steps of The New London Arts Museum. A minute later, the Escalade pulled up, and Mom and Dad emerged.

Inside, we asked for Gabi, and once again, were escorted to her office. This time, she was sitting at her desk, looking off into space and ignoring the stack of papers in front of her.

She rose quickly when the host announced us. I introduced my parents to Lady Gabriella Peake Jones, and she seemed relieved to meet them. Especially my dad, who Marina had told her was on board to help sort things out.

Gabi was in on the plan that Dad was here to meet Dame Rosemary Harris, ostensibly to discuss the idea of a small endowment from Hamilton Capital.

Since he wasn't supposed to know about the problem with the Gentileschi, he would keep the conversation focused on finance. That was his forte, and he'd know it if Dame Harris slipped up.

"Rosemary is in the main gallery," she said. "We're going to be joined by Stella Manning, who is the Managing Director." She smiled at Dad. "Like the CEO of a top firm. She's been apprised of the situation," Gabi added in a worried tone, suggesting Stella Manning was decidedly not happy. "Let's go over and have you meet them, shall we?"

"Is Mia around?" I interjected. "I'd like to speak with her."

She picked up the phone on her desk and punched in a few numbers. "Mia, hi. Can you pop over to my office? Nick Donahue and Marina DiPietro, the investigators helping us with our situation, have a few questions." She listened to the young woman's reply. "Great, see you in five then.

"Now, Mr. Donahue, shall we proceed to my gallery?"

Both Marina and I caught the word 'my.' I knew Gabi was worried it wouldn't be hers for much longer.

"Elizabeth," Marina said to Mom, "why don't we wander a bit and catch up to Nick and Michael after they finish?"

"You go ahead, Marina. I need a minute to speak with Nick."

What did I do now? I hoped she wasn't going to ask if I'd given any thought to quitting playing Blackjack and doing something else, like banking. I hadn't.

"Nick," she said, "don't look so worried. I need your help."

This was a departure. I was generally considered the prodigal son, not the helpful one.

"Is there something wrong?" I asked, taking her hand. It was icy cold and gripped mine tightly.

"I'm not…sure," she replied, shaking her head. "Your dad was very upset after his meeting yesterday. I don't know what happened, but it's so unlike him."

I nodded in agreement. Dad was the definition of unflappable. Apparently, Oxford Alliance Ltd had caused him some concern. "What can I do to help?" I asked.

"That person who was staring at you when we were at Fortnum and Mason's?"

She made it sound like a question, and I looked at her warily.

She sighed. "I know you don't think so, but I do notice what's happening around me." She paused. "Anyway, your father mentioned that Cargill had introduced himself to you at the casino and that he worked for the company Dad was meeting with. But I thought something was off when he showed up at tea."

I had no idea that Dad ever told her about his professional dealings. Dad always kept his personal and business lives separate. It took me a moment to remember that Mom and Dad had met at Georgetown, where they were both enrolled in its finance program. They married right after earning their degrees and entered the investment world. I like to think I'd followed in their footsteps. Blackjack often required a knowledge of high finance, although I knew Mom wouldn't see it that way.

After they were married for a few years, Mom decided to quit working and start a family. I'd bet the bank that she had no idea what she was in for. Keeping track of stocks and bonds wasn't as hard as keeping up with two overactive young boys.

Looking back, it wasn't unreasonable to think that Dad had always confided in Mom and counted on her opinion. Only this time, I sensed the situation was different—call it my gambler's intuition—and I didn't like it that Mom was involved. Not to mention as jittery as a player down to his last chip.

By now, she was shaking her head. "Can you find out if I'm right, Nick? See who this Cargill is and what he wants?"

She was worried about Dad. That much was certain. I drew her in for a hug. "Of course I will. Don't worry. It's probably something about their business practices that seemed off to Dad." The words *crooks, frauds, and thieves* crossed my mind. "You know what a straight arrow he is." I took a step back and smiled at her. "I'm sure it will turn out to be just fine.

"Now, why don't you catch up with Marina? And I'll meet you in the café after I speak with Gabi's assistant." Another link to Cargill, but one I couldn't mention.

Mom smiled. "Alright, see you a little later, Nick." She kissed me on the cheek and left the office.

I wasn't sure at all. Windsor Smythe and his cronies were up to something. Whatever it was, he had tweaked Dad's bull shit meter, and knowing him, he wouldn't let it go. And, if he needed my help, neither could I.

Chapter Eighteen

Five minutes later, Mia Fondsworth entered Gabi's office. She held out her hand to shake mine and still appeared as nervous and jittery as the first time we'd met.

She seemed to take hold of herself and arranged her face into a calm mask before speaking. "Lovely to see you again, Nick. Gabi said you wanted to have a chat." Her deep blue eyes were open wide, and she looked directly into mine, smiling up at me.

It was a 'nothing to hide' look, which I'd noted many times before at the Blackjack tables. Card counters were fond of employing it. It hardly ever worked.

Mia was wearing what I thought was a conservative style for a young assistant curator. It was a blend-into-the-background kind of look. She'd tucked her hair back behind her ears, and her face was almost bare of makeup. There wasn't much pizazz in the black, long-sleeve dress that was fitted at her waist and fell below her knees. But what did I know? It probably came from a famous designer and cost several thousand pounds, which might be too expensive on an assistant curator's salary. I'd have to ask Marina.

"Mia," I said. "I want to discuss your thoughts on the Gentileschi."

"Oh, of course. What would you like to know?"

"You accompanied Gabi to New York three times to view the painting. What was your initial impression?"

She nodded and seemed willing to talk. "I thought it was splendid. A wonderful representation of Gentileschi's work. A strong image of a strong woman." A look of bitterness flashed through her eyes and was gone a second later. "There was a bit of damage to the upper part of the canvas and a few nicks on the frame, as well as a layer of dirt, which you'd expect if it hadn't been properly seen to. Nothing that we couldn't repair. Overall, I thought it a magnificent painting and a brilliant addition to the show."

She tilted her head to the side and waited for me to continue, her eyes dimming slightly with suspicion. She'd most likely surmised I already knew all this. "Had you met the New York forensic art expert Meade and Medina brought in, Jerome Benedict, before?"

"No," she replied quickly, "but I've heard of him. He's very well-known as an appraiser, and I've read several articles he's written about various paintings and their provenances."

"How about Jose Bidenstock or Dame Harris? Had they met him before?"

"I wouldn't know." She frowned slightly, signaling her annoyance. "You would have to ask them directly."

She crossed her arms over her middle and suddenly seemed jittery. I thought she might be lying, but I let it go.

I wanted to bring up Cargill, but if she were up to something with him, it would tip my hand since he hadn't been mentioned in connection with the Gentileschi.

We spoke for a few more minutes, and then she returned to her own office.

I thought about the interview and wasn't satisfied. I left Gabi's office and went in search of Marina and Mom. I found them sitting at a small table in the modern Café d'Art, sipping tea and eating pastries. Both women seemed at ease, and I was happy to see Mom smiling. I might have had something to do with that since our talk a little while ago.

"Hello, ladies," I said as I took a seat at their table.

"We're enjoying 'Elevenses' Marina told me. "It's the mid-morning tea break onboard the English luxury liners." She lifted her not-very-delicate mug and held out her pinkie.

"At home, we call it a coffee break," Mom chimed in, picking up a small creamy-looking tart, taking a bite, and licking her lips in satisfaction.

"Everything okay?" Marina asked. I knew she was referring to my conversation with Mia.

"Fine," I replied, shrugging and snarfed up a pastry of my own. We'd discuss it later

"Why don't we look at more of the art while we wait for Dad and Gabi to finish their chat with Dame Harris and Managing Director Manning?"

I cut my eyes toward Marina, and she understood that I could hardly wait to hear what he'd have to say.

Chapter Nineteen

Gabi delivered Dad to us in the Impressionist Gallery. After she proudly showed us the Monets, Manets, Seurats, and Cezannes, which we could hardly refuse to view, we hustled out to the waiting Escalade and back to the Connaught.

It was a quiet ride, with all of us keeping our cards close to the vest until we were back in the suite.

Dad ordered a lunch of sandwiches and salads from room service. We got right to it once we were seated around the suite's roomy dining table.

"So, Nick, what did Mia have to say for herself?" Dad started the conversation.

"About what you'd expect." My mouth tightened in consternation. "She gave me the usual art speak: believed the painting was genuine, as did the experts who evaluated it. Etc. etc."

"And?" She continued.

"I couldn't get a really good read on her," I replied. "There was something going on under the surface."

Marina lifted an eyebrow. "No, tell, that you noticed?"

"Honestly, except for a few brief moments, she maintained her composure. That got me wondering." I paused. "I mean, if you had been one of the people who signed off on a seven-million-dollar painting being genuine, wouldn't you be more concerned about discovering it was a fake?

"She accompanied Gabi to the Meade and Medina Gallery three times and still missed that something was wrong." I lifted my shoulders in a shrug that said I wasn't buying it.

Marina chimed in. "Do you think she was influential in convincing Gabi that the painting was a genuine rediscovered Gentileschi?"

"No," I shook my head. "I think she'd keep her opinion low-key, especially if she knew something she wasn't telling.

"We need to speak with Gabi again and learn more about her relationship with George Colabello."

I sat poking at the food in front of me, which remained practically untouched, before I spoke again. "You know, I met with Marc Rivers about how this could be a giant, long con." I continued without explaining all the roles and people involved, and confusing things even more. "Based on what he told me, I'm convinced it is. And that George Colabello is a key player."

I let that sit there for a moment.

"What about Dame Rosemary Harris and Stella Manning?" I asked Dad. "What was your impression of them?"

He sat back and blew out a short snort, which certainly got our attention.

"Dame Harris is quite a piece of work. She addressed me as Mr. Donahue and Gabi as Lady Peake Jones." A frown crossed his face. "So, of course, I felt obligated to address her as Dame Harris." He shook his head. "So pretentious."

Marina bit her lip to keep from laughing and cut her eyes my way.

"She had that Grace Kelly look. You do know who Grace Kelly was?" He looked at Marina.

Mom rolled her eyes. "Really, Michael?"

"A beautiful, thin woman with a very blonde updo. Princess material." He glanced at Mom to make sure he got that part right. She shook her head at him. "That's where the comparison stops. Dame Rosemary has the coldest blue eyes, which she focused on me like lasers, and she never smiled. Just looked down her nose as though she were a member of the Royal Family." He paused. "Although, I don't think they'd be so snooty." He looked at Marina. "What exactly is a Cultural Trustee?"

Marina snatched up her laptop, clicked on her files, and found the one on Dame Harris. "The trustees all have different backgrounds. Most have experience in areas that can benefit the museum, such as finance, development, planning, and journalism.

"According to her credentials, Dame Harris possesses none of these traits. What she does have is the kind of reputation for knowing the right people who could offer support with either money or cachet.

"Her background is upper-class English. Think of the Middletons before Kate married William. She's been on several smaller museum committees over the years, but The New London Arts Museum is a big step up for her." Marina stopped to consider the ramifications. "There's a lot of tricky stuff here. A well-to-do family and a once well-to-do husband who lost most of his money speculating on wild schemes. Somehow, though, she's held onto hers while divesting herself of him."

I didn't dare look at Mom. I could see the word *Blackjack* flashing through her mind. Marina hadn't mentioned gambling. I'd ask her later about those schemes. Instead, I said, "So how did she get this appointment?"

Both Marina and Dad replied at the same time: "Connections." They were kind enough to leave off the 'Duh'.

It's the same everywhere, I thought. Who you know is more important than what you know.

"Is Cultural Trustee a paid position? I asked.

"It's an appointment from the Prime Minister. An influential party member most likely referred her, but I'm not sure if there's a substantial salary attached." She scrolled through her notes. "I'd have to ask Gabi if she knows how much that is. I can't think it's enough for a very lavish lifestyle, which Dame Harris seems to enjoy."

Marina left the thought hanging. Could Dame Harris be part of the con, the Second Inside Man? A crooked Trustee looking to enrich herself? If she were, it would explain a lot.

"What about Stella Manning?" I asked.

Dad thought about it for a second. "She's about the same age as Dame Harris, maybe a few years older, but a little shorter and stockier. She kept her distance and let Harris take the lead. Mostly, she nodded, clasped her hands, and acted as if she wished all this would disappear. I sensed a certain disconnect from the problem."

"But she's the head of New London. Do you think she wanted to distance herself and her position from the forgery?" I asked

Dad shrugged. "I'm not sure. I felt there was a nervous energy under her calmness that she was trying to control; maybe to stay in charge, although she didn't behave like she was. She seemed frightened." He paused. "This can't be good for her career either."

Especially since she's the boss, I thought.

* * *

It was a beautiful day, and we decided to take a break from thinking about the Gentileschi. The four of us headed out to Hyde Park, the largest of the Royal Parks. It's close to the hotel, and the day was perfect for a stroll. Besides enjoying the sunshine, its reputation for beautiful flowers and greenery was well deserved. And it would give me an opportunity to ask Dad about his meeting at Oxford Alliance Ltd. From the look on Dad's face when I'd mentioned it earlier, I could only imagine how that well had gone.

Chapter Twenty

I slung my arm around Dad's shoulder as we entered the lush, green park and asked, "So how did your meeting go?" I made sure Mom, who was a few steps behind us with Marina, heard the question. I wanted her to know I was on the case.

"There's something very peculiar going on at that firm," he shook his head as he replied. "Do you know how hedge funds work?" he asked.

"Just the basics," I replied. "Big investments. Quick turnaround. Huge profits."

"Most of the time. After the pandemic, the market changed. Many investors pulled their money out of the funds, which took a big hit.

"Oxford Alliance Ltd and its CEO, John Windsor Smythe, were talking a big game about how they've regrouped and shifted to the new hot art sector."

Everything was revolving around art. A week ago, I barely knew anything about it. Now I was practically an expert. I just couldn't figure out how it all fit together. Did Oxford Alliance somehow tie into the fake Gentileschi? Had they, with a little help from the inside, arranged the switch?

Dad continued. "Windsor Smythe is a big guy, a looming presence. Flowing black hair. Big square jaw. Wide shoulders. Big handshake. And a booming voice. He showed me report after report on the art market sector and how Hamilton Capital clients could benefit from an alliance. And he intimated that I would benefit personally, as well. He assumed he could bribe me." His scowl showed what he thought of that.

Dad turned to me and continued. "He presented everything but his client list, which he said was proprietary."

"What if you'd agreed and told him you'd steer some of your clients' investments his way?"

Dad nodded. "He'd have to put up or shut up, but I sensed that would be a battle, which made me even more leery.

"I explained that Hamilton Capital collects art to add to the bank's overall portfolio and that our event next Monday is meant to showcase the firm's latest acquisition for our London office. I added that most of our clients are invested in debt and equity securities, real estate, and derivatives. I knew art wasn't something they'd be interested in pursuing in any major way."

Besides, most of Dad's clients already had significant art collections of their own. If they were going to buy art, all they'd need to do was call in at Sotheby's or Christie's.

"What did Danielle Burkett think?" I asked, referring to his London partner, who was the head of the firm here and had accompanied Dad to the meeting.

"She thought he was full of…hot air. And she didn't miss the reference to profiting personally. Danielle looked at Windsor Smythe as though he'd slapped her."

It was good to know his second in command was standing up for the company.

"We sat through his presentation for over an hour, and he kept pushing. Finally, I told him we had another appointment, and it was time to leave, or we would be late."

"Of course, I understand," he said, *"putting one of his big, beefy hands on my shoulder and squeezing too hard. "It's unfortunate that I couldn't persuade you. It could be very lucrative for all of us. He shot another look Danielle's way. Maybe he thought she could convince me.*

There it was again. Inferring an under-the-table payment.

"Perhaps we can discuss this further at your firm's celebration on Monday evening. We'll be happy to host the after party at the Free Port, where we keep our art holdings. It's an impressive space, and once you see what I'm speaking about, I'm positive you'll be motivated to do business with us." Then, he shook my hand and added, "London can be dangerous, Mr. Donahue. Make sure to keep safe." He

gave my hand one more hard squeeze. "I hope you and your wife enjoy the rest of your stay at the Connaught."

"Something about how he said those words made my hackles rise. I felt, no, I knew, that it was a threat. And how did he know where we were staying? Does he have someone watching us?"

Probably, I thought, but kept that to myself. I'd ask Marina to ask her operative at the Connaught if he'd noticed any outside interest in my parents.

"Will you go to his 'after party'?"

"No," Dad said emphatically, his face furrowed into a frown. "And what the hell is a Free Port, anyway?"

Fortunately, I'd asked Marina to explain Free Ports to me and was delighted to share my knowledge.

"They're basically fancy warehouses in certain free trade zones, usually at airports, where wealthy people store their valuable assets—think art, precious gems, antiques, gold, and wine collections—while deferring taxes. There's one at JFK in New York and others all over the country. Not to mention the world."

"So, that's where the one percent stash their goods?" Dad asked the question with a good amount of snark.

He was getting quite an education since he arrived in London. "From what I understand, the spaces can be quite lavish, with private offices and large conference rooms where people can conduct business or have a party. Buy. Sell. Make boatloads of money without the bother of paying tariffs. That is, if the goods never left the premises.

"I'm sure the space is large enough to display Oxford Alliance Ltd.'s art holdings in the most lavish way possible."

"So, the items, in this case, the art, would have to remain there until it was sold and removed. Then the taxes would be due?"

Dad had grasped the concept immediately. He shook his head. "I don't see how that would benefit my clients. They prefer their assets to be more liquid and readily available, not hidden away in some warehouse, as swanky as it might be.

We both recognized a boondoggle when we saw one.

We'd been wandering through the Hyde Park Rose Garden with its spectacular array of colorful blooms. He glanced over to where Mom and Marina were admiring the climbing magenta roses that had been blooming in the same spot since they were planted there in 1861.

I understood why Dad was so rattled. Any threat against Mom, or his family, wouldn't be tolerated. He stopped and turned to me. "Nick, will you attend the Gala with me and help me figure this out?"

I nodded. It was a sure bet I couldn't say no.

* * *

We caught up to Marina and Mom and exited the park. I gave her a wink to let her know I'd kept my promise and spoken to Dad. I noticed a look of relief spread over her face. I tried to project a positive feeling that things were under control. Yeah, as under control as betting on the wheel of fortune in a casino and expecting to win thousands. We walked my parents back to their hotel, and I filled in Marina as we headed home.

"Your father is right to be worried. Windsor Smythe sounds more like a thug, thief, and a scammer than a banker."

I was frowning; my poker face had slipped down to my stomach, where it was doing backflips.

"C'mon." Marina stretched up and planted a kiss on my cheek. "You'll figure it out."

I hoped I could. Dad hadn't mentioned meeting Cargill, who I presumed wasn't at the meeting. He was one more unknown piece of the puzzle that needed to fit in.

We arrived at our flat and heard music playing and ice cubes clinking as we entered.

"The children are home," Marina said. "Let's see what they've been up to."

Chapter Twenty-One

Alex and Simone had enjoyed another great day wandering around London. Tonight, they were going to a gastropub some friends in New York had recommended.

Marina and I were on our own. Except, we needed to meet with Gabi to discuss everything that we'd discovered.

She picked up immediately when Marina called and said she'd be down shortly. I looked at Marina. No way was this going to be easy. We were going to accuse Gabi's friend of art theft and more.

The awful look on Gabi's face said it all as she entered. "What happened?" she asked, looking from Marina to me. "You can tell me."

Marina took her arm and led her to the couch, where she sat expectantly.

I took the lead. "Gabi, we've discovered some things about the fake Gentileschi and how this all transpired." I raised my hands to include everything around us. Then, I explained about the long con and how her friend George Colabello had set the whole thing up with the help of what was known as a Shill.

"The Shill is the person who befriends the Mark, gets close to them and ultimately insinuates themself into his life, and slowly leads him to what he wants most, which is, in this case, a connection to a valuable artwork."

Gabi was looking at me as though I'd lost my mind. It seemed elaborate, but then again, a lot of money was at stake. Seven-million-dollars.

"I don't understand," Gabi said. "What has George got to do with this?"

I looked at her face, which had filled with worry, and continued. "We believe George Colabello's what we call the Grifter, the person who sets the wheels in motion and finds the art that will satisfy the collector.

Gabi was shaking her head. "How do you know this?" she demanded. "Why would George do that to me. I thought we were friends?"

The easy answer was money. Also, he was a lying scumbag. But I knew she'd realize that soon enough on her own.

"To make a con like this work, takes a lot of time, and a lot of people in the right place at the right time." I paused. "Meade and the gallery were, and still are, part of it."

Gabi collapsed back on the sofa and looked stunned. I offered her a glass of brandy, which she accepted.

"I was prepared to accept the Gentileschi was a fake, but having George behind it, I can't wrap my head around it."

"He's not the only one involved." I looked over at Marina, who had just clicked off her cell. "We're pretty sure someone at The New London Arts Museum is in on the con, too."

Now was not the time to upset Gabi even more by explaining all the roles involved in the scam. We'd get to that as soon as we found the Second Inside Man there. She was having enough trouble processing what we'd told her so far.

Marina turned her attention to us. "Nick, don't be cross with me, but I called Marc Rivers before he left town and asked him to help once he was back in the city. I had an idea he could ferret out some information for us."

"Okay," I said, not sure exactly how I felt about Marina going around me and asking Marc to step in.

"That was him on the phone. He still has some contacts from…the old days. He put out some feelers and asked around." She looked at Gabi before continuing and chose her words carefully.

"Marc knew a woman he'd worked with a while ago who was able to help. She'd heard on the street that someone had been planning a big art con, and she knew one of the players. Marc believes she's the Shill, a woman named Natalia Kosova, a con artist from Russia, who's been in the game for a long time. A tall, beautiful brunette, she goes by Natalie Stapleton, and Marc's informant says Natalie has let too much information slip. Maybe she was bragging about the big score they would make, or just trusted the other woman?" Marina shrugged. She understood people couldn't always resist a little self-aggrandizing.

"Marc had some people follow Natalie, who, it turns out, is living with George Colabello."

"What?" Gabi's face turned ashen, like a ghost had taken over her body. I wondered if she thought of George as more than a good friend. Maybe a former lover before she committed to Sydney?

"Quite the coincidence, wouldn't you say?" Marina continued. "Marc had someone tail her. For the last three mornings, Natalie's left George's apartment and met up with a good-looking guy in his thirties, Brian Ahern, who we're positive is the Mark."

Marc's people said Natalie was all over him. Lavishing him with hugs and kisses, and whispering in his ear, as if she were reassuring him that things would be okay." Marina's voice dripped with sarcasm.

"Mr. Ahern is wealthy, a trust fund baby. It appears he's been looking to start an art collection to grace the walls of the East 64th Street townhouse he purchased a year ago." She consulted the notes she'd made while speaking with Marc. "It's right next door to the one where Ivana Trump lived. An expensive, upscale street."

Marina raised one eyebrow, indicating the con artists had done their homework.

"I think Natalie and Colabello had been on the lookout for someone just like Ahern. Marc tells me Ahern and Natalie have been seen around the city for many months and appear to be more than friends."

Marina paused. "The rest is all conjecture, but I believe it, or something very similar, is true."

I'd double down on her being right, I thought.

"Natalie probably 'met' Brian Ahern at a gallery, or art exhibit where she was looking for a Mark like him and struck up a friendship. It seems reasonable to assume that after a while, Ahern confessed his desire to find a masterpiece painting to Natalie, who, I'm sure, professed an appreciation of art while pretending not to know anything about it at all. After stringing him along for months, she eventually 'remembered' a very old acquaintance, George Colabello, who knew the people who owned the Meade and Medina Gallery and introduced them.

"George must have explained that Meade and Medina just recently acquired a rediscovered Gentileschi. He probably billed it as a stunning addition to the Gentileschi canon and a coup for the discerning collector."

Marina shook her head at the thought. "He made the introduction to Maxime Meade, who was happy to sell the Gentileschi to Ahern. Then, he was persuaded to loan the painting to New London, hopefully increasing its resale value after the exhibit. All the while, Natalie was by his side, adding her encouragement."

"Why is Natalie, or Natalia, still seeing this Ahern?" Gabi asked. Wouldn't she have disappeared by now?"

"That's part of the scheme. She couldn't just disappear from his life. It would look too suspicious. She needs to be around to commiserate with him and 'help' him through this trouble."

Gabi covered her face with her hands. "This is even worse than I thought. Jonathan is dead. Other people are at risk. This could ruin us." Her anguish seeped through her voice. "How are we going to fix this?" she asked.

Marina bent over and took her hands in her own. "We'll figure out how to make this right."

I didn't know how she planned on doing this, but I'd lay odds that she would.

Chapter Twenty-Two

After Gabi left, Marina and I sat for a while, each with our thoughts. I didn't want to sulk about her contacting Marc Rivers without telling me. It was juvenile, but I felt proprietary about our friendship. It had been a good move, and we got the information we needed.

What had happened was clear, but we'd have to prove it. It would have been easier if I could clone Marc Rivers, but that wasn't in the cards.

The best I could come up with now was to work out how the forgery had come to be and where it had been until it was switched for the original.

No one on that team would admit to it. They'd invested too much time and effort to let it go.

Marina had been right from the start. Those in on the con presented an original: the genuine, rediscovered Gentileschi 'Weeping Magdalene.' Meade and Medina had shown it to Gabi, the museum people, and the experts. Then, in a cunning move, they switched it after it arrived in London.

By now, the original was stashed away someplace, waiting for the right buyer to appear. Someone who would never display it on their living room wall but would keep it hidden away and view it purely for their own pleasure. A buyer who would pay triple or quadruple what Ahern had paid.

"Hey," I said, as I slid closer to Marina. "I've been thinking about all this."

She put her head on my shoulder. "You have. Have you?" There was a playful tone in her voice. "Are you upset that I contacted Marc about the case?" she asked more seriously, turning her luminous green eyes up to mine.

"No," I replied. "He knew just what to do, and it was critical." Then I changed tack. "Do you remember when you were sure the forgery was switched for the real painting?"

Marina nodded into my chest. "I do."

"Well, I believe you're right. At least a half-dozen experts in New York and here marked the canvas as genuine." Even Marc thought they'd used the original to lure in Ahern." I paused. "I think the original canvas was shipped to The New London Arts Museum. Then, once it arrived and was examined and went through all the tests of dating the canvas, looking at the pigments and the brushstrokes, someone switched it." I thought about the young art restorer who'd died.

"Jonathan Hudson was giving it another look when he discovered the funky signature. I believe he was meant to find it. To set off the alarm bells. And then he was silenced."

"So, it was definitely an inside job," Marina said, "planned by one of the museum's own."

I nodded in agreement. "Someone painted the fake, probably months ago, and the gang had it ready to substitute for the original.

"The plan was to expose it as a forgery sometime before the exhibit—" I began.

"—and cause the doubt and chaos that's transpired since," Marina finished.

I sat up straight. "We need to find the forger who painted the Gentileschi and the person who hired him. There are only a few people in the world good enough to do this kind of work, and I seem to remember one of them retired to England after getting out of his legal troubles in the States."

Far enough away to hide from prying eyes, I thought.

The forger was adjacent to the con, a paid participant, not precisely part of it, but not out of it either. "He's our ace in the hole, and we need to play him if we're going to win."

Chapter Twenty-Three

"Good morning, Nick," Dad said into my cell, which had woken me from a deep sleep.

"Hey, Dad," I replied, shaking the cobwebs from my voice. "You're up early."

"Your mother has a full day of sightseeing planned." He barely concealed the sigh hovering on the edge of his voice.

Poor Dad, I don't think he had any idea what he was in for when he left New York. Especially the weird meeting with Oxford Alliance Ltd.

"Anyway, Nick," he continued. "I've planned a surprise for everyone for Saturday night, and I need your help."

Something must really be wrong if I was being the helpful son yet again. "Sure," I replied. "What can I do for you?"

"I got tickets for the family for Elton John's performance on Saturday evening at the Royal Albert Hall. It's a private benefit concert in support of Prince William's Royal Foundation Charity. As I understand it, the charity benefits environmental issues, early childhood development, mental health, and homelessness, among other projects."

I was still working on Elton John, as in going to a private concert at which he was playing. His performances were legendary, but he didn't perform much anymore, and I knew this would be a memorable event—as well as a very expensive one.

"I want this to be a surprise for everyone else. So, please don't mention it to anyone, especially Alex. He'd blab it to Simone right away."

"Okay," I replied, laughing. "Does Mom know about this?"

"She does not, and I want to keep it that way."

"Got it." Mom had been a big Elton John fan since she was younger and still listened to his music. I remember seeing her dancing around the kitchen to 'Crocodile Rock.' I'm sure she'd be over the moon to see him perform live in his hometown.

"I'll text you all the details. I booked a table at Côte Kensington, which is nearby and has an excellent reputation. We'll meet there.

"Got to go." I could hear Mom in the background calling his name. "Remember not a word to anyone."

Wow, I thought. Those tickets must have cost Dad a small fortune. I started to laugh. He was spending like a drunken sailor, as an old friend of mine would say, and he didn't seem to mind.

Marina walked into our bedroom. "Nick, why are you still in bed? She bent over and planted a kiss on my forehead.

She looked at her watch. "I'm leaving for New London to interview Jose Bidenstock, the art handler.

"An interview or surprise attack?" I asked. She was dressed for the latter in a fitted black suit and heels that made her almost as tall as me. I'd be impressed. Maybe even scared.

"He's a person of interest. Exceptionally high interest."

"Oh?" I replied. "Why is that?"

"He was in the best position to switch out the real Gentileschi."

"So, he is your prime suspect?" I asked.

"Just a suspect…for now."

She cocked her head to one side and listed his duties. "His job has a lot of moving parts," which she recounted: "The packing and unpacking of works of art, preparing and moving them, and installing them in the appropriate gallery." Marina considered his position. "Jose had the most contact with the Gentileschi after it arrived in London, and once Jonathan Hudson had finished his inspection, he would have been the one to install it in Gabi's exhibit."

I trailed Marina into the living room. While she gathered up her laptop, notebook, and phone in preparation for leaving for the day, I thought about her notes on Jose Bidenstock that I'd looked over. He'd been doing this type of work for about ten years at various galleries and exhibition halls in London, and there were no incidents or bad marks against him. Could be he'd never been caught.

But…and you know whatever comes after the but is important…it seemed he had the ideal job and perfect opportunity to switch the original for the forgery. I just wondered where the original 'Weeping Magdalene' was stashed. Wouldn't it be interesting if it was still in the basement storeroom, crated and hidden in plain sight?

I mentioned this to Marina just as she opened our front door. She shook her head and said, *"Tu sei pazzo,"* for my trouble. I wasn't crazy. Well, it was possible, wasn't it?

"Okay, Nick, enough with the theories. It's time to get going and find the bad guys. *Andiamo,"* she added in Italian and closed the door behind her.

"On it," I shouted toward our doorway as I headed for the shower. Contrary to what Marina might think, I had a scheme to find the forger. I planned to start at The London Library.

After I showered, had coffee, and dressed in my best business casual attire, I clicked on the link to join this esteemed literary institution. A hefty five hundred sixty-five pounds later, I was the bearer of a yearly membership. I printed out my receipt and tucked it into my wallet.

Armed with my laptop and lots of enthusiasm, I left for the library. I know. I could have done my research on the computer, but this library was one of the most unique in all of London, and I hadn't set foot inside it in all the time I'd been living here. Who knew what I might find?

It was billed as one of the world's greatest lending libraries, contained over one million books in its collection, and even had Helena Bonham Carter as its President. I was sure one or two of those volumes in their stacks would yield some information on the art forger I was in search of, Luke Chimini, and maybe even divulge his current whereabouts.

I called an Uber and twenty minutes later, I reached my destination. I presented my receipt to the librarian at the front desk, who swapped it out for a plastic card with a Rembrandt on the front. I asked where I could find books on Luke Chimini, the art forger. A few clicks on her computer and she directed me to the art crimes section, where I located several volumes that included information on him. And one he'd written after the statute of limitations on his crimes had run out.

Luke Chimini has conned everyone. No one was exempt. Not renowned experts, super galleries, major auction houses, or affluent buyers, all of which he detailed at length in his book, BUYER BEWARE. I thought his title could have been a little more interesting for someone so creative and imaginative.

About ten years ago, the FBI had been ready to close in on him, but abruptly curtailed their investigation, the scope of which would have rocked the art markets around the world. His 'masterpieces' were unparalleled and included paintings by European and American Masters that were so technically perfect that they were never discovered as fakes.

Meaning he was never caught out.

As I looked through the names of the great artists whose works he'd forged, I was astounded at the scope of his compositions. Only the artist's names were listed; his copies, which were hanging on walls all over the world, weren't shown. After all, who'd want to remind anyone that their prized Martin Johnson Herde or Picasso was a forgery?

I was sure he would have fooled me, along with everyone else. And, he had. No paper trail, or fake provenance was assigned to any of his paintings. They spoke for themselves, and the experts gobbled them up.

Only one detail was missing: his current whereabouts. At the time all of this went down, Chimini was living in a small town in Maine. It's cold winters and short summers probably got the best of him. Eventually, he just disappeared. Where to was the question?

That was something I could find out with one phone call. Well, Ana, Marina's assistant, could.

I replaced the books I'd been looking through and walked outside into the bright sunshine of St. James Square, clicking on my cell phone as I headed toward the bus stop.

Ana answered on the first ring. "MDP Investigations," she said.

"It's me, Ana," I replied. "I need a small favor."

"Nicky," she exclaimed. "Anything for you, Luv." Her voice turned make-believe sultry. "You know that."

I wasn't sure Marina would agree, but I made my request anyway.

"That shouldn't take too long. I'll get back to you in a jiff," she said and clicked off.

I'd owe her the next time I was at Gatwick's Duty-Free shop.

* * *

A few minutes later, I had an address for Luke Chimini in Bath. He wasn't trying to hide. Why would he? He currently sold art as his own reproductions and included the real artist's signature on many of the works. It wasn't a fraud. Not unless someone represents a copy as the original, which he wasn't doing. *At least,* I thought, *until the Gentileschi.*

Chimini wanted the world to believe he'd pulled a blinder over his art forgery career and that going legit, or sort of, meant nobody was after him. Something he thought of as a sure thing, which, as we all know, is laughable.

Chapter Twenty-Four

Bath was one of the most beautiful cities in England. Marina and I had gone there for a long weekend and explored as much of it as possible. A world heritage site, it's built along the River Avon. Ancient Roman world-famous hot springs and the thermal waters of their baths tempted visitors and were layered among historic homes like The Circus, where, according to Ana, Luke Chimini was a freeholder of a Georgian townhouse at number seven.

The Circus consisted of thirty homes, arranged in a perfect circle with three separate entrances. Pricey for sure, but with the money Chimini had made with his forgeries, he could afford the house and an extravagant lifestyle. I decided I'd like to see his home for myself.

I called Marina's cell, and it went straight to voicemail. "Hi," I began, I'm going to Bath, following a lead. I should be home in time for dinner. Don't worry. I won't get into any trouble."

Undoubtedly, Ana had mentioned that I'd asked for a favor, and Marina already knew where I was going and why. At Paddington station, I caught the next straight-through train to Bath, which would get me there by lunchtime.

As the train left the city and moved through the English countryside, I opened Mr. Chimini's website and viewed his current offerings. There was a beautiful Matisse of a woman with red hair sitting on a settee with bright flowers in front of her. It reminded me of Marina.

I pulled out my cell and punched in the number on his contact page. I hoped he was at home and would pick up.

After two rings, he did. "Luke Chimini," he answered in a low baritone.

I was ready. "Hello. My name is Nick Donahue, and I'm interested in purchasing one of your paintings." I'd almost said one of your fake Matisses but caught myself in time.

I continued. "I'm going to be in Bath at lunchtime, and I was hoping we could meet to discuss the painting." I paused. "It'd be my pleasure to take you to lunch."

I'd metered my tone and hoped I sounded like a serious buyer and not like a first-timer at the Blackjack table. "Can you suggest somewhere we could meet?"

He could and he did. We agreed to meet at 1:00 p.m. at The Blue Bird Café. I looked up the address and it was close to The Circus, where he lived. After lunch, I would ask to see the painting and get a look at his home. I'd inquire about the prices for his pieces and eventually, get around to discussing my love of Artemisia Gentileschi and see where that led me.

Chimini famously said that people see what they want to see, and buyers believe what they want to believe. If that were the case, I'd have to make him see me as a person hungry for a Gentileschi and a buyer who could afford one. That's if he didn't laugh in my face.

* * *

The Blue Bird Café did a lovely lunch, as our housekeeper, Mrs. Carmichael, would say. Set on a side street filled with small shops, it had an artisanal feel with fresh organic food that seemed appropriate for Bath. A décor of wood, glass, and plants and pottery added a homey touch. After a crisp salad, homemade toasted bread, and a glass of Inspector Remorse Porter, the talk turned to art.

"I'm sure you know who I am, Mr. Donahue," Chimini said, getting straight to the point. A tall man with silver-gray hair, piercing blue eyes, and a thin, narrow face, I'd recognized him on sight. He was dressed casually, with a loose, white linen shirt, khaki pants, and sneakers. Still, I was glad I'd opted for business casual. I was the buyer, after all.

"Yes," I replied, dipping my head in his direction, "your reputation precedes you." I was still going for cultured Nick, not Blackjack Nick. It was more complicated than you might have imagined.

"So, which of my reproductions are you interested in?"

I shot my cuffs and sat up straighter. I noticed Cimini was careful how he phrased his question. "The Matisse of the woman with red hair in the purple robe," I replied. "It reminds me of my girlfriend," I added with a sheepish grin.

He probably thought I was some romantic fool trying to win over a woman. That was fine with me.

Chimini pushed his chair back from the table and reached for the check. I stopped him.

"No, please, this is on me."

He shrugged in assent. "I live close by. Why don't we walk over, and you can have a look at the canvas?"

It was about a ten-minute walk to The Circus. Seeing the area in real time was impressive. His house, number 7, was a few buildings from the east entrance. Since all the houses faced straight ahead, he had a magnificent view of the green in the middle.

At the front door, he bent down and retrieved a key from under a small stone. He must trust his neighbors, or maybe his reputation had preceded him, and they just kept away.

The four-story house had high ceilings and was furnished in a clean, modern style. It was decorated with paintings on every wall and over the fireplace on the entry floor. I recognized some of the more famous ones, especially the Van Goghs. I wondered how many copies of those he'd sold as the real deal and who owned them.

I followed him as he walked through the lounge and down a long hallway with a curved wooden staircase to the left that led to the upper floors. "My studio is in the back of the house," he said and led the way. "The Matisse is there."

He flipped on a light, and I stood there stunned. Paintings lined the walls from top to bottom, and several works in progress rested against easels in the middle of the large room. To my mind, it was like having a representation of the best art in the world all in one place. Too bad it was all fake.

Even so, a "wow" escaped my lips, and Cimini smiled. "Please have a seat." He pointed toward a settee along the wall where we entered. "Let me show you the painting you're interested in."

He touched a switch on the wall opposite, which opened a door concealed by stripped wallpaper and held several paintings. The door swung open and led to what I assumed was a large storage closet. He stepped in and, a moment later, emerged with the Matisse replica in hand.

My view was limited, but I wondered how many of those were stacked up inside that space. Well, I guessed he could sell as many copies as he had buyers. And always paint more.

He handed me the painting. His woman in the purple coat was stunning. The colors rich and glowing, the anemones on the table in front spilling over each other in a burst of light and shadow. It looked just like a real Matisse. Or so I thought. I knew Marina would love it. Of course, I was going to buy it, and I had a feeling it was going to cost me big time for this 20" x 24" piece of replica art. It was a good thing I'd been winning at the casino.

I had to buy in for my plan to obtain a Gentileschi to succeed. It was the only way he'd take my request seriously.

Chimini offered me tea, which I accepted, and we sat down to discuss price. I didn't haggle with him and managed to suppress a gulp at the thirty-five-hundred-dollar price tag. He quoted me dollars instead of pounds not surprisingly assuming I was an American. I nodded in agreement and pulled out my credit card.

While Chimini carefully wrapped the painting for me to take home, which I insisted upon—he had my real name, but he didn't need to know where I lived—I began to speak about how much I would love to be able to purchase a work of art created by the actual painter.

"Nothing against your craft," I said with a smile, "but it's always been a dream of mine to own an original masterpiece." I halted briefly. "I recently heard of a rediscovered Artemisia Gentileschi, two in fact, a 'Weeping Mary Magdalene' and a 'Lucretia' that have come on the market. I can't imagine how expensive either would be...but still." I raised my eyebrow and stopped to gauge his reaction.

"Two?" he replied, swiveling around to face me. "Where did you hear that?" he demanded, his bright blue eyes drawing together and causing his face to crease into a frown. Was it surprise I saw, or anger?

I'd upped the ante, and he'd more than matched it.

Chapter Twenty-Five

"Two!" Marina's hands flew up toward the ceiling. "Why did you tell him there were two paintings?" She sounded annoyed as she shook her head at me, completely ignoring the Matisse I brought her as a gift.

"I figured he'd already painted the copy of the 'Weeping Magdalene' that's now being touted as a fake and that he'd be extremely interested to know more about the 'Lucretia.'"

"There is no new rediscovered 'Lucretia' on the market," she said, her tone more exasperated. "The only original was sold a few years ago."

"I know that—I'd done my research—but he may not." I thought he'd be pissed that the gang had kept him in the dark about another rediscovered painting, and wondering if they were shafting him.

"After Chimini masked his surprise, his questions became very pointed. 'Are you sure about this?' 'Any idea who owns the paintings?' 'Have you seen them yourself?' He kept speaking about them as if there were two, being cagey. I gave him vague replies and non-committal answers.

"By then, I was certain he was the forger for the team running the con." I paused. "I could see he was angry at the thought of the gang cutting him out of another original Gentileschi. One that could provide an additional payday.

"I'm sure the minute I left his home, he was on the phone to whoever hired him for the 'Weeping Mary Magdalene' job."

"I'm not sure I like this, Nick. You used your real name. It wouldn't be hard for him to find you…us." Her eyes clouded over with anxiety. "That was not wise."

I nodded. "That's why we're going to call Nigel and ask him to help. I know this is your case, but we could use his team to work on the Chimini aspect. It could be something Interpol would be interested in."

To my way of thinking, colluding in stealing a priceless work of art and creating a duplicate billed as the actual painting was forgery and had to come with major jail time.

Nigel Phillips was a good friend and our go-to spymaster, well, the King's. He was a bigwig in MI6. How big would always remain a mystery. He had access to all kinds of operatives and intelligence that we mere mortals did not. The kind that had kept us from being killed in Monte Carlo when mob boss, Tommy 'B' Bonnannaio, had murder on his mind, not to mention helping us take down the Salafi cell in Dubai, saving our butts, and the world from a weapon of mass destruction. Of course, his efforts, altruistic as they might have been, came with a Knighthood.

If these were the spymaster missions that he could speak about, Nigel would dine out on them for years. However, his actions were all top secret. Only a few of us knew some of what he had accomplished.

Marina, smart woman that she is, agreed that Nigel would be an asset. She would call him in the morning and set up a meeting.

I finally realized that the flat was quiet and that we were alone. "Where are Simone and Alex?" I asked.

"They left a note and said they were spending the day in Brighton and would stay overnight.

"We have some alone time." She smiled at me, finally relaxing into the softness of our couch and picking up the Matisse I'd given her. "It's lovely, Nick," she said, reaching for my hand and pulling me down beside her. As we snuggled, I asked about her interview with Jose Bidenstock.

"We met in Gabi's gallery, where the rest of the paintings from the Italian, Spanish, and French Masters were already in place. It was weird to see one empty space on the wall surrounded by all those other magnificent pieces of art. It was like an open window without a view. A view Jose Bidenstock was standing in front of.

"Or, I should say blocking. Jose is a big guy." She puffed out her chest and pulled her shoulders up. "He looks more like a linebacker than someone who deals with art, but since he's the one who moves the art around the galleries and installs it, heft is a plus."

Her eyes focused inward as she continued. "He has café au lait skin set off by such dark eyes they seemed to absorb all the light around him, making it hard for me to read his thoughts. He was wearing an Arsenal team tee-shirt and baggy jeans. I think he exaggerated his Jamaican accent to throw me off. With a head full of dreads pulled back and tied at his neck, he didn't seem like your typical New London Arts Museum worker."

I thought of the impeccable Gabi and her assistant, Mia. "Well, he does all the heavy lifting," I said. "He doesn't have to be chic."

"You're right, but that's not it. It wasn't just his clothes that were casual. It was his attitude. He came off as a little cocky, with lots of implied shrugging and evasive replies as he answered my questions about the Gentileschi. Of course, he'd seen it and was waiting for Jonathan to finish with the restoration before he could install it. That kind of thing."

"Do you think he's the Second Inside Man?" I asked her.

"It's a strong possibility, but I'm not sure yet. Bidenstock needs further looking into. I asked Nikki to do a thorough background check on him, and to recheck everyone who's had contact with the Gentileschi, including the two major players, Billings and Manning."

"Even Gabi?"

Marina nodded slowly.

No one was above suspicion, I thought. I wanted to know if that included me.

"What's our next move?" I asked.

"I'd like to know more about Mia and Cargill's relationship. Why is she involved with someone so dodgy?"

"Love," I ventured. "Or sex?" *Or maybe money?* I thought.

"From what your Dad said about his firm, I don't trust him. He could be using her to feed paintings to Windsor Smythe." She cocked her head and looked at the Matisse, which she'd placed next to her. "I have to find out how much is real and, more importantly, how much is fake."

With Ana and Nikki conducting a deep dive into all The New London's employees, and Marina planning her strategy for when the Meade and Medina people and their lawyers arrive, I thought I'd take on that task.

"Let me handle that," I said, holding up my hand before she could protest. "I'll be discreet." The look on her face said she wasn't convinced that was possible.

Chapter Twenty-Six

Marina had already left to meet with Gabi and New London's solicitors. They were preparing for the pushback from the Meade and Medina attorneys arriving the next day.

I had my laptop up and running and was flexing my fingers like a piano player getting ready to play a concerto when my cell beeped, flashing Marc Rivers' number across the top.

"Are you jonesing for more Blackjack already?" I asked, laughing into the phone.

"I wish," Marc replied. I'd rather be in London than fighting off the sharks who are giving me a hard time about a new property I'm trying to buy."

"How much of the city do you already own?"

"Not enough. But that's not the reason I called. My friend who dropped a dime on the lovely Natalie Stapleton had more information to share."

I wondered how much Marc was paying for her help. Or maybe he was gifting her a new apartment, rent-free.

Marc continued. "They were partying at a very private club in SoHo— think mega big celebs like Gaga, and high-level politicians, like Hizzoner— when Natalie let it slip that she and her new boyfriend, BriBri, were leaving for London the next day for a very important business trip that could net her a lot of money."

"I think she's in the wrong profession, "I replied. "For a Shill, she seems to have a very big mouth. Or maybe she's just dumb." I paused and shook my head even though Marc couldn't see it. "Is that what she calls him? BriBri?"

"Apparently so," Marc replied with snark. "Anyway, if Colabello finds out she's been giving out TMI, he won't be pleased."

Marc's voice lowered. "This is the kind of thing that can make a con go sideways fast." His tone became more serious, "And someone could get hurt before, or even if it gets back on track.

"Watch out for Marina, Nick. I know she's fierce and likes to get close to the action. Don't let anything happen to her. And tell your friend, Gabi, to watch her back. Let's keep each other posted. We'll talk soon."

After Marc rang off, I remembered something my Grandpa Robert, who'd lived through World War II, told me he used to say when he wanted to keep something secret, "Loose lips sink ships. Don't forget that, Nick."

These people were dangerous. And, with seven million dollars on the line, they were playing for keeps.

I'd tell Marina about Marc's call and his warning. But if there was one sure thing I could bet on, I knew she wouldn't back off.

* * *

It was time to begin my deep dive into Clive Hastings Cargill. I'd already done a cursory Facebook and Google search on him and Oxford Alliance Ltd. There were the usual links you'd expect and some photos with buddies of his, one of whom I'd 'friended.' I'd rethought that ploy.

I needed to go deeper. Following him at lunchtime had yielded the surprising info that Cargill was somehow connected to Mia Fondsworth, although friend or foe hadn't been exactly clear. Well, except for the kiss, which was confusing. Now, it was time to make sure the odds were in my favor.

Marina's company used the LexusNexus service to gather information on people involved in her cases. I had her passcode, which gave me access to the reporting data and, more importantly, the information I was looking for. I logged on, typed in Cargill's name, and waited for the report to load. It didn't take long.

As I scrolled through the information, I found the evidence I'd hoped for. Clive Hastings Cargill didn't have a stellar reputation. Hedge Funds in the

UK are more strictly regulated than in the United States. As a manager at Oxford Alliance Ltd, a license was mandatory to sell stocks and financial instruments. Unfortunately for him, he'd never gotten one. He'd also filed for bankruptcy a few years before joining the company, which, given the apparent laissez-faire management style of the firm, Windsor Smythe either didn't know about or didn't care. These 'black marks' should have precluded him from working for the firm and managing any of their clients or anyone else's money.

As information continued to load onto my laptop, I discovered Cargill owned a tony high-rise flat on the south bank of the Thames. His neighborhood was snootier and pricier than Mia's, and he was the freeholder, along with his wife, Caroline Wickham Cargill, to whom he'd been married for five years.

He was a cheater. And in more ways than one. I wondered if Mia knew he was married. From the scene I'd witnessed on Canary Wharf, I suspected she did. I also questioned if he was involved in the Gentileschi fraud and if he had involved her in that, as well.

It was time to find this guy who'd stalked me at the casino and Fortnum's and turn the tables on him.

I looked at the city map for Southwark and found a few pubs near his home. I planned to head to the Assembly House, which would give me a great view of his building right next door.

Initially, I was going to go for surprise. But then I thought I'd make him sweat a bit. I called Oxford Alliance Ltd and asked for him.

The disbelief in his voice was apparent. "Mr. Donahue…uuh Nick, what can I do for you?" he asked.

I paused for a moment before answering. "I have a proposition for you that your company might be interested in."

I wish I could see the look on his face as he answered. Suspicious? Pondering? Alarmed? "What might that be?"

"Why don't we meet after work at your local, The Assembly House, next to your building? We can discuss it then."

I thought he was going to turn me down. Or at least ask how I knew where he lived. Instead, he agreed. He didn't seem to mind that I also knew where he drank. "Sure. How about 6:00 pm?"

"See you then," I replied, pausing before I added, "By the way, maybe Mia would like to join us, or your wife if she's free." I clicked off before he could respond. He'd have all afternoon to wonder what this was about.

I was sure I'd be able to whip up something tasty to wet Cargill's appetite.

Chapter Twenty-Seven

"Is this what you meant by being discreet? Meeting with Cargill at his local? And, asking him to bring along Mia, and hey, while you're at it, why not your wife?" Her words poured out like a stream of white water raging downriver. I could only hope they'd hit a giant rock and slow down long enough for me to respond. "Oh, Nick." The frustration in her voice was as thick as a London fog.

This wasn't the reaction I'd expected when I called to explain my plan to Marina.

"It will be fine," I replied. "I'm sure Cargill won't invite his wife or Mia to join us." At least, I hoped not. "I'll just float some thoughts about how coming clean about Oxford Alliance Ltd.'s plans regarding Hamilton Capital could benefit his career. Or, on the other hand, could sink it. I'm not sure if he'll admit the company's plotting some scam, but if he's scared enough, he might twig to it.

"Then, I'll mention Mia and see how much he knows about the Gentileschi. I suspect she might have confided in him, even if just out of worry for her job."

Marina sighed deeply and long. "You're a regular Sherlock Holmes, aren't you?" I was glad I couldn't see her face. I imagined it was scrunched into a snarl.

I changed the subject. "So, how is it going with the Meade and Medina people and their lawyers?" I asked.

"About as well as you'd expect. So far, blame and recriminations are flying back and forth like a traveler trying to rack up bonus miles." She paused.

"They are adamant they sent the genuine Gentileschi, which, at this point, we know they did. Not that anyone at The New London Arts Museum will admit that.

"They want the board of directors to cough up the insurance money and an additional payment for all the bad publicity their Gallery is receiving. The only hope is to find the original painting as quickly as possible and the person who stole it."

I refrained from telling her again that I thought whoever had replaced it with a fake had stored it somewhere in the museum itself. The more I thought about it, the more sense it made. I could be wrong, but I didn't think so.

"To make matters worse," she continued, "the once anonymous owner, Brian Ahern, has come forward. He and his gal pal, Natalie Stapleton, are in England and are planning to join the discussion next time the board meets."

I could hear the frustration in her voice, and I didn't want to add to her worries, but it was crucial to tell her what Marc Rivers imparted.

"Marina, I said calmly, "Marc called today, and the news isn't good." I let that sink in for a minute. "He found out that Ahern's girlfriend was at a very upscale club and was very drunk. She started blabbing to Marc's contact about coming to London with her boyfriend and cashing in on a big deal. They'll be at the meeting tomorrow. I have a feeling Ahern will make a big show of the forgery, no doubt egged on by the girlfriend.

"He wanted me to warn you to be extra careful. Gabi, too. These are very dangerous people who won't stop at anything to get what they want. He said it could get ugly if this breaks bad for them."

Marina kept her voice calm and low. "That's good to know. I'm prepared, and I'll watch over Gabi. The more I think about it, the more I'm convinced she has nothing to do with the con.

"We're regrouping with all parties concerned in ten minutes, so I need to ring off. The museum's Exhibits Director, Lloyd Bennings, is participating, as well. He's finally taking an interest, which I find suspicious."

She didn't sound happy at the prospect.

"Is he on your list of possible suspects?" I asked.

"He is now. The rank of Exhibits Director doesn't automatically preclude him from being a thieving scumbag. He's responsible for the poor security, whether by omission or commission, remains to be seen." Her voice had turned hard. One of the signs she was becoming angry. "He's also very chummy with the Royals, which could be a problem pegging him as a suspect. He has a stellar reputation, at least on paper, and has consulted with the King on the Royal Collection at Windsor Castle. He may be status-rich and cash poor, which can be a motive for thievery. We should know more soon. Ana and Nikki have shared up our suspects, and I believe Ana drew the short straw with him."

I sensed a slight lightning in her tone. "See you tonight after you meet with Cargill."

Cargill wasn't the only reprobate on my mind. Chimini was also on the list. I'd check in with Nigel later this evening to see if his people had discovered anything more. Or if the former forger had contacted George Colabello, who we were sure was the Grifter. I'd bet a stack of chips he had. I smiled to myself. I'd riled him up pretty good. Now, I'd have to see if it paid off.

Chapter Twenty-Eight

J ust as I was about to leave to meet Cargill, the door burst open, and Simone and Alex flew into the lounge carrying an armful of packages. "Nick! Hi, how are you?" Simone didn't give me time to reply, just launched into details of their stay in Brighton. "We had a wonderful time. We visited the Royal Pavilion, the seaside resort of King George IV. His father was George III, the Mad King, who was married to Queen Charlotte, just like in *Bridgerton.*"

I nodded, even though I had no idea what she was talking about, but she continued undaunted. "It is so beautiful." She glanced up at Alex. "I wouldn't mind living there."

"In your dreams." He smiled at her and took over the convo like he'd been doing it for years instead of months. "We also had fun at the Palace Pier. You must have been there."

I nodded. I had, and it was fun.

Alex continued. "So, you know it's filled with rides, games, food stalls, plus hordes of people." His voice dipped at the last mention. I knew Alex didn't like being in crowds unless they were his fellow bankers, but he'd made an exception to make sure Simone was happy. He was being a good husband. Probably learned that from Dad, as well.

"I see you made time for shopping, too." I pointed to the bags they'd dropped at their feet. I recognized some of the logos on the shopping bags, but some were new to me, like Wolf and TOAST. Simone's style was what I'd call classic. Simple and elegant, and she always looked great.

"We did." Alex scrunched up his face, probably thinking of all the money they'd spent. "But it was worth it. And we met a great couple from Manhattan, Brian Ahern and his fiancée Natalie Stapleton. Natalie had never been to England before and wanted to stop in Brighton to see the Royal Pavilion."

Simone nodded and said, "It was gorgeous."

Alex continued. "They said they were planning to head to London this afternoon to check out some of the new art galleries and museums. He's a collector. We decided to travel together on the train to Paddington, and we're going to meet them later for dinner at Manju's. Brian said it's the best Indian restaurant in the city. Do you know it?"

I looked from Simone to Alex, trying to keep my expression neutral and my mouth from dropping open while they related their story. They'd been targeted for sure by Natalie, who'd found out they were related to me—probably from George Colabello—and, by extension, close to Marina.

For once, I was at a loss for words. "So, where did you meet them?" I finally stammered.

"At the bumper cars on the Palace Pier. Natalie and I kept bumping into each other, and we started laughing and couldn't stop." Simone paused. "After the ride was over, we started chatting and realized we all lived in Manhattan. It was one of those weird connections that happen from time to time," she added.

"Those two hit it off," Alex said, gesturing to Simone, "so we're having dinner tonight."

"That's nice," I replied, nodding at him easily while wanting to throw up and punch Natalie Stapleton in her lying face. Alex had no idea about the forged Gentileschi and the couple's involvement. This was bad. Worse than bad.

"Do you know where they're staying?" I asked, hoping I sounded casual. I'd have to get this information to Marina immediately.

"At the Peninsula Hotel in Belgravia." Simone raised her eyebrows in awe. "I Googled it and it's one of the city's most expensive and modern hotels."

No doubt, I thought. I was sure Natalie knew how to play her cards right. Especially when it came to her Mark, BriBri.

Simone must have seen the troubled look that flew across my face. "But we love staying with you and Marina," she said. "It's so much nicer to be here than in any hotel."

My head was throbbing. I couldn't let Simone and Alex see how upsetting this news was. I looked at my watch. "Glad you guys had fun, but I have an appointment. Enjoy yourselves at dinner, and we'll see you later."

Once I was outside, I walked around the corner and sent Marina a 911 text. It was our signal that something momentously bad was happening. Like losing every cent I owned at the casino. Only, this was worse. It seemed like hours instead of minutes before she called back, and I was able to tell her what was going on.

"Nick, stay calm. I'll send someone to cover the restaurant and keep an eye on Simone and Alex. I have a contact at the Peninsula who can report what Natalie and Brian are up to and if they get any visitors.

"Marina, he's my brother…if anything happened to him…"

"I promise," it won't. It's the gang's way of letting us know they know we're on to them. It's their insurance."

"Okay," I said, my voice shaky as a gambler about to make his first bet. "I'll trust you on this."

"Good. Our meeting is almost over. We haven't made any progress. The art expert from New York, Jerome Benedict, and the authenticator from London, Tamara Capitani, have very different opinions on what could have happened." She paused. "They pulled out their respective copies of all the tests they'd done on the painting they initially examined, including the AI report, carbon dating, and X-rays that showed the under-painting. It all pointed to the Gentileschi being an original. Neither could explain how or when it was switched for what they were looking at now.

"They all seem to be forgetting that Jonathan Hudson is a casualty, murdered by whoever did this. "This is more than art forgery and theft." She paused. "I believe whoever stole the painting is also responsible for his murder. We need to find that person or persons and put them away."

I couldn't miss the bitter tone in her words. I know she meant to be reassuring, but it made me worry more about Alex and Simone.

"Don't you have your meeting with Cargill soon?"

"I'd better get going," I said.

"Make him sweat, Nick. Then wring him out to dry."

That was my girl. Ice in her veins when she needed it. And fire in her soul to match.

Chapter Twenty-Nine

I Ubered to The Assembly House pub on Kentish Town Road and sat near the window where I could watch for Cargill's approach. It was a typical English pub, homey and inviting, with a wood-topped bar, plank flooring, and a skylight. A large selection of canned and bottled local beers was displayed on the back bar amongst bottles of premium liquor. A chalkboard advertised the daily specials, which I was sure we wouldn't be ordering.

A few minutes later, Cargill slouched along and entered. He had the look of a scared rabbit, but the moment he saw me, he shifted into defensive mode, lifting his head and pulling his shoulders back. He tried to tough it out, like a pit boss staring me down when I was winning. It never worked then. And it didn't work now.

"What the hell do you want, Donahue?" he asked as he took a seat opposite me.

"Hello, guys," a waiter said, arriving at our table and interrupting Cargill mid-rant. "What can I get you?"

We both ordered beers, and I took over the conversation once he was gone.

"I think you've got that backward," I replied. "What do you want? Or should I say, what does Oxford Alliance Ltd want?"

"I...I don't know what you're talking..."

I cut him off. "First of all, what's their real interest in Hamilton Capital? Anyone who'd done their research would know their clients are not interested in investing in art. Why the push?"

For a moment, I didn't think he'd answer me, and I thought he might get up and leave. He didn't have to speak with me, but he sensed there might be trouble if he didn't.

Before he replied, he glanced around the busy pub, making sure no one was listening. All the other patrons were engrossed in their own conversations. He took his time answering, and I sensed he was trying to tell me as little as he could get away with.

"My boss, Windsor Smythe, thought Hamilton Capital would be an easy sell." He shrugged. "You know, a good firm with rich clients who appreciate the finer things in life."

"What could possibly have made him believe that?"

"Research," he replied too quickly.

I pinned him with my eyes. He was lying. "Try harder," I demanded. "Or, there'll be consequences you'll regret."

He took a swig of his beer, put it down, and looked even more defeated.

"Well," I said, "what's it going to be?" I took out my cell and asked Siri for the number of the FCA. I started to punch it in, but Cargill begged me to stop.

"Wait…please." Sweat had broken out on his forehead, and I knew I had him.

He looked even more defeated. "I, umm, think someone from Hamilton Capital may have mentioned it at a party or an event." He paused. "I'm not sure. Something like that."

It was another shock to my system. Was there a traitor at Dad's firm? Who would go behind his back to deal with someone like Windsor Smythe?

I kept my expression neutral as I continued. "So, would their investments be used to purchase works of art that would be held until your company could move them at a profit and reinvest that money on behalf of Hamilton Capital?"

"Yes, that's it," he replied excitedly, his voice rising as if he'd wormed his way out of a hole.

I shook my head slowly. "I don't think so. I do think that Windsor Smythe would never use any investment from Hamilton Capital to purchase genuine art. For our money, you might show us a few masterpieces, probably excellent forgeries. The same paintings you'd shop around to attract other investors to a mirror portfolio." I thought about Luke Chimini and all the paintings lining his studio walls.

I drummed my fingers on the table to punctuate my point. "If Hamilton Capital wanted to, say, liquidate their portfolio and take their money out, they would find it would be gone in some catastrophic blip or market downturn that couldn't have been foreseen. It seems to me that's what's called a Ponzi scheme." I paused. "Am I right? What do you think?"

Cargill had turned as red as a man about to have a stroke while I was talking. And, I wasn't finished yet.

"I know you don't have the required license to work as a Hedge Fund Manager, which your thieving boss has most likely conveniently overlooked. I'm sure the FCA regulatory commission would be interested in knowing this. All I have to do is hit send." I waved my phone under his nose.

"Then there's the question of Mia Fondsworth and her position at The New London Arts Museum." His brown eyes were now flickering with fear. "Have you ensnared her in your little scheme and caused her to become a partner in a crime?"

He was shaking his head from side to side like a ball on a string. "No, no," he said. "I would never do that to her. I...I care about her. And," he gulped, "I think she cares about me."

I wanted to say there's the little matter of your wife, but didn't.

He looked down into his nearly empty mug. "I was at a pub in Shoreditch with some work pals and got to talking with Mia. She lives nearby, and I offered to walk her home. One thing led to another..." He trailed off.

I had no actual proof that he'd used the Gentileschi to entangle Mia into his firm's Ponzi scheme, or if Mia was working the con as the Second Inside Man. That would take a little more probing.

All I knew was that we couldn't trust her, and we'd have to let Gabi know about her ties to Cargill and his firm.

Cargill finished his beer and stood up to leave. "What are you going to do?" he asked me, his voice shaking with anxiety.

"I'm not sure yet," I replied. "I'll let you know when I decide." It was not the answer he wanted. But the only one he was going to get.

I watched him leave the pub, more worried and downtrodden than when he entered. Then, I paid the bill and headed home.

Chapter Thirty

Marina was waiting for me in the kitchen, working on preparing dinner, which smelled delicious.

"Taste," she said, offering a spoonful of her Chicken Cacciatore sauce.

"It's very spicy…but delicious," which was the correct response even as I turned away and waved my hand in front of my mouth to cool off my palate.

"I called your parents, and they'll join us for dinner in about an hour. "She held up the wooden spoon she'd been using to stir the sauce like it was a baton.

I poured two glasses of Brunello wine and handed one to Marina. "I have a lot of information for Dad—not all of it good—and I'll tell you when they're here, so I don't have to repeat it."

"Your meeting was that good, huh?" She put her finger under my chin and tipped my face up to hers.

"There might be a traitor working in the firm," I said, holding out my hand. "If there is, it will be hard for Dad to accept."

Her beautiful green eyes opened wide in surprise as I spoke, and she saw the disappointment on my face.

"Okay, Nick, we'll discuss it with him. But you know your father. He's strong and honest, and he'll be able to figure this out."

We had a while to wait for my parents, and I moved outside to the deck with my delicious, ruby-red Tuscan wine. Before joining me, Marina checked on the chicken simmering on our classic AGA stove.

I took her hand in mine and asked, "So, what's on the agenda for tomorrow?"

A small, derisive 'humph' escaped her throat. "We'll be starting late, at eleven-thirty, to give the new arrivals from New York time to rest and gather their thoughts before meeting," she said sarcastically. "We're the only ones who know they've been in England for a few days. It's not something we can share."

I was sure she was thinking of Simone and Alex.

"*Puttana*," She spat out in Italian, which did not need a translation.

"Any new suspects?" I asked.

"Everyone. The people from New York are still front and center. Also, Mia Fondsworth, Jose Bidenstock, Stella Manning, Dame Rosemary, and Lloyd Bennings." She took a big gulp of wine. "Suspects for Jonathan's murder, too. It's a nightmare, Nick."

"I'm not sure you have to worry about—" The sound of the doorbell chiming cut off my words.

"That must be your parents. I'll get it."

* * *

Everything that had happened with Cargill, Simone, and Alex was weighing heavily on me. I felt the need to tell both my parents the whole story.

After I hugged them, I asked them to sit, handed each of them a glass of the Brunello, and explained what was on my mind. It was time to let Mom in on the account of the long con that was playing out around us.

The hardest part was telling them the gang had tricked Alex and Simone.

Marina, who had regained her composure, spoke softly as she sat opposite my parents. "Elizabeth, Michael. I know it will be futile to tell you not to worry, but I promise you will be safe."

"Where are Simone and Alex?" Mom asked apprehension evident in her words as she looked around the apartment as if expecting them to appear. "Are they still in Brighton?" Her voice rose. "Shouldn't they be here?"

Marina shifted her gaze to my Mom, who was trying to take it all in. "There are some things you aren't aware of, and I think it's time you should

111

be."

I took up the conversation and told them about the fake Gentileschi at The New London Arts Museum, the murder of the young restorer, and the people in the con who were responsible for all this. Dad already knew most of it. But when I finished, Mom looked like she was in shock.

Protecting her family, her immediate reaction. "What about Simone and Alex?" she asked again, looking at each of us in turn.

Marina replied. "One of the people running the con, the Shill, a young woman named Natalie Stapleton, arranged it so that she and the Mark would 'accidentally' meet Simone and Alex in Brighton. She'd 'befriended' the Mark in New York and made herself indispensable to him." Marina's mouth pulled tight. "His name is Brian Ahern, and he's very wealthy. Brian Ahern is the victim here. He believes the Gentileschi he purchased was an original 'Weeping Mary Magdalene' that has now been switched for a fake by New London. Alex and Simone are having dinner with them this evening.

Mom was shaking her head from side to side. "Oh my God! How could this happen?" she asked.

The short answer was that there was no way we could have known they'd target Simone and Alex, but she wouldn't want to hear that.

"Nick, you have to keep them safe…he's your baby brother."

Marina reached over and took her hand. "We, Nick and I, will make sure of that. I have top-notch people watching Simone and Alex, and nothing will happen to them. Or, to you."

"What about those people that Dad met with?" Mom pinned me with her eyes. "The hedge fund group? Are they part of this, too?"

"I've been looking into them." I hesitated before I continued. I had done what she'd asked me to, but I didn't want to worry her further. "I met with one of the employees earlier this evening. "We don't believe they're involved.

"Although we aren't a hundred percent sure. It seems to me they're running a Ponzi scheme." I paused and took a deep breath. "One of them intimated Hamilton Capital was targeted and that they were getting information from someone on the inside."

"What?" Dad jumped up from the armchair he'd been occupying. "Who?

Someone in London or in New York?"

"The guy I talked to, Cargill—you remember him from Fortnum's, right?—didn't know." I paused. "You'll have to think about who would be willing to betray the firm." *Who needs money and might be after your job,* I thought.

My parents looked overcome by news they hadn't expected to hear. Dad was shocked at the idea of betrayal, and Mom was worried about her family. Marina came to the rescue. She stood up and beckoned everyone to the table. "I made a special chicken recipe for dinner. You wouldn't want it to go to waste? We'll figure this out after we eat, okay?"

Along with good detective work, food was her cure for almost everything.

Chapter Thirty-One

Everyone was subdued for the rest of the evening. We discussed everything again and tried to reassure Mom and Dad that their family would be safe.

They stayed with us until Simone and Alex arrived home. Mom's relief was so intense that I was surprised Alex didn't take one look and demand to know what was wrong.

Instead, he launched into a blow-by-blow of their meal and their great time with their new friends. I wanted to poke him for being so self-absorbed. Unlike his older brother.

"I'm a little sad, though," Simone said. "Natalie and Brian have back-to-back gallery visits tomorrow, and then they're leaving first thing the next morning for Paris and Geneva. We won't spend any more time with them until we're all back in New York."

Natalie knew we'd gotten the gang's message: they could get to the family anytime they wanted. They wouldn't be a further threat to Alex and Simone. I hoped she wouldn't be too sad when she realized she'd never see the couple again.

Yippee, I thought, and did the internal happy dance I do when I win big at the casino.

Marina cut her eyes to my parents. "That's too bad," she said, ensuring Mom and Dad got the message and didn't give anything away.

In this case, ignorance was bliss, or at least safety, for the young marrieds.

"Hey," Alex said, turning toward our parental units. "We plan to take a day cruise on the Thames to Greenwich tomorrow and visit The Royal

Observatory. I'm looking forward to standing on the Prime Meridian Line with one foot in the eastern hemisphere and one in the western. We can also have lunch at one of the cafes nearby. Why don't you come with us?"

Before they could disagree, I piped up. "That's a great idea. A day on the water will be perfect." *And, you'll be away from prying eyes,* I thought.

Mom said yes before Dad could say no. "That will be lovely. Count us in." I knew she thought it was a good way to watch out for them.

Before my parents left, Marina pulled Dad aside and told him she'd have two former Special Forces friends on the boat and at each site they visited. They'd all be safe.

* * *

Alex and Simone headed for their bedroom. "Night," he said. "See you guys in the morning."

"Hey, Alex," I replied. "Thanks for including Mom and Dad in your plans for tomorrow."

"I was happy to. It will be fun."

Maybe he wasn't so self-absorbed as I imagined. He had Simone to think about, as well.

I sank into the couch and put my feet up on the coffee table, relieved that this day was over and grateful that my family was safe. "Thank you," I said to Marina. "For everything."

"Of course," she said with a smile and leaned over to kiss me. Then she became serious. "I want to speak with Gabi before the meeting tomorrow." She picked up her phone and sent her a text asking her to join us for breakfast.

"Nick, I want you to come to the meeting with me."

"I was planning to," I replied. "I want to see these thieves and liars face-to-face."

She nodded. "Good. I'm counting on your superior powers of observation," she smiled, then continued, "or your gambler's mojo to out the Second Inside Man or Woman."

115

With that, she rose and pulled me up. "I think it's time to turn in."

As we headed to our bedroom, we heard whispers and giggling from the guest room. *Ah, young love,* I thought, and pulled Marina close to me as we walked down the stairs in sync with each other. Old love wasn't bad, either.

Chapter Thirty-Two

Gabi knocked on our door at 8:00 a.m. and entered with a frown marring her beautiful face. "Did something else happen?" she blurted out, clutching her hands.

Marina reached for her and soothed our young neighbor. "Nothing we can't handle."

Gabi's expression said she didn't believe it. "Are you sure?"

Marina nodded and led Gabi to the dining table, where I was ready with a large pot of coffee. We had decided not to tell her about Alex and Simone's 'chance' meeting with Natalie and Ahern in Brighton or dinner last night. We wanted her to be calm and confident for the upcoming meeting.

I poured the coffee and took a seat between the two women. Marina began to speak. "As you know, Ahern and his girlfriend, Natalie Stapleton, will join us for the meeting." She paused. "I'm sure they'll push for The New London Arts Museum to pay the seven million dollars the painting is valued at, plus a ten percent fee in damages.

I know all the lawyers will argue about who's responsible for losing the original Gentileschi, assigning blame, and sticking the museum for the settlement."

She shook her head. "That is not going to happen…at least not today." She gazed at Gabi, who had her hands wrapped around her mug. She was staring into its depths like they might reveal the secrets of the universe. "We're going to push back against the experts, the lawyers, the gallery. And especially George Colabello and Natalie Stapleton."

"How do you plan to do that?" Gabi asked.

Marina cocked her head to the side and smirked just a little. "First, it's imperative that I sit next to Natalie, which I need you to arrange. "While everyone is 'discussing' who is responsible, etc., I plan to drop my phone right at her feet. Accidentally. When I bend down to pick it up, I'll make sure she sees several compromising photos of herself and George." Marina pulled up a very graphic shot of the couple, and a loud "Oh" escaped Gabi's lips. She looked at us in despair. "How could he betray our friendship like this?"

Marina's expression softened as she continued. "I'll keep the phone low and be very discreet." She paused and tossed me a glance, and I rolled my eyes. "I'll make sure she's the only one who sees the photos. If I'm right, she'll get the message in living color."

"Where did you get those?" both Gabi and I said at the same time. She hadn't shown the images to me, and I tried not to let her know I was a little miffed.

"I have my sources," she replied.

I bet, I thought. Marc Rivers had come through again.

"Do you think that will stop them?" Gabi asked. "It's just a few photos she could explain away."

"Maybe. But I don't think Natalie would want the whole room to see them. Especially Ahern. All I'd have to do is forward the images to everyone's cellphones."

If that happened, I could imagine the pinging and beeping around the table. It would cause quite a stir.

Marina licked her lips like a cat who'd just swallowed cream. "I think it will deter her, at least for a while, until she can regroup with her cohorts, especially Colabello. I guarantee she'll say she doesn't feel well. Or make some other excuse and look pleadingly at Ahern, who will insist they postpone the meeting.

"Gabi, that's when I want you to make a tremendous fuss about wasting everyone's time over this supposed forgery. Get their team riled up. Complain loudly and get really, really, angry. Push your chair back, stand up, and act like you're losing it. Tell them to get out. Scream as loud as you can." She hesitated before speaking again. "Will you be able to do that?"

Gabi, the quiet assistant director and curator, seemed to undergo a transformation. Her eyes turned inward, and her mouth clamped into a grim line before she answered. "It would be my greatest pleasure to toss each one of them out of my museum on their lying, thieving arses. As Nick would say, 'I'm all in.'"

It didn't look like she'd have a problem becoming angry. Colabello's duplicity had rocked her faith in their friendship.

Marina continued, "Once they're gone, tell your people it's pointless to continue the meeting without the New York people. Leave the room and ask me to join you in your office."

Marina turned to me. "Nick, this is where you come in. Please act like a pit boss who never stops watching. Get eyes on everyone on the museum's end, especially anyone who seems overly angry or furious about calling off today's meeting. Use your gambler's insight to find their tell. I hope it will give us a clue to who the Second Inside Man is."

Gabi nodded along to Marina's instructions to me. "I'm sorry, Gabi, that this is taking such a toll on you, but we're working on every angle, and we'll find out the truth."

And the real Gentileschi, I hoped.

* * *

Gabi left us and returned to her apartment, no doubt to catch Sydney up on the latest developments. The young women didn't deserve the misery of this scam interfering with their upcoming marriage. This should be a happy time for them. Not a disaster they had no part in creating.

Marina and I were alone, finishing our coffees and reviewing her plans for the meeting. "So, Marc came through again?" I asked. "Didn't he?"

"I didn't mention it because I wanted to see how you and Gabi would react. I expect the people in the room would be as shocked as the two of you were."

I stood and grabbed the coffee carafe, holding it up for a refill, which Marina declined. "I get it. It's a great ploy and one the gang deserves."

119

I sat at the table with a full cup of the rich Harrod's Blend 49 Coffee I'd become addicted to. I inhaled deeply, letting the aroma soothe my ego, and moved on.

"Is there any word from Nigel?"

"Yes, but not enough for any substantive action against Chimini." She waited a beat. "This is all pretty hush, hush, Nick."

She leaned forward conspiratorially. "They're tapping his phone, a rare occurrence in England. They need a special warrant to do so, and Nigel had to get the request approved by one of the Ministers. Thankfully, it's a friend who didn't ask too many questions."

"I'd expect no less." I knew my tone was sarcastic.

Marina matched it. "Shall I continue? Chimini's made several calls to the Meade and Medina Gallery in New York." She gave me a winning smile. "Paintings were mentioned, mostly in abstract terms. As in, which clients might be interested in a copy of a Picasso, a Rembrandt, or a Gentileschi, etc. He was fishing for information about the "Lucretia," I expect.

"Meade, who Chimini was chatting with, seemed a tad confused. He was careful in his response but told Chimini that there weren't any requests for new replicas of artworks. He'd be in Bath the day after tomorrow and see him at his studio. It's something, but Interpol and MI6 need more before they act."

"Will they be able to surveil them when they meet?" It would certainly help our case if we could definitively prove that Chimini had created the fake 'Weeping Magdalene.'

"That's the plan. They'll tape their conversation, and with any luck, have what they need to bring Chimini in, at least for questioning.

"Nigel also confirmed he has someone looking out for your family in addition to my guys." She took my hand in hers. "I don't want you to worry about them today. They are safe. Trust me."

I put my other hand over our clasped ones. Trusting her was the one thing I could always count on.

Chapter Thirty-Three

While Marina was reviewing and perfecting her plans for the meeting one last time, I took the opportunity to call Dad.

His phone beeped a few times before he answered. "We just boarded the boat at the Westminster Bridge stop and are getting settled in. London looks different from the water. It's nice to see it from this vantage point and imagine how it used to appear with quayside taverns and warehouses."

I knew he'd be taking it all in, imagining the history and the turbulence that once had been such a part of the city.

"Westminster is behind us, and we're just about to pass The London Eye." He paused. "I think we'll disembark at the Globe Theater on the way back and watch a performance. Mom and Simone want to see the Crown Jewels in the Tower. We'll be gone all day, and I'll need a big Scotch at the end of this. Wait, hold on." He put his hand over the microphone, and I could hear a muted voice in the background. "Nick," he said in an aside. "That was Mom." He lowered his voice. "She's still worried about everyone's safety. I can't spot the people Marina sent."

I could imagine him looking around furtively. "They're there, Dad. Stop searching. They're undercover." I emphasized the word. "That's the point." I didn't dare mention the people from MI6. If anyone from the gang was onboard, I didn't want them to notice the family's protection. "They'll go to wherever you go, the Globe and the Tower included.

"Tell that to your Mother." I could hear the frustration in his voice, and I imagined the shrug of his shoulders.

I already did, I wanted to say. But it was time to change the subject.

"We're leaving for New London in a few minutes. I'll fill you in after the meeting.

A more serious tone crept into Dad's words. "Nick, be careful.

"Always," I replied. The word flashed through my mind. I'd be like a hawk hovering over the meeting, swooping in if the atmosphere morphed from contentious to dangerous. And no one could stop me. Well, it was nice to dream.

* * *

The New London Arts Museum was housed in a stately four-story Georgian building close to the city's center. The outside still maintained its classic proportions of an Italian villa with quadruple chimneys easing out of its garret roof, but inside, it had been totally renovated into a modern, spacious open design plan with one gallery flowing into the next. Its white walls and natural lighting showcased the art to perfection. Gabi told us the unique design was meant to give the art 'room to breathe' and the viewer the 'space to take it in'. You couldn't miss the pride in her voice.

Marina and I arrived just shy of eleven thirty and asked for Gabi. After we entered the renovated 'piano nobile' on the first floor, we were again escorted to the private elevator that sped us to the third floor and into a large conference room, where Gabi greeted us and showed us to our seats around a large oval table.

All our 'suspects' were there. Well, almost all of them except for the two key players.

The Managing Director, Stella Manning, had decided to join us and took a seat at the top of the oval, defining her position as chief. She was flanked by Lloyd Bennings, Mia Fondsworth, Jose Bidenstock, and Dame Rosemary Harris. The museum's solicitor and Tamara Capitani, the London art expert, were further down the row. The opposition, as I'd taken to calling them, Meade and Medina, and company, were seated opposite.

On the other end, Gabi had left one open seat next to Brian Ahern's legal counsel and one on the other side of her for Natalie Stapeleton. Then came Marina and me. Marina claimed the seat next to what would be Natalie's, and I sat back in a second row behind Marina as an observer. Gabi had done exactly as we agreed and arranged the seating for Natalie to be between her and Marina.

Of course, the couple was late and arrived with much fanfare and many apologies. Gabi showed them to their seats and prepared to start the meeting. Natalie, who'd spared no expense—well, it was Ahern's money after all, was dressed in a very sexy, slinky dress with a double-wrapped belt sporting the double 'Gs' of a brand even I recognized. She settled herself with a loud huff and made it clear she was extremely miffed that she wasn't seated next to her BriBri, where she could whisper encouragement in his ear. Ahern didn't notice, which probably made her even more annoyed. He was already in the midst of a conversation with the gallery's lawyer and wasn't aware of her posturing or the sour look that contorted her beautiful face.

Gabi began the meeting by asking everyone to be considerate while presenting their thoughts on how and when the Gentileschi had gone from an original to a copy. Lloyd Bennings started by saying he believed Meade and Medina were involved in a conspiracy to defraud New London with the 'fake' that they substituted once the painting had been authenticated. Maxime Meade countered that the museum was responsible for the switch.

It only escalated from there. Voices ramped up. More people joined in the fray. This was Gabi's cue to stand up and make a royal fuss. By the looks of her performance, it seems she missed her calling. Screaming and yelling ensued.

"You. All of you. She was pointing to the New York contingent. Get out! Right now. Go!" She raised a trembling hand and pointed toward the door.

While Gabi was giving a Master Class in theater arts, Marina accidentally knocked her cell, which had been face down on the table, to the floor.

"Sorry," she said to Natalie as she bent to retrieve it and turned it so the young woman could see the images of George and herself that Marina quickly scrolled through on the phone. Natalie's face grew a bright shade of red, and her mouth gaped open like a fish desperate for air. She looked around to see if anyone else had noticed. But everyone was staring in shock at Gabi, who was still insisting, well, screaming, that they all leave.

I saw Marina take her time to sit up and whisper a curt message in Natalie's ear as she did so.

By now, Natalie had composed herself, and as she made a show of gathering her things, she turned and spoke quietly to Marina, her face a mask of rage. Before anyone else could see her anger, she managed to tamp it down. Then, she stood, rushed around the still combative Gabi, took Ahern by the arm, and departed in a swirl of put-on sympathy for him. I could hear the words "Oh, honey, I'm so sorry this happened" as she led him from the conference room.

Everyone on the museum's team stared in shock and disbelief at Gabi, who was still on a rant. When the Meade and Medina team were finally gone, she turned to her people and told them it was pointless to continue today. "Marina, please come with me to my office." She made her tone contrite before she spoke again. "Everyone might as well get back to work."

My gambler's eyes had been scanning the table the whole time, watching the staff as Marina had asked. At first, all of them were surprised and stunned into silence by Gabi's outburst. *Where is our Gabi?* I could imagine them thinking. *Who is this stranger?* A few people tried to intervene. Murmurs of "Gabi, please." "And, what's this?" floated over her tirade but didn't land. Mia's mouth opened in surprise. Dame Harris looked appalled. Bidenstock folded his arms and sneered. The solicitors and art experts shook their heads as if they couldn't believe what they heard. Lloyd Bennings sat there, slowly turning stroke-out red as he snapped the pencil he'd been holding clean in half. But only one member of the team, Stella Manning, sat perfectly still and composed, sphinx-like, her hands folded on top of the table, a woman in charge.

And then there was Mia. Her focus never left Jose Bidenstock. It was a high-wattage laser-like beam that flamed hot enough to melt him. I'm sure Jose could feel it, but wouldn't lift his eyes to meet Mia's. It didn't matter. Her gaze was relentless, and she rose from her seat and started to move toward him. He finally felt the heat, looked up at her, and quickly left the room.

Another piece to add to the puzzle.

* * *

Marina and I had decided we wouldn't share my observations until we were alone. I knew I had a little time to kill while she debriefed Gabi on her ploy with Natalie. I figured I could use it wisely: I'd go search for the original 'Weeping Magdalene' that I still believed was somewhere on the premises.

The private elevator would take me to any off-limits-to-the-public floor. I entered and pushed the button for the basement. I exited into a space filled with more paintings, sculptures, furniture, and crates filled with art, silver, and glass than I could have imagined. If The New London Arts Museum had this much art in storage, I could hardly imagine what the Met in New York had socked away in its lower levels. I remembered reading somewhere that about ninety percent of their objects were in storage rooms. Very little was on display at any time.

I didn't think the Gentileschi would be sitting there in plain sight, so I thought I'd start with the crated paintings that were slid side-by-side into vertical cabinets. The spine of each crate had a numeral and abbreviated names written on it. I tried to match the initials with artists' names, such as SBot for Sandro Botticelli and Rem for Rembrandt? They were the only ones I recognized. I'd need to know much more about art than I did to figure this out.

Not that my lack of knowledge stopped me. I was searching for any crate marked with the initials AGen, although the thieves wouldn't make it that obvious, would they?

I was working my way down the first row when I felt a hand grip my shoulder and spin me around. "What the hell do you think you're doing here, mon?"

I knew who the voice belonged to even before we were face-to-face. Marina had told me about Jose Bidenstock's slight Jamaican accent. His face was still a mask of anger from his encounter with Mia, and he hadn't calmed down. He was looking at the stored crates behind me as if he was their protector. Art he could never possess as a lowly handler. His passion was palpable. And unfulfilled.

"I asked you what you're doing?" he repeated, eyes still scanning the crates to make sure I hadn't disturbed the precious contents.

"Just looking," I replied like any seasoned New Yorker who'd rebuffed the unwanted attention of a salesperson. I looked down at his hand, which was still on my shoulder, until he removed it. "And, just leaving," I added, making for the door.

My snooping hadn't gleaned anything of substance. Maybe my theory was just that. A theory. But I'd learned something about Jose Bidenstock. I just wasn't sure what it meant.

We still had a painting to find, not to mention a murderer, and time was running out.

Chapter Thirty-Four

I was waiting for Marina when she arrived home, excited to divulge my findings. She placed her computer and bag on the sideboard while I poured us both a double Scotch. It was time for a drink.

"So, what do you think?" she asked, kicking off her shoes and settling into an armchair with her feet tucked under her. She swished the golden liquid around the tumbler.

"I'd put my money on Lloyd Bennings as the Second Inside Man. It was obvious, to me anyway, that he was just posturing when he accused Meade and Medina of substituting a fake."

"Maybe he just wanted to act like the big man. Take charge."

"Could be, but once Gabi started her performance, he began to look apoplectic. By the time she asked them all to go back to work, I thought he was going to have a convulsion right there, and we'd have to call the paramedics."

"And everyone else?" Marina raised her eyebrows.

"The surprise and shock you'd expect and an eerie calm from Manning, almost like this was above her, and a smoldering attitude from Bidenstock.

"Mia looked like she wanted to kill him, and I'd like to know why."

"How was Gabi after her performance, which was stellar by the way?"

"She was completely wrung-out." Marina looked pensive. "I'm not sure what we gained by this charade. I'm hoping it will make the gang rethink their position. If somehow, the original 'Weeping Magdalene' was 'found', I'm sure the board would pay a good faith finder's fee to make it all go away before the exhibit opens."

She smiled at me. "I'm pretty sure Natalie Stapleton could make that happen."

"What exactly did you say to her while she was viewing her indiscretions in living color?

"I told her the photos could go out to Ahern with one click, and I was sure he'd be surprised."

"And her reply?" I asked. I'd seen her whisper something back to Marina.

"She warned me off." Marina paused for a moment. "But the threat was lacking in depth. I think she was concealing the fear that Ahern would go ballistic over her and Colabello's relationship. Then, drop her faster than a grenade about to explode.

"Let's give her some time and see where she lands."

I wasn't sure she'd back out. She might have a big mouth and a penchant for oversharing, but she had a lot to lose if the con went south.

"What about the rest of the gang? It took almost a year to plan this down to every detail. Do you think they'll fold just like that?"

"We might have to force them to do it, although it seems unlikely." She shook her head. "Bennings might be our best bet to get at the truth. We need more intel on him and his lifestyle.

"Nigel?" I asked.

Marina nodded. "It's tricky. Since Bennings is close to the Royal Family, we need to tread carefully." She rolled her eyes. "This is right up Nigel's alley.

"As for the rest of the gang, they have a lot of time and money invested in this. It would be hard to give up the seven million in addition to reselling the original 'Weeping Magdalene,' and getting Ahern to invest in another masterpiece." She rubbed her hand across her eyes, and her wariness showed.

"What did you do while Gabi and I were debriefing?"

"I explored the basement storage rooms."

She laughed. "Looking for the Gentileschi?"

"Yes. Following a hunch." I described what I'd noticed, and the crated paintings stacked in slots beside each other.

"No Gentileschi?" she asked wryly.

"No. Just Bidenstock invading my snooping. I thought about the passion I'd sensed in him how protective he'd seemed for the art, and how unfulfilled he must be as just a handler.

I rose, refilled our glasses, and then settled back in the matching armchair. "I spoke to Dad before we left. They planned for an eventful day on the water." I smiled. "He's going to need another vacation after this one."

"My guys and Nigel's are still watching them." She held up her phone. "I just got a text that all was well, and he heard your folks discussing stopping at The Globe for a performance on their way back from Greenwich."

"Dad better spring for cushions for the stalls, or he'll be sorry." I remembered attending a play there and sitting on those hard wooden boards for hours. My bottom began to ache again at the memory.

Marina looked at her watch. It was already late afternoon. "Why don't we take a break and nap?" she asked suggestively, pulling me up and leading me toward our bedroom.

Who was I to argue? A nap sounded just about perfect right now.

Chapter Thirty-Five

ap time over, Marina went off to call Nigel regarding Bennings while I sat on our deck nursing a glass of wine. Being outside with the greenery that surrounded me was calming and relaxing after the day we'd had. We'd decided to dine out at our favorite neighborhood French restaurant, Bistro du Monde. I was looking forward to a juicy, rare steak and frites with a glass of burgundy when my cell beeped, interrupting my vision of an excellent meal.

"Nick?" the voice was tenuous. "It's Mia. Do you have a few minutes to speak?"

"Mia, hi. Of course," I replied, wondering if a confession about the Gentileschi would be forthcoming.

I could hear her take in a massive breath before she began. "I want to explain about Clive. Clive Hastings Cargill."

This was unexpected. "Okay." I knew I sounded tentative. "What about him?"

She spewed it out quickly. "Clive told me he spoke with you. That you knew about us." She hesitated before going on, emotion coloring her voice. "It's true, we're together. I know he's married, and it's —"

"Mia, stop. I'm not judging you. Your relationship with Clive is your own business."

"That's just it. We love each other, and he's going to divorce his wife." A low sob escaped her lips.

Tell me another one, I thought.

She might have been reading my mind. She sniffled and continued. "I know how that sounds, but it's true. I just want you and Marina to know we had nothing to do with the 'Weeping Magdalene' forgery." She paused again before she continued. "I only met Maxime Meade when he arrived in London. I never heard of him or his gallery before.

"Clive's company…they wanted him to sound you out about your dad and Hamilton Capital. I know it isn't cricket, but that's all it was. His job is on the line. Please understand."

"All right, Mia. I get it, and I'll relay your message to Marina, as well. Thank you for telling me this." I clicked off and thought about what she'd said. She'd lied about knowing Meade. Why would she do that? She probably didn't realize that Gabi had told us Mia had been with her in New York.

Marina came out onto the deck and gave me a curious look. "Why so pensive?" she asked.

"Mia just called. She wanted to come clean about her and Clive Hastings Cargill."

"Really? What did she say?"

"That neither of them had anything to do with the Gentileschi, and Cargill's boss sent him to the casino to fish for information."

"It could be she didn't have anything to do with the switch. But his company is another story. They may be involved, somehow."

"No. There's more going on with her. I need to find out what that is".

She snatched up her handbag. "C'mon. *Andiamo!* We can discuss this after dinner. I'm starving. Threatening Natalie was hard work."

Ten minutes later, we were at the restaurant, being greeted like old friends by the owner, Michel. He led us to our usual table and left us to look at the menu. Soon, our waiter appeared with two glasses of the house Burgundy, which was produced in a small vineyard in the

Côte de Nuits district that Michel and his partners owned. Michel knew we both enjoyed this wine. I lifted my glass to him in thanks, and after a few sips, I felt the wine work its magic. I began to relax. We both ordered: for me, the steak and frites, and for Marina, the moules meuniere.

Dinner was restorative, and we laughed and joked while we ate. Marina needed a break from searching for the 'Weeping Magdalene.' Our dinner was just the right move.

We both had another glass of wine, and I asked Marina about her conversation with Nigel. It was just as she'd thought.

"He said he had to be very circumspect in investigating Bennings."

I raised my eyebrows. I didn't think Nigel knew the meaning of the word.

Marina caught my skeptical look. "As I mentioned, Bennings is chummy with the King. An advisor on his art collection and purchases," she said. "If the King got wind of it, he could shut it down."

I didn't think the King would interfere. I knew Nigel would find a way around this, so I said so. After all, now that he was knighted, I imagined he could foresee an Earldom or Dukedom in his future. "He'll come through."

Marina agreed. "He will, but I hope he can fast-track this, as you Americans say. We don't have much time left." She paused. "Gabi was forced to call the Meade and Medina people and apologize for her outburst. Stella Manning insisted on it. They're coming back the day after tomorrow to restart negotiations."

What were they planning for tomorrow? Why wait an extra day, I wondered.

"That makes me even more suspicious. If Bennings is involved, as I suspect he is, it's in his best interest to keep things moving along. We need to find out if he needs money. That would make a difference."

"And Stella Manning?" I asked. "Where does she fit in? She's been pretty laid back until today."

"Gabi said she's quiet; lets people get on with their jobs without too much interference. She's been at various art institutions for the last twenty years before she was offered the position of Museum Director."

"Does she have a family?"

"A husband who's a top analyst at MI5." She paused. "We'll find out more about them."

Marina switched subjects. "What about Mia?" she asked.

"I told you everything. I caught her in a lie. Cargill and Oxford Alliance Ltd are another matter. If they know about his relationship with Mia, he may be a pawn in their game." I pondered the connections for a moment.

"Somehow, I'm sure they're involved, but I haven't worked out how they fit in. Plus, we need to prove it." That wasn't going to happen tonight. I'd have to confront Cargill again.

I asked for our check and paid. Then we walked out into the night, arms around each other, gazing at the few stars we could see far above, and back to our home.

Chapter Thirty-Six

Marina noticed it as we approached our building; the front door was slightly ajar. "Nick, did you lock up when we left?"

"Of course," I replied. As native New Yorkers, we always locked our door when we left the apartment, even though there was always a concierge and a doorman on duty for each shift. No sense making it easy for someone to break in.

We walked up the short flight of stairs, wary of what might be in front of us. "Maybe Alex and Simone are home and forgot to close the door."

"I don't think so," Marina whispered. "It's too quiet." She paused to listen, then pulled out her cell, ready to dial 999 if we encountered an intruder inside.

With the tips of my fingers, I gently pushed the door open and peered around it. We waited a beat, entered slowly, and saw that the apartment appeared empty. Keeping the lights off, we checked both floors and realized nothing was missing or out of place.

Marina knelt in front of the safe in her closet. She removed a red hair she always placed on the bottom where the solid steel door met the frame. "Still in place," she said, casting it aside and entering the combination that released the door. Her computer, notes, and jewelry were undisturbed, as was her gun. Alex and Simone's room looked normal, with their clothes and possessions scattered around.

We made our way back upstairs to the lounge and turned on all the lights. That's when we noticed it. The Matisse painting I'd bought for Marina was propped up in front of the window, sporting a slash across the front.

Marina turned to me. "Natalie's threat wasn't as empty as I thought." She gestured to the sliced-up canvas, and her eyes became as dark as thunderclouds. "Ruining the painting was spiteful and not too bright. It's stupid with all her boasting to her friends and her affair with Colabello."

Marina opened the photos app on her phone and pulled up the shots of Natalie and George Colabello having sex. "I could get even with her in one second. I have half a mind to send these to Ahern right now." She scrolled through the images and stared at the cell, finally clicking on her home page and looking over at me. "It's so tempting to bring her down, but I don't want to escalate the situation." Her expression turned hard, her face growing red. I knew she was seething with anger. "But believe me, these won't go to waste. We won't let them get away with this…with any of this."

"Should we call the police?" I asked, gesturing to the cell still in her hand.

"No. Nothing was taken, and I don't want them involved. We can't afford a leak about the situation at New London. That would be enough to cause a scandal."

I could imagine the repercussions throughout the art world. Other works of art the museum owned might be called into question. Gossiped about. Inspected. It would be monumental. I now understood why the authorities had dropped their investigation of Chimini.

Marina tapped in a number on her cell. "I'll get a contact I know to watch the house anytime we're not here." Someone answered, and she gave them instructions. "He'll be ready when we need him. In the meantime, let's put the Matisse away. I don't want Simone and Alex to see it and ask questions."

"Are they…?" I started to ask.

"They're fine, still with your parents. The team is watching closely.

"You're calling in a lot of favors for this, aren't you?" I asked.

"They're good people, and know I'd do the same for them." She took a deep breath. "This is exhausting. I have a few notes to make, then I'm going to bed. I'll fill in Ana and Nikki in the morning and get them looking further into Manning. Hopefully Nigel will have some answers for us by then.

"I want to nail these people. They can't get away with this. Too many people will be hurt." She left the lounge and headed to our bedroom. I understood this was personal for her, and she wouldn't let it go.

"I'll be down in a little while," I said. I wanted to wait for Alex and Simone to return home. I knew they were being watched, but still, I'd feel better if they were here with us. Just as I started to relax, that old quote from the "Jaws" movie popped into my head: "Just when you thought it was safe..." The da dum da dum theme that went with it filled my brain and was anything but reassuring.

* * *

Once the junior members of our family were in the house and expounded at length about their incredible day, they were finally knackered enough to head for bed. I decided to have a nightcap on the deck—for medicinal purposes only. I thought about the conundrum of the fake vs. not fake, original vs. copy of the painting. How we would determine who did what and when was still eluding me. Well, I was not going to figure that out tonight.

I listened to London's nocturnal sounds. It was very quiet in this part of the city, with just a slight breeze swaying through the trees and a distant buzz of traffic from the main road. I appreciated the silence and the feeling of the darkness. I drained the last sip of Scotch from my glass and was headed inside when my cell buzzed with a text, breaking the spell.

It was from Nigel.

It was just like Nigel to be so cryptic.

Be at my office at 9:00 a.m.
We're going on a field trip.
N

Field trip. What field trip?

I hit send and waited for a reply. No little dots appeared under my message. I didn't expect they would. I'd have to wait until morning to find out what was afoot.

Chapter Thirty-Seven

At 9:00 a.m. on the dot, I was outside the majestic MI6 building at Vauxhall Cross on the south side of the Thames, home of Britain's Secret Intelligence Service. It was tasked with gathering information from far and wide under the leadership of George Davies, its chief. Known as Control, just like in John le Carré's novels, he runs the show, and Nigel Phillips is one of his highly placed intelligence officers. 'Indispensable,' as Nigel might say if asked.

His amour-plated Mercedes was idling at the entrance. The driver stepped out the moment he saw me and ushered me into the back seat next to Nigel, who pointedly looked at his watch.

I ignored his show of impatience—I was on time—and turned to face him. "Where are we going on this field trip of yours?" I asked.

"Of ours," he replied. "To Bath, where we are meeting the surveillance team watching Luke Chimini's house." He uttered all this in an 'are you satisfied now' tone. "As I understand it, a certain Maxime Meade will be arriving shortly to discuss the fine art of forgery or something of that nature."

"Will there be video?" I asked just to tweak his nose a bit. "And popcorn?"

He gave me a withering look before he continued. "Cameras and microphones were placed inside the building yesterday while Mr. Chimini was absent. Nothing much was going on. Today, it should be a different story, and we will be able to see and hear all."

Nigel liked to flaunt his power and could be a bit, umm, pompous. But he owed Marina from an incident when she'd been working for him, and he'd made good several times.

"Now, Nick, why don't you inform me about the case. I'd appreciate all the details forthwith," he added as though I might hold something back.

I took him through it, from Gabi's first plea for help to the information on the con and the gang from Marc Rivers to my visit to Chimini to the meeting at the museum.

Nigel nodded while I spoke. "It's very elaborate but well planned. And, of course, there is the money."

It's always the money, I thought.

He looked pensive. "If they pull off such a major con, they'll be sure to try it on another unsuspecting victim." He turned to me. "No one wants that to happen, do they?"

"What about Chimini?" I asked. "This time, he colluded with thieves to steal a painting, forged it, and signed Artemisia Gentileschi's name, breaking the law."

"Many laws," Nigel replied, nodding. "And several agencies, including ours, will line up to arrest him. He won't get away with it this time."

Interpol and the FBI would probably want in on that.

"It certainly would be better if we could get our hands on this original Gentileschi, 'Weeping Magdalene,' he added. "Any idea where it might be?"

I shook my head. "I wish I knew. Another company, Oxford Alliance Ltd, a hedge fund, might be involved, but I have no proof. One of their managers is dating an assistant curator and has been sniffing around my dad."

"How are they connected?" he asked. "I thought their focus was elsewhere, such as defrauding their overly greedy clients."

I wasn't surprised that Nigel knew all about them. His pudgy fingers were in every pie.

I explained the high-powered pitch their chairman, John Windsor Smythe, had given Dad and the implied threat he'd made. "They've been after Dad to offer Hamilton Capital's investors a stake in their new art market sector. Dad turned them down, but I don't trust them. My intuition tells me they're up to something."

"Undoubtedly they are," he replied. "But so are we."

* * *

We arrived at Chimini's home and headed past a catering van parked at the end of his road on The Circus. The caterers were making a show of unloading chairs, tables, and assorted crates of glasses and dishes. It appeared that they'd be there for some time. Nigel's limo followed the road to the far side of the enclosed garden in the middle and parked.

He opened his laptop, logged on to the communications equipment in the van, and spoke to one of the operatives. "We're good to go, Sir," the agent told Nigel. "Let me take you through the setup."

Several windows opened, and we roamed through Chimini's house, painting by painting and room by room. Nigel looked surprised at the number of art works on display.

"You weren't kidding, Nick, were you?" he said to me. "Bugger all, it's like his own private gallery in there."

A minute later, the doorbell chimed, and we watched as Chimini greeted Meade and invited him in.

"Let's speak in my study," Chimini said as he led the way up a staircase to the floor above. The hidden cameras captured it all, and it wasn't pretty, except for the art.

Meade looked furious and didn't waste any time getting down to business. "Listen, Luke, things are critical right now. I don't have time for any screw-ups. Don't make me sorry I hired you," he said, his voice rising with every word.

Chimini interrupted. "You're the one who's screwing up, trying to cut me out of another Gentileschi," he said, poking Meade in the chest.

Meade pushed him away. "I already told you, there is no other 'Lucretia.' I don't know where you heard that, but it's bullshit." He walked around the study. "You already got an installment for forging the 'Weeping Magdalene.' Don't try to scam me on this, Luke, or you'll be sorry."

He turned, walked down the stairs, and stormed out the front door, shouting over his shoulder, "Don't call me again."

* * *

"That went well," I said as we pulled away and headed back to London. Nigel spoke to the men in the van and told them to pack up. We had the proof that Chimini had been paid to forge the original painting. "So, what's next?" I asked as the Mercedes merged into the flow of traffic moving West.

Nigel steepled his hands and tapped them against his chin. "I'll send one of my men to take him in for a little chat after we give him an hour or two to stew. We'll see how cooperative he is after a day in a cell."

I'd heard about the detention cells in the basement of MI6. Dark, dreary, isolated spaces. I had no desire to ever see one.

Nigel was pondering the situation with Chimini. "We might have to release him—"

"You can't—" I started to reply.

Nigel held up his hand. "Just temporarily so as not to tip off the gang before we bring Meade in."

"Will you be able to hold either of them?" I asked.

"Chimini committed a crime on British soil, so yes. But we may have to have the U.S. extradite Meade.

"I'd feel much better about this if we had the original painting in our possession."

So, would I. Much better.

Chapter Thirty-Eight

When I arrived home, I found a note from Marina. She'd be staying late at her office with Nikki and Ana, catching up on other cases. My woman was in demand and busy, and she'd been devoting a lot of time to Gabi and the museum.

Even though we'd gotten what we needed from the surveillance on Chimini—guilty as charged of forgery—I was more drained than excited. It was time to regroup and recharge. A visit to the casino was just what I needed after a bacon cheeseburger and fries in my favorite pub, The Elephant and Castle.

I walked in and could feel my spirits begin to immediately revive. The atmosphere was casual and welcoming. The barman recognized me when I slipped onto a stool at the bar and placed a lager in front of me with a nod of his head. I tipped my glass to him, took a sip, and ordered.

While I waited for my lunch to arrive, I reviewed what we'd gotten from Meade's visit to Chimini. By calling him to meet, Chimini had misplayed his hand and turned an ally into an enemy. The gang was ruthless. They'd never let a threat against the operation stand.

I debated calling Marc Rivers again, but decided against it. If he had more information, he'd let us know.

Instead, I called my dad.

"What's going on with the case?" He asked.

I filled him in. "Nigel is sending an agent to bring Chimini in for a talk. That should scare him enough to spill about more of the operation. He's obviously done this before."

I didn't mention that Meade might ensure he never did it again.

I was going to invite Dad to meet me at the casino, but Mom would not appreciate that, so I let it slide. Instead, I asked, "What are you and Mom up to this afternoon?"

"We'll be having lunch at the Lanesborough near Hyde Park Corner, which the hotel concierge recommended, then visiting the Victoria and Albert Museum."

The concierge was one of Marina's contacts. He'd let Marina know where the parental units were heading.

Dad sounded tired but happy. "Then, a nice quiet evening in front of the fireplace." He laughed. "Mom loves this suite. We both do. Watch out, Nick. She might want to move here."

I closed my mouth firmly before I said anything mean. They'd had quite a vacation so far. A little more R and R for them would be welcome. Moving to London, not so much.

"How are Simone and Alex?" he asked.

"They were still sleeping when I left. Probably knackered from all the excitement of dashing around London and Brighton."

"Thank God that woman and Ahern told them they were too busy to see them again." Stress suddenly filled his voice. "They belong behind bars."

"That's where they'll be as soon as we find the Gentileschi and the person who stole it." I reveled in the thought of rounding them all up and carting them off to jail. I had no clue if Ahern would be charged with anything except being a patsy. Natalie was a different story. I'd like to see her get put away for a long time. I wondered how she'd look in orange.

Dad's voice changed as he whispered into the phone. "Don't forget about tomorrow night and the concert. You haven't told Marina, have you?" Now, he sounded worried.

"Of course not. It's going to be a great surprise,"

"Good. Let's keep it that way. Gotta go."

"Good-bye to you, too," I said into my silent phone just as my food arrived.

Chapter Thirty-Nine

I paid my tab and was walking toward the Tube when Nigel rang.

"Nick, we have a situation. Chimini is missing."

"Missing?" I repeated like a parrot. "How is that possible? Your people are monitoring his every move."

"We replaced the van with a car stationed on the other side of the road behind the green. It was less obtrusive. He was in his studio for a while. The video feed showed him sitting there and drinking. Then he went out back into his garden, where we hadn't set up for sound or video since it was enclosed.

"My watchers thought he'd just gone out for some air and weren't too worried about it."

A mistake. Chimini was a disgruntled and now desperate man. Who knew what he'd do?

"When my agents arrived an hour later to pick him up and bring him in for questioning, he was gone. He must have scarpered over the back fence. I have a team looking for him."

"He's worried about Meade," I said. "And any retaliation."

"Correct," Nigel replied. "And right to be. He'd be much safer with us."

I was sure he didn't see it that way. "Let me know when you find him." He had my name, and as Marina had pointed out, it wouldn't be too hard to find my address.

It was one more thing to worry about. I had to let Marina know.

Thoughts of Blackjack flew from my head. Instead, I headed home, hoping I wouldn't encounter a crazed artist when I arrived.

* * *

Fortunately, all was quiet at the flat. I texted Marina regarding Chimini's unknown whereabouts and settled in for the evening. Once again, Simone and Alex were out enjoying the city. Since there wasn't anything to do right now, I picked up a novel I'd been meaning to read, and was in the middle of chapter two when there was a knock on my door.

I rose to answer it, knowing Chimini wouldn't be so subtle. I opened it, surprised to find Syd, our neighbor, standing on the threshold.

"Hullo," she said. "Can I come in?"

"Of course," I said and led the way into the lounge. It was then that I noticed the tears on her face.

"Syd, what is it?"

"Oh, Nick. It's Gabi."

My eyes darted from Syd to the door. "Is she…where is…"

Syd nodded. "She's fine. Not quite fine. She's gone for a walk to think things over."

My stomach clenched. Not the wedding, It couldn't be.

Syd noticed my horror-struck face and read my mind. "No, it's not us…not our upcoming nuptials, anyway. It's her work. She breathed in deeply and shuddered it out, trying to compose herself.

I led her to the lounge and offered her a seat. I held up a bottle of brandy and a glass. Syd nodded yes. "Why don't you tell me what happened?"

"Lloyd Bennings rang her earlier and told her the board had decided this forgery business had to end. The New London Arts Museum has agreed to pay Ahern, Meade, and Medina the full value of the painting, seven million dollars, plus fees for the inconvenience. He told her the vote was unanimous. That they could not afford to have a scandal, or any bad publicity that would taint the rest of the exhibit."

She paused and took a swallow of her drink. "Gabi is to meet with Stella Manning, who will represent the board and all the other parties tomorrow, to draft a memo of intent to pay the money." I couldn't miss the rancor in her voice.

Sounded more like a ransom to me.

Syd continued. "The lawyers will need a few days to review it. Once they do, they'll regroup at the museum to sign the paperwork. Then, accept a transfer of the funds.

"Do they want the forged Gentileschi, as well?" I asked. It was the seven-million-dollar question. I left off 'so they can sell it again.'

Syd shook her head. "Not as far as Bennings knew." She raised her hands to her face, bangles jangling down her arms. "Oh, Nick, what are we going to do?"

I had no answer for her. Gabi's life would be shattered, possibly her career and reputation, as well.

I took Syd's hands and placed them in my own. "We have a few days. There's still time to figure this out." Was I blowing into the wind? It all depended on finding the original 'Weeping Magdalene,' and the people who had it. And I wasn't forgetting about Jonathan Hudson and the person who murdered him. We'd have to double down to get this done.

Chapter Forty

Marina arrived home, and we got down to business. Syd had left shortly before, and I'd heard the outer door open and close, alerting me that Gabi had returned.

I tilted my chin toward the ceiling. "There's a lot of grief up there right now."

"Did Syd tell you why the board made the decision today? We were supposed to meet again tomorrow for further discussion."

"They wanted to put this in the rear-view mirror and avoid a scandal." Or at least that's what I assumed.

Marina was pacing around in panther mode, on the hunt for prey. She stopped and turned to face me. "Bennings never mentioned a word of this at our meeting. Someone is putting on the pressure. He's just the messenger, but it came from the top, from Stella Manning."

"And the board, I presume. Wouldn't the members all have something to say about this?"

Marina seemed unconvinced and shook her head. "I wonder who influenced them?" she mused. "They seemed willing to let the negotiations continue."

"We'll need to speak to Gabi to find out exactly what happened," I added. "Maybe tomorrow morning rather than now." I cut my eyes to the ceiling, sure she could use some private time with Syd right now.

"Meanwhile, Chimini's disappearance doesn't bode well for finding the missing original. He might not know who stole it or who has it."

"If he does, Nigel will get it out of him."

You know that old saying: 'Speak of the devil, and he shows up on your doorstep.' Or, in this case, he rings your cell instead.

Marina swooped up her phone and put it on speaker so I could listen in. "Nick and I are here together. What's going on?"

"We've located Chimini. In a bar, as you might expect." His voice was thick with contempt. "He's lucky we found him first before the gang decided to do something about his threats."

He lowered his voice as if someone else might be listening to the conversation. "We sent our Hounds to round him up and bring him to our secure basement facility." He sighed in exasperation as only Nigel could. "I'm confident we'll…discover…everything he knows about the forgery. I really must go now. Speak soon."

The conversation hadn't been funny, but Marina and I started laughing. "The Hounds?" she said.

"Like the MI5 security Dogs," I added. "No wonder he was whispering. Doesn't want the head of 5 to know what he's up to."

We sobered up quickly. We were still looking for the truth and getting nowhere fast.

* * *

The next morning, Marina rang Gabi and invited her for a coffee before her meeting. She walked through the door and immediately burst into tears, leaving her already red-rimmed eyes even more inflamed. "I can't fathom this has happened," she said through her sobs.

We both consoled her and explained we believed there was still time to make things right. I hoped Marina had a plan for this because I sure didn't.

Gabi was due to arrive at New London in an hour and was instructed to come alone. Marina shot me a look. She was not pleased with this latest command. Our friend would be flying solo without any backup. Only Stella Manning, representing the entire board, would accompany her to face the New York contingent.

Marina told Gabi to stay focused and unemotional. Easier said than done, although the young curator nodded in agreement. She also instructed her to record the whole meeting on her cell, which we would listen to when she returned. "Just click on the app and leave it in your pocket. It will pick up everything," Marina added. Then we both hugged her and sent her on her way.

"Well?" I asked. "What do we do next?"

She smiled her Cheshire cat grin at me, crinkling her eyes before she spoke. "Ana and Nikki found piles of info on everyone at New London and uncovered some delicious gossip. It might turn into evidence rather than gossip. Seems like one or two of our suspects have a dirty little secret."

"Who?" I demanded with more force than I intended.

She made me wait for it before she answered. Seems like mister straight arrow, Lloyd Bennings has a bit on the side, Jose Bidenstock."

That surprised me. It seemed like a mismatch. "Is Bennings married?" I asked. I hadn't seen any mention of that in the reports we'd looked through.

"No," Marina answered. "He does, however, have a partner of five years. You'll never guess who." Again, she played out the suspense. "Dame Rosemary Harris, whom he lives with in Mayfair."

"So, you think Bennings is in cahoots with Bidenstock? I thought of the big, powerful, younger Bidenstock and the very average-looking Bennings. Who knew what attracted one person to another? Just look at Marina and me. Not exactly two of a kind.

"Who enticed whom to swap out the painting?" I asked. "I'd put my money on Bidenstock." I didn't know what kind of money an art handler made, but it must be less than one of the Directors. "I'm sure he'd like a bigger salary and a better job, a little higher up the rung," I added.

"I'm not certain about Bidenstock," Marina shook her head. 'In fact, I'm not sure it's either one of them. Or that they're responsible for Jonathan Hudson's death."

"Really?" I know I sounded incredulous.

"They both might be getting set up to take a fall." She paused. "I'm not certain yet."

Her last statement was unexpected. Doubting herself wasn't her style.

"Do you think Dame Harris knows about Benninngs's extra-curricular activities with Bidenstock?"

"I doubt it." Her mouth quirked up. "She doesn't appear to be the type that would accept disloyalty. If she did, he'd be out on his bottom, as she might say."

I remembered what Dad had relayed about her: icy, cool, and snooty. She had gotten rid of her deadbeat husband and made a name and career for herself. What was she doing with someone like Bennings, who looked almost rumpled next to her?

Thinking of Dad reminded me of the dinner and surprise concert this evening. I didn't want to get Marina's radar spinning, so I kept my approach low-key.

"I think we should get dressed up for tonight's farewell dinner for Simone and Alex. Have a bit of a celebration."

"I'll miss them," she said, "even though they've hardly been here."

"Don't worry. Those two will be back for sure." Simone had fallen in love with London. She liked us, too, so I knew she'd convince Alex to take her here again.

"Where are we meeting?" Marina asked.

"Dad found a place your concierge friend recommended. The Côte Kensington." I had no idea if Dad had asked at the hotel, or not, but it would keep Marina's worry meter from moving into the red zone.

Little did I know dinner would be the least of our problems this evening.

Chapter Forty-One

The food was spectacular. At the prices they were charging, it should be. Very French- Inspired and incredibly delicious. Dad was in his element, enjoying the pleasure being with his family gave him. Not to mention his favorite: rib-eye steak and frites. He went a little off the reservation and ordered a rosé negroni as a pre-dinner cocktail. Then, he instructed the sommelier to produce a classic Gamay with Beaujolais undertones for dinner.

Everyone had taken my advice and dressed up for the occasion, even though our destination had yet to be disclosed. Somehow, we Donahues and our partners knew we were in for something special, which I had kept secret. We three men all wore suits, with cuffed shirts and ties. Marina was in a bottle green sheath that set off her eyes. Mom had chosen a tan silk shift and a long Burberry jacket that looked great on her. And Simone was in a strapless gold jumpsuit that matched her glowing good looks.

We had a great time eating, drinking, and ribbing Dad about how much money he was spending on this trip. He didn't seem all that amused, which made us goad him even more.

"So, are you going to expense Hamilton Capital for everything?" I asked, opening my arms wide to encompass all of us and London itself.

"Not if I want to remain Chairman of the firm," he replied and smiled. "Some of it, of course. After all, we are here for business." He looked over at Mom and smiled. "And let's not forget shopping."

She rolled her eyes at him and shook her head. She knew how to play the long-suffering wife even if she didn't mean it.

"Anyway," he added, a smile lighting up his face. "I have a surprise for all of you, so drink up."

I ignored my family's questions of "What is it?" "And what are you talking about?" and did as Dad suggested, drinking the last sip of the delicious red wine in my glass. "I'm ready," I said, plunking down the wine goblet on the table and standing up. Marina gave me one of her 'behave yourself' looks, and I retook my seat.

Dad was geared up for his big moment. He reached into his jacket pocket and pulled out a white envelope from which he removed six tickets and fanned them out. Mom leaned over to get a better look and gasped in surprise when she saw the name printed on the tickets.

Her reaction couldn't have made Dad any happier, and he beamed as he said to the rest of us, "We are going to see Elton John at the Royal Albert Hall." He paused and checked his watch. "In fifteen minutes. So, let's go."

Marina took my arm as we walked the few blocks to the venue. "You knew about this, didn't you?" She asked.

"I was sworn to secrecy. I couldn't tell anyone, even you."

Her mouth closed in a moue of discontent, then she laughed. "Imagine that. Nick Donahue keeping a secret."

I let it slide. I was Dad's insurance that his surprise would be a winner.

A few minutes later, we were seated next to the Royal Box. The seats couldn't have been better, and my family was as anxious for the show to start as a roulette player waiting for the next spin.

The stage went dark, and the sound system came to life, with the words: "Ladies and Gentlemen, Mr. Elton John." Sir Elton did not need an opening act, and neither did the crowd, which went wild.

With the spotlight on him and his piano, it took a few minutes before the clapping and cheering stopped, and Elton could play his first song, *Rocket Man*. To say it only got better from there would be an understatement.

People sang along to their favorites, especially Mom, who was rocking her seat. Dad had done good. It was a great concert in a legendary concert hall.

At intermission, we left the box to get some drinks. The Champagne was on me, and the bubbly wine only added to the magic of the evening.

Marina was first back into the box, and I heard her gasp in surprise.

"What's wrong?" I asked.

Her face was ashen, and her hand shook as she handed me a photo left on my seat. It was a shot of Mom and Dad walking on the Brompton Road with Harrods in the background. Unremarkable except for the bullseye that had been drawn on Dad's face.

It was a warning, plain and simple, to keep away from the case. First, Simone and Alex are befriended and set up, and now Mom and Dad are being threatened. As I slipped the photo into my jacket pocket out of sight from Mom, a bright red "Danger" sign began flashing through my mind. I looked around the box in desperation, but I knew whoever had left the photo was long gone. Someone had slipped in during intermission. I moved into the corridor to find an usher and asked if they'd seen anyone going in while we were at the bar. Marina noticed what I was doing and distracted Mom. Dad cut his eyes toward me and watched as I left.

As I expected, no one had noticed anything.

Chapter Forty-Two

I couldn't figure out why the gang was doing this. Tomorrow, they would have an agreement to obtain the seven million dollars they wanted. And keep the original Gentileschi, I was sure they were hiding. This was all about revenge. Natalie's spiteful threat to be sure we wouldn't out her, in collaboration with the lying thief Colabello. I looked at Marina, and I knew we couldn't step back and that no matter what, we'd have to find a way to keep my family safe.

When I returned, I tipped my head toward Dad and motioned him to the side of the box. I turned my back to the others and showed him the photo. His face furrowed into a frown so intense, I could see deep lines like parentheses forming from his nose to his mouth. His voice was hard as steel as he spoke in a whisper that belied his feelings. "Do not let your Mother see this." I nodded in agreement. "We'll speak about it later."

We took our seats, and he reached for Mom's hand and held on tight. If she was surprised, she didn't show it.

It was fortunate she couldn't see Dad's eyes or the fear in them—not for himself but for her and us, her family.

After the show, we made sure Mom and Dad were safely back at their hotel. Marina had called her man there and told him to be extra vigilant.

Alex and Simone decided to go for a nightcap before returning to the flat. I thought they'd be okay since the gang had already made sure we understood that they could find them again whenever and wherever they wanted. Hopefully, one threat at a time was enough.

I told Alex we'd be up early to see them off. I guess I didn't manage to keep all the worry out of my voice.

"Anything wrong, Nick?" He asked.

"Just tired." I smiled and changed the subject. "How's it going working with Dad at Hamilton Capital?"

His expression became thoughtful. "I wasn't sure it would work out. You know, the father-slash-son nepotism thing. I thought maybe the other employees would resent me." He shook his head. "That hasn't happened. I think they can see that I'm working hard and not playing the family card. Not that Dad would ever allow that."

"No, he wouldn't," I replied.

He nodded as Simone joined him and they left. By now, Marina was steaming, anger flooding out with her words. "We can't let them get away with this." She whipped out her cell, her finger hovering over the images in her photos. "I'm going to send Ahern those photos of Natalie and Colabello." She looked at me with fire in her eyes. "If he doesn't dump her, he's a bigger fool than I thought."

"Don't do that. Please," I said. "It could backfire. Simone and Alex will be gone soon. Safe. On their way home."

She moved her hand away from the screen and turned toward me, her shoulders relaxing slightly and her voice calmer than moments ago. "What about your parents?" She asked.

Her worry was warranted. "They'll be okay once the deal goes through. It's just a few more days, and the gang would be stupid to allow anything to jeopardize it. This is on Natalie. If the deal crashes and burns, she'll be the one they blame." I'd make sure of that.

Marina reluctantly agreed. But I could see what it was costing her. "I swear to you, when this is over, I'll make that *puttana* wish she'd never been born.

She was all in, and I was right there with her.

Chapter Forty-Three

Our home seemed empty, with Simone and Alex gone. We'd kissed them goodbye, promised to visit them in New York soon, and showed them into the waiting Escalade SUV for their trip to Gatwick.

After we closed the door, Marina slumped against me. Her beautiful face was pale, and worried lines edged around her mouth and furrowed her forehead. Her usually shining red hair was limp. She was bone tired, and it showed.

"I'm going to review everything we have so far on the New London staff," she said, opening her laptop and pulling up the files. "One of them is guilty. There must be something I've overlooked."

I doubted it, but didn't voice my opinion. Marina was as methodical and as thorough as a casino cashier counting out at closing. She'd work through the information in her own way.

I left her in the lounge and slipped away to call Dad.

"Nick. I just heard from Alex. He and Simone are at the airport and have boarded. They'll be leaving shortly." His 'thank God' was implied in his relieved tone. "Any news on the gang?" he asked. "Or who might have left the photo?"

Dad knew about Alex and Simone being set up in Brighton by Natalie and her dimwit boyfriend, Ahern. And that I suspected her of being responsible for the photo at the concert.

"Not yet," I replied. "I'm going to speak with Nigel and see what he got from Chimini." Dad knew who Nigel was and how he'd helped Marina and me in the past.

"Good," he said. Keep me up to date." He sighed in the way only a long-married husband could. "Your Mom wants to find a spot for brunch, then walk to Hyde Park and go back through the flower gardens. I'd rather we'd stay in, but I can't tell her why."

I understood his dilemma. "Go out, Dad. Those people…it's just a scare tactic. They won't do anything now that the money is almost in their hands." They could taste victory, and it was up to us to snatch it from their grasp. "Go anywhere Mom wants to go and enjoy the day." I paused. "We'll catch up later."

Thinking about scaring someone gave me an idea.

I called Marc and asked him for another favor. Syd's idea about me ratting her out to Gabi had resurfaced in my brain. Maybe it had been there all this time. It was slightly crazy and slightly out of his wheelhouse, but I knew the former King of the Con would love my idea. He did and laughed at how diabolical it was.

"You're full of surprises, Nick. I guess a few of my tactics rubbed off on you," he said as he agreed to the plan I proposed.

Let's just say Meade and Medina wouldn't know that the shit was about to hit the fan until it was too late to stop the splatter.

* * *

New York City had an unprecedented rat problem. The furry creatures were taking over—roaming the park, nesting under garbage cans on Park Avenue, scampering through bodegas in the Bronx, and hopping the ferry to Staten Island. Some people even gave 'rat tours' in the late evening hours, prime time for viewing the vermin in their favorite habitats.

The citizens were up in arms, calling it an epidemic and demanding that the administration do something about it. The Mayor, who had his own problem with rats on his Brooklyn street, not to mention with his constituents, appointed a Rat Czar to tackle the problem. That the person who was now in charge, a former New York City public school administrator, had no experience and no plan with which to combat the pests who nearly outnumbered the city's inhabitants seemed to be immaterial. When I asked Mom about it, she tskd. "Another brilliant idea from Hizzoner."

The city had changed garbage pick-up times, mandated closed bins, and rodent-repellent plastic liners, but the furry friends squeaked in delight as they gobbled up the goodies. Rat tours…how demented was that?

That's where Marc Rivers came into play. With a wide network of former miscreants, Marc had no problem in contacting a rat tour guide who would nab a few bagsful of the pesky pests and let them loose in the Meade and Medina Gallery on Spring Street in Soho.

Imagine everyone's surprise when passersby noticed dozens of rats running around the gallery's windows. Like good New Yorkers everywhere, they marked the sight of the infestation with cellphone photos and posted them liberally all over social media.

"Well, well," I said to Marina, holding my phone up to share the Facebook and Instagram posts that kept popping up with her. I think Maxime Meade might be a touch preoccupied today, dealing with this unforeseen event at the gallery."

She leaned over and asked, "Is this your doing?" Was that pride I heard in her voice?

"With a little help from a friend," I replied. "Wait until the *New York Post* gets wind of this." It would be an epic story and a sure business downer. No one would want to enter the space for days. Even then, I could imagine the cringing that would ensue if anyone set foot across the threshold. A huge smile spread across my face. I know, I was gloating as if I'd just broken the bank in Monte.

I'd bet Meade was fielding a call from his father right about now. Their artists were most likely freaking out. I wondered if rat poop would be hard to remove from oil paint?

Well, that wasn't my problem. I know my trick was petty, but it was what the gang deserved, and I hoped it would be distracting enough to buy Marina some time to figure out who the people involved in the switch were.

* * *

There was a knock on our front door as I savored the feeling of one-upmanship along with my cappuccino and croissant.

Gabi arrived, beautifully dressed for work but excited and flustered. "Good morning," she said in an upbeat tone. "I just heard from Stella that the meeting has been delayed for a few days." A moment later, she bit her bottom lip in uncertainty. "I'm not sure what happened, but there's some kind of problem at the Meade and Medina Gallery in New York, and Maxime has to fly home to deal with it."

I cut my eyes to Marina, who was brewing Gabi a coffee. "Really?" I said with as much of a poker face as I could manage.

Marina gave me the stink eye, which I ignored.

"Yes," Gabi continued. "The meeting has been postponed, although no one has explained the reason to me." She paused. "Please, don't misunderstand. Of course, I'm delighted to have another few days to try for us to outwit those people," she added with a touch of venom. "Especially that…that tramp, Natalie Stapleton."

Those photos had really gotten to her. George, whom she thought of as a good friend, had not only let her down but also betrayed her trust. Gabi plopped down in one of our comfy dining room chairs, looking deflated. Marina handed her a mug of fragrant coffee, which she inhaled. It seemed to settle her emotions.

"The emergency? It was our doing." I held up my laptop and showed her the posts and videos of the rats scurrying around the gallery windows and all over the paintings. Our rat tour guide must have left some tempting tidbits for the vermin to nibble on. They looked very contented.

Her beautiful, dark eyes widened, and her mouth opened wide. Then she began to laugh. "Nick, you are quite the devious gentleman, aren't you?"

"I try," I replied, wondering if Maxime Meade had smelled a rat.

Marina rolled her eyes at me. "Yes, it was a good ploy, but it's only temporary. She sat down next to Gabi. "I may be onto something, but I'm not sure yet that it will amount to anything." She took Gabi's hand in hers. "If it does, I will let you know."

"Are you going into work on a Sunday?" she asked.

Gabi checked her watch. "Yes. There's no such thing as a weekend until the exhibit launches. I'd better get going. Even without the Gentileschi, there's still so much to do."

"One more thing," Marina added. "Don't let anyone know about the situation at the Meade and Medina gallery. If someone mentions it, act surprised, okay?"

Gabi nodded and rose to leave. "I will positively keep mum about the whole episode," she said, biting back a smile. "Thank you both for being such good friends."

* * *

As soon as the door closed, I turned toward Marina. "What are you onto?" And, I asked myself, why hadn't she told me?

"Don't look so aggrieved, Nick. I just want to do a little more digging, and then I'll share. Why don't you carry on with your plans for the day?"

My plans were sketchy, but I couldn't sit around doing nothing. Nigel's name flashed across my brain. I'd pay him a visit and see what, if anything, his people had gotten out of Chimini or if the forger had known about the photo of Mom and Dad. That might be a long shot. The gang was tight-knit and probably didn't trust him enough to tell him about their scare tactics. He was the forger, not a full-fledged player. The guy knew how to keep his cards close to the vest, but by now, he might be frightened enough to make a play.

Chapter Forty-Four

I found Nigel where I knew he would be: sitting at his imposing antique desk in his large office at MI6 at Vauxhall Cross, surrounded by a mound of the Sunday papers. Behind him was the requisite portrait of the King, and a sideboard held silver-framed photos of Nigel with everyone who was anyone in the government, along with several A-list English celebrities. The Beckhams and Paul McCartney looked happier than I might have expected. What had Nigel done for them?

He peered over his glasses as I entered his domain. "Donahue, what do you want? I'm busy." He lifted his hand in a shooing away gesture as if dismissing an over-friendly pet.

My skin was thicker than that. Nigel hadn't barred me from entering the building or being whisked up to his office, so I took a seat opposite him, crossed my ankle over my knee, and waited for him to look up.

"Donahue, you are aware you are one of the most irritating people I know."

That couldn't be true, I thought. He knew every member of the Royal Family and the Cabinet, and I'd bet they gave him grief from time to time.

"Have you learned anything from Chimini?" I asked, leaning forward.

He placed his elbows on his desk and rested his chin on top of his hands. I was all set for a big reveal. But all I got was nothing.

"We pushed him as hard as possible, but he didn't know much," he replied.

The anticipation that had gleamed in my eyes was at a lower wattage now.

"Cheer up, Nicky. We're not finished with him yet."

Instruments of torture that I'd seen in spy thrillers flashed across my mind, and I gulped.

Nigel sat back in his big, luxurious leather chair, and a small smile parted his lips. It was as though he knew what I was thinking. "The only person he admitted to having contact with is Maxime Meade." He lifted a sheet of paper from a stack on the corner of his desk. "Who, as I understand it," he continued, "is now at Heathrow awaiting a flight to New York."

He set the paper back down and leveled his gaze straight at me. "I believe there is some kind of problem at his father's gallery. Something to do with a vermin infestation." His eyebrows rose to meet his patrician forehead. "You wouldn't know anything about that, would you?"

I didn't trust myself to answer. I shook my head and made what I hoped was a horrified face. Nigel's instincts were good, well, the best, and I wasn't sure he believed me.

"No, I don't suppose you would," he said with a heavy dose of sarcasm.

It was time to change the subject. To get back to Chimini.

"Are you sure he didn't say anything else? Did he mention George Colabello or Brian Ahern?

Nigel steepled his fingers and shook his head from side to side. "Not either of them, but he did intimate that some upper-crust English snob with a title had been tapped to pay the down payment he received to start the project."

So, he got part of his fee upfront. Interesting. He hadn't trusted the gang completely, even though they'd done business before. "Did he know who it was who ponied up the advance?" I asked.

"He may have, but he hasn't told us that…as of yet."

Nigel believed he would get the information out of Chimini in time. "Have you searched his house for paperwork or tapped into his bank accounts?"

That earned me a withering look from my friend that said, 'what exactly is it that you think we do around here?'

It was time to depart, as they said in Ancient Rome. Only, I was just leaving the building, not planning to commit suicide…not yet anyway.

* * *

While I'd been with Nigel, an idea had popped into my brain. MI6 was done with Chimini's home in Bath. I was sure they'd scoured it from top to bottom, but I had an idea about something they might have overlooked. What harm could it do if I took another poke around?

None, as far as I was concerned, although Nigel might not agree. It was still early in the day, and Marina was at her office with her staff. No one would miss me if I was gone for the afternoon. I stepped outside onto Vauxhall Cross and hailed a cab to Paddington Station. I'd take the next train to Bath and see what I could turn up.

Number 7 at The Circus was precisely as I remembered it. There was no blue and white 'police do not cross' tape across the front door. In fact, there was nothing to suggest that any police action had taken place there a day ago.

I walked up to the front door and bent down toward a rock on the side of the path. Underneath, the key that Chimini had used when we walked back from the pub was tucked in its regular hiding place. I looked to either side to make sure no one was watching me, or the house, put the key in the lock with a slightly shaking hand, and let myself in.

Breaking and entering isn't all it's cracked up to be on TV. Although, technically, I was just entering. Still, I had a horrible feeling that someone was watching and would surprise me with a bang on the head any minute. Shaking it off, I slid the house key into my pocket and looked around.

The ground floor was a mess. Paintings had been removed from the walls and were stacked in multiple piles on the floor. Lamp shades were tilted, and cushions were overturned as though Goldilocks had been looking for just the right one to plump up.

Walking around the debris of the police search, I cautiously made my way to the studio where Chimini and I had conducted business. The closet where he kept his replicas and works in progress stood open. The searchers had made a mess of it, too. There were several more copies of the Picasso I had purchased, and I was tempted to take one with me. I picked a canvas, then sighed and set it back down.

The striped wallpaper that had concealed the closet door was intact, although the paintings were scattered around. I remembered that before

Chimini had opened it with a slight push, he'd started to reach for a spot right above the switch on the right side, then stopped himself. It had looked like an unconscious gesture, and I hadn't thought it was significant at the time, but now I realized it might be.

Looking over my shoulder again to ensure there weren't any police lying in wait, ready to jump out at me, I took a deep breath and pressed the spot Chimini had almost touched.

A moment later, a narrow panel clicked open. Camouflaged by the stripes of the wallpaper, you would never have noticed it. Using two fingers, I pulled it open fully. It was about twelve inches high and five inches deep. Just the right size to hold the thick stack of hundred-pound notes I found there. On top of the banknotes was a folded letter with a note that looked like it had been scrawled in haste: *Hope this is sufficient to get you started on our project.*

There was no signature. But I knew who'd sent it and the money to Luke Chimini.

I'd seen the same letterhead with the crest of the Peake Jones family before on the wedding invitation that Gabi's parents had posted to Marina and me. I opened my cell and snapped a photo of the note and the money. Then, I put them back where I found them, closed the panel, and retraced my steps to the front door. I opened it a few inches and cautiously looked out. My hands are shaking for real now, like a player who'd have to face his family and tell them that he'd lost their home in a winner-take-all poker game.

For me, it felt worse than that. I'd have to tell Marina what I found and the implications for Gabi. There was no good time to do it, even though I had to. I was lost in thought as I walked back to the station. It wasn't until I boarded the train back to London that I realized I still had Chimini's key in my pocket.

I hoped he'd have a spare if Nigel ever let him go.

Chapter Forty-Five

On the train back to Paddington, I realized I needed to discuss this with someone I could trust before I brought my evidence to Marina.

I called my dad. "How's your day going?" I asked.

"What's wrong?" He replied, cutting right through my affable question.

"Nothing. I just wanted to see if you and Mom enjoyed brunch and your walk in Hyde Park."

"We did." His tone said he didn't believe me. "Your Mom decided she wanted to shop some more at Harrods, and I declined. I'm just heading downstairs to the bar for an early cocktail. I think you should join me." I could hear the concern in his voice for me.

He didn't have to ask me twice. "I'll be there in about twenty minutes."

When I arrived, Dad was seated at a table for two in the stylish silver and grey bar. He was sipping one of their famous Martinis with a twist poured tableside from a trolley.

"No Jameson's today?" I asked as I joined him. "I heard these were really good," he said, lifting his glass. Would you like to try one?"

I nodded yes, and the barman with the trolley appeared as if by magic. Cocktail in hand, I tipped my glass toward Dad's, took a sip, and let out a contented sigh.

Dad noticed my satisfied expression and nodded toward my drink. "Glad that could help lighten your load."

"I wish a drink was all it took," I replied. Then I told him about my recent trip to Bath and what I'd found in Luke Chimini's hidden cubby.

"You think Gabi's father is the royal snob funding part of the con?" he asked in amazement.

"The note I found with the cash would suggest so." It made me angry, and I could feel my face growing hot. "How could he do this to her…his own daughter? He's put everything she's worked for on the line, including her reputation. She's already been betrayed by someone she thought was her friend, and now by her father. If anyone in the museum finds out about this, there'll be no coming back from it."

Dad took another sip of his drink and then spoke. "Someone there already knows. The person who's—what did you call them—the Second Inside Man. They know exactly what's going on. They're setting up Gabi to take the fall."

"You got that right." I nodded. "We still don't know who that is, and we're running out of time if we want to get the original Gentileschi back and catch a murderer."

"Nick, tell Marina what you discovered as soon as possible."

"I'm planning to the moment I get home," I replied. "But I wanted your opinion first. You know how much I value it."

"Thanks." He lifted his empty glass and signaled for another. I shook my head, no. I needed to be clear-headed when I spoke to Marina.

"I need you to do me a favor, Nick."

"Sure," I replied. "Anything."

"Reassure your Mom that those Oxford Alliance people are all smoke and mirrors and not dangerous criminals. She's very concerned about them coming to the Hamilton Capital Gala. She's got it into her head that they're planning something. I told her they wouldn't do anything untoward."

I wasn't so sure about that. Had Mom mentioned to him that she'd already spoken to me? I didn't think so. I nodded to Dad and said that I'd get on it. "Of course," I replied. "I'll tell her everything is fine."

Was it the truth? Excluding my gambler's intuition, I had no way of knowing.

Chapter Forty-Six

Marina had beaten me home by a few minutes. When I entered, she was hanging up her favorite bright red bomber jacket.

I hugged her and kissed her lush lips, then stepped back, taking her in. Her eyes were troubled. Their usual sparkling green dulled with worry.

"There's something I have to—" I began at the same time as she said, "Oh, Nick, I found out—"

We both stopped mid-sentence. "You first," I said to Marina. I had a sinking feeling she would tell me what I already knew.

"I've been looking into everyone at New London, top to bottom, including Gabi." Taking a deep breath, she continued. "It's not her I'm worried about. It's her Dad."

I nodded at her in agreement, and she gave me a strange look. "You know this? How?"

I explained that after visiting Nigel at his office, I decided to have another look around Luke Chimini's home. I told her what I found: a stack of hundred-pound bills and the note and letterhead with Gabi's parents' crest sitting on top of them. I showed her the photo I'd taken. "There's no getting around the fact that he's involved. If he were standing here right now, I'd punch his lights out. For starters."

"According to Syd, Gabi's Dad is in dire financial straits because of his unsuccessful winery." *And, living the high life,* I thought.

Marina was nodding along. "That's what we found, as well. He'll lose the estate If he doesn't pay off some of his loans very soon. She looked at me.

"A man like that? Who knows what he'd do to keep up his lifestyle?"

"For starters, he's willing to sell out his daughter," I replied. "I'd bet the flat he's never seen the original 'Weeping Mary Magdalene,' so he must be working with someone at New London who could insure he'd get part of the take for staking the operation."

My money was still on Bennings, Royal connections, and all, but I kept that to myself.

Marina had a cock-sure smile on her face. "What?" I asked.

"I'm positive the gang used him for the upfront money to pay Chimini's deposit, and that they have no intention of cutting him in. Why would they? There's not much he could do about it after the fact. If he went to the police, he'd be arrested for aiding and abetting a crime. He'd surely have to hand over the estate and the winery, and his status will suffer."

"He'd become a pariah amongst the gentry. Someone who let it all slip away."

He wouldn't be the first. If it became public knowledge, it would ruin Gabi's life, nonetheless. "Should we tell Gabi what's going on with her father?" I asked. If we did, I was afraid it would destroy her.

Marina demurred. "Not yet. Since the meeting was postponed, we have a few more days to work this out. "I'm not sure we can avoid hurting Gabi, but we can try. I'm not finished with the museum's personnel. I have several more people to re-investigate."

We'd both taken seats at the kitchen island while we discussed what we'd uncovered. "Let's order in some Thai for dinner," Marina said. "It's going to be a long night."

I agreed but told her I had plans for later in the evening.

Over the years, I'd heard rumblings about many players, including Duke Harrington Peake Jones. The rumor was that he was fond of playing Blackjack at a few of the smaller London casinos. They weren't as polished as the city's famous spots. Shabby might be a better way to describe them. Like a run-down toff in a suit with shiny spots on its elbows. More like the casinos in Vegas that were way off the strip, downtown.

These gambling emporiums had a more lenient policy of extending credit to the gentry. From what I heard, the owners were rough, and if you didn't pay up, they had ways of making sure you did. Default, and you were in deep trouble. Unless you anted up. If threats didn't work, estates could be seized, or family members threatened. Violence was always an option.

I hadn't encountered the Duke anywhere I played, but it would be easy enough to find out which casinos he frequented and how much he owed at each. I made a few calls and got what I needed.

After dinner with Marina, I dressed in my Blackjack tuxedo and headed to the Kensington Gaming Club. It was a small, discreet casino on a side street near Hyde Park. Nothing flashy or obvious. It would appear to be a member's only club if anyone noticed. A fifty-pound fee was the tariff to become a member, which I handed over to a gorgeous blond at reception who was there to tempt potential patrons to join.

The club had seen better days, like I said. If you looked closely, you'd notice the faded wallpaper and slightly threadbare carpet. Although, I didn't think the members seated around the Blackjack table cared about the amenities.

Mostly, they appeared to be hell-bent on losing their shirts.

I watched for a while and thought the games might be rigged. Especially Roulette. But watching wouldn't get the job done.

I'd looked up the Duke on social media and recognized the man sitting at the high-stakes Blackjack table. My hands immediately balled into fists. Not a good start. Calm down, I told myself. Just sit down and play. That's the way to get what you need.

Fortunately, the anchorman's seat was vacant, and I slid onto the chair and nodded at the dealer. The other players, including Peake Jones, barely acknowledged me. I was okay with that. I wasn't here for chit-chat. I was here to watch. And do my best to make sure he lost.

He didn't need any help from me. After a few hands, I was on to him. He was using a camouflage technique, raising and lowering his bet randomly when the count was good without giving it away. The problem was that he drank quite a bit and played erratically. It felt like he was losing the thread of when to bet high and when to go low, and his stack of chips dwindled quickly. He called for the pit boss and had a whispered conversation. A few minutes later, he signed a chit, and a new pile of chips appeared in front of him.

No wonder the family was in dire straits over their finances. The estate needed repairs, and the winery was a drain. This wasn't the only casino Peake Jones played at, and I knew he was losing at all of them. He was a fool and a reprobate.

I gathered up my chips—I'd won a few pounds—and left the table. I headed for the bar and kept my eye on Gabi's Dad. He lost his second set of chips and had asked for another. The pit boss leaned in and whispered in his ear as he shook his head no. Usually, a casino will extend credit to a longtime player, but he must be at his limit. No more chips until he paid up.

My stomach was roiling at the thought of how much he must owe and what he was doing to Gabi and his family. It was apparent he didn't care. His face turned bright red. His dark eyes flamed with fire as he turned to the pit boss and croaked out a slurred warning. I only caught part of it: "…make sure…be sorry…" before he stumbled from the table and toward the cloakroom, trying to look imposing and failing miserably.

I followed him out of the casino and watched as he lurched toward his waiting car, all the while thinking of our friend and the scumbag who she had the misfortune to call father.

How would she take the news of his betrayal? Not well, I thought.

Chapter Forty-Seven

"Is Gabi in?" I demanded of Marina, looking up at the ceiling, anger rolling through my body in waves. "I need to speak with her."

She took a step back. "What happened, Nick?"

"Her father. He's what happened." My voice was shaking.

Marina took my hand and led me to the couch. "Sit. Talk to me."

I shook my head. "He's a drunk, and he's gambling away his daughter's future." I could hear the fury in my voice. I took a deep breath and calmed down enough to continue. "He lost big tonight and would have lost a significant amount more if the casino had extended additional credit.

"We need to tell Gabi about his involvement with the Gentileschi." I paused. "It's going to break her heart."

"I think he's already done that," Marina replied. "She knows the kind of man he is. Not a good one." Marina raised her eyes to the ceiling. "There's no good time for something like this. They're home, but let's wait and tell her tomorrow. I'll be meeting with her to discuss everything I've learned."

I'd calmed down a bit and sunk back into the couch. Marina rose and made us each a cup of herbal tea. "Was there any new information?" I raised my mug and inhaled the fragrant aroma.

"Yes. It appears Dame Harris is very friendly with the Duke. More than friendly."

I sat up straight. "So, you think she's the Second Inside Man?

"If she is, she's playing a dangerous game. She could stand to lose everything."

"Yeah, well, she's tough. She got rid of her deadbeat husband, kept her money, and used her influence to get her position; she must have contacts who could be giving her helpful information," I said. "She could have something on Bidenstock. Be blackmailing him."

"Or," Marina added, "it could be the other way around. Listen, he's all over the galleries, and sharp enough to know everyone's business and who's playing with fire."

"Do you think he knows about her relationship, whatever that is, to Gabi's father?"

"I'm certain he does, and he's not above exploiting it. Although, maybe not as far as stealing the original Artemisia for her." Marina made the universal gesture of rubbing her thumb and first two fingers together for money. "If he's in, it's for some cash. Plus, he's got a cushy job at New London and may be angling for a better one."

The gang would have to split the take too many ways, even though it would be at least seven million, plus damages. I wouldn't put it past them to eliminate some of the players. But which ones, I wondered? I knew Marina would eliminate Natalie Stapleton without batting an eye.

"Has Bidenstock been in any legal trouble?

My question was rewarded with a Cheshire grin. "Interesting that you should ask. He was sent down for a minor drug charge when he was a juvenile."

"Wouldn't that have been expunged?"

"It was, but I talked to the right people and found out about it." Her grin grew wider.

"Ana or Nikki?" I asked. The young women who worked for her knew how to elicit information. No one seemed to turn them down. Marina had trained them well.

"Ana," she replied. "Niccolo knew somebody who knew Jose way back when."

Niccolo, Ana's boyfriend, had a wide orbit. "Your network is almost as good as Nigel's."

"Speaking of the man, has he learned anything more from Chimini?"

"Not yet. He's still working on it. Nige is optimistic the forger will take the government's protection over being bumped off by the gang.

"I'm just not sure he's smart enough to do that."

Marina rose to make us each another mug of tea. When she returned, she said, "I spoke to your dad today."

"You did?" I couldn't keep the surprise from my voice. "I had a drink with him at the hotel, and he never mentioned a word about talking to you."

"He's worried, Nick."

"I know that." I shook my head. "He's concerned about Mom and the threats against our family. He asked me to reassure her again."

"There is that, although I convinced him the photo with the bullseye was just another scare tactic, and we'd make sure everyone was safe." She took a sip of her tea and continued. "It's more about the idea that there could be a traitor in his company."

"Did he ask you to investigate this for him? Any idea if it's true?"

She nodded. "It might be. I have business acquaintances in New York who know your dad's firm." Her deep green eyes lit up with admiration. "They assured me it has one of the most stellar financial reputations.

"Hamilton Capital uses its company to run background checks on its employees every six months. Everyone at the New York office is clean. No red flags. All above board."

"So, it has to be someone here, in London?" I asked. "Someone who knows Oxford Alliance Ltd and has an allegiance with Windsor Smythe."

"I agree." Marina's red hair bobbed up and down as she nodded. "Your dad's postponed the company gala for a few days until he can find the traitor and put this behind him. He's furious, Nick. He feels betrayed."

"He asked me to have several of Hamilton Capital employees followed."

"Which employees?" I asked. There weren't that many people in the London office, and I didn't know any of them well, so could hardly venture a guess.

"I'm sorry. I can't reveal their names. Your father requested that I keep this confidential."

"From me? His son?" I was sure my expression telegraphed that I wasn't happy about being excluded.

"It's probably for your own protection," she said, her face devoid of any expression that would help clarify Dad's reasoning.

I got it. Although I didn't like it. Dad didn't want me poking my nose in and putting myself in danger.

"I've got several people working on it now. We're certain that Windsor Smythe is somehow involved with the gang from New York."

"Of course he is," I said, nodding in agreement. I remembered being approached by Cargill at the casino and Dad's retelling of the meeting at Oxford Alliance Ltd. "With their supposed 'collection of masterpieces,' they could take the original Gentileschi, reposition it, and move it to a new buyer for a hefty commission. Unless we get it back first."

"I imagine Windsor Smythe is getting nervous with all the delays. And I wouldn't be surprised if his contact from Hamilton Capital, who also stands to profit, wants a quick resolution. Windsor Smythe may be pushing for a meeting with this person to help move things along and influence your dad. If the traitor acquiesces, we'll know who it is by the end of the day."

Once again, I thought there were a lot of people sharing in the payoff. I know seven million dollars plus sounds like a huge sum of money, but the gang seemed to be growing exponentially, and the share of the pot becoming smaller. Unless another forged Artemisia was hanging around that the gang was also planning to sell as the real deal.

I hated that Hamilton Capital had become embroiled in this mess, even on the fringes. I could imagine how Dad felt. Another betrayal of trust. Another punch in the gut. Dad didn't deserve this. It was bad luck, but I knew it could be turned around. And I intended to make sure it was.

Chapter Forty-Eight

We couldn't put it off any longer. It was time to tell Gabi about the extent of her father's treachery and duplicity. Just thinking about the drunken, entitled Duke made me want to make him eat every single one of the chits he'd signed from each of the casinos where he owed money. Literally swallowing his lies and deceit with his substandard, overpriced wine would just be the beginning. I...

"Nick?" Marina interrupted my inner musings. The vile look on my face must have given me away. "Please, focus. On Gabi. Not her Dad." She had read me perfectly, just like always.

"Gabi and Syd will be down in a few minutes. She insisted that Syd come with her. I'm sure she knows that what we want to discuss isn't good news."

"Okay, I'll keep it together," I replied. At least, I'd try to. I took a few deep, calming breaths and put a neutral expression on my face. Believe me, it wasn't easy. Anger was bubbling right below the surface.

Just then, there was a tentative knock on the door. Marina opened it, and the two women walked in. Their faces were ashen, and they looked nervous.

Bad news seemed to have a way of letting your body know it was coming even before it arrived. I'd bet neither of them had had much sleep last night, or any night recently.

Marina hugged them and invited them to sit with us around our dining table, where tea bags, mugs, and a kettle were waiting.

Gabi took a seat, looked at Marina and me in turn, and burst into tears. Syd rose to comfort her fiancée and put an arm around her protectively. If only it were that easy. Her body shook as the other woman held her, finding little comfort in her embrace.

"Have you found out who replaced the Gentileschi?" she asked, sniffing through her tears.

Marina reluctantly answered. "Not yet. But we're closer." She shot her eyes at me. "We have a lead we're pursuing with someone involved."

"Who? Who is it?" she demanded.

"Gabi, it's your father. He's financed part of the con and paid the upfront money to the artist who forged the painting."

Her face drained of all color. This was the embodiment of what people meant when they said someone turned pale as a ghost. She swayed in her seat and probably would have fainted if Syd hadn't been holding her so tightly.

"My father?" she asked, skepticism in her voice. "Are you certain? Why would he do this to me? I know he can be a bastard. But this is beyond even what I thought he was capable of. When did he decide to ruin my life? And, on purpose. Why? Why?"

The easy answer was entitlement, which had started long ago, and no one had curbed. From the unchecked gambling debts, the vanity winery, and heavy drinking, the Duke had gotten away with it all. Until now. Now, it was time for him to face up to his actions.

"Gabi," Marina leaned across the table and took her hand. "We have proof that he can't refute. I'll be taking it to someone in government who's helping us. He'll make sure your father pays for what he's done. I promise you."

Would that really do any good, I wondered? Had too much damage already been done to this promising young woman. A reputation was hard to repair once it was broken.

The color had begun to return to her face. She took in a deep breath. Syd also looked relieved and stepped back to pour her partner a cup of tea. The steam curled up and filled the kitchen with a calming fragrance.

Marina posed her next question carefully. "Do you think your mother knows about any of this?"

Gabi shrugged. "She certainly knows about the gambling and the drinking. It would be hard to ignore that when she sees the results nearly every day. I know she hates it and probably him for carrying on that way."

"She lives with the man," Syd interjected. "At least most of the time," she added snidely.

Gabi continued. "Him working with a forger and ruining me and my career? She'd never allow that. She'd probably threaten to kill him."

It would be justifiable homicide, I thought.

"Since we've been making plans for our wedding, I've questioned her about if they could afford to spend so much on such a lavish event. *"Don't be silly, of course we can, darling,"* was her reply." Gabi hesitated. "It was what I expected she'd say, avoiding the real problem."

Her mom was in self-imposed denial, I imagined. For the benefit of her child? Or for the survival of her own marriage. Such as it was.

"I suppose I wanted it to be true, so I ignored my feelings that it was too much. Honestly, everything has been very off for as long as I can remember." She paused. "The money is Mother's, inherited from my grandfather. The estate belonged to Dad's family and was passed to him. I know she's given him loads and loads of cash to keep it going, especially that awful winery." Gabi shook her head, and her sleek black curls tumbled around her face. "It was foolish of her to leave it to Dad to manage things. He takes his privileged upbringing seriously and always thinks he's in the right."

Syd gently squeezed her shoulder, and Gabi gazed up at her. "We certainly won't be doing what her parents did," she said to Marina and me. "We plan to share our lives always."

These women had the right attitude. I hoped life wouldn't derail them and that it would always be like that for them—the way it was for Mom and Dad, and Marina and me.

Chapter Forty-Nine

Marina shook her head after the two women departed. "Gabi's mother is trapped."

"No one is trapped if they really want to be free," I replied.

Marina turned to me and considered her words before she spoke. "She probably still loves him on some level. I believe she's trying to protect her child, and she's afraid leaving him would do more harm than good."

"How so?" I asked.

"Leave Gabi more vulnerable…to his machinations." She shrugged. "I don't know for certain, but I believe he's the kind of man who thrives on cruelty to those he believes he can control and would try to get even if his wife left with her money. Take it out on his daughter."

Her green eyes had gone as dark as the bottom of the sea, and I could see she was thinking of other men and their cruelty. Had she experienced this kind of behavior herself? I prayed she hadn't.

She looked up and returned to the present, squared her shoulders, and picked up her cell. "It's time to tell Nigel about the note and the money."

* * *

Marina put the cell on speaker and let Nigel know I was part of the conversation. "Now what, Donahue?" he huffed out.

Marina didn't give me a chance to answer. She laid it all out. "We have proof that Duke Harrington Peake Jones is involved with the forged Gentileschi." She explained that when I went back to Chimini's house, I'd discovered a secret compartment filled with cash. And a note that was written on the Duke's letterhead.

"Where exactly did you find this, Donahue?" Nigel seemed extremely annoyed that his team had not discovered the hidden cache.

"It seems your agents didn't look hard enough," I said with a bit of snark, then toned it down and gave him specific details on where the compartment was located. "If you'd like, I could meet your people at the house. Fortunately, I still have the key."

"That won't be necessary," he replied. I could almost see him drumming his fingers on his desk in frustration. "My team will take care of it."

Marina chimed in. "In the meantime, I'll send you Nick's photo of the note and the money."

"Yes, please do," he replied. "And I'll be speaking with Mr. Chimini again quite soon."

"What about the Duke?" I asked, leaving out all the expletives that were floating through my mind.

"Don't worry, Donahue. We'll see to him, as well."

Then he was gone.

Finally, a break in the case that made me feel hopeful. I smiled at Marina. I could imagine Chimini's reaction when Nigel's men showed him their new evidence. He'd have to fold. And the Duke. Nigel might have to tread carefully, but he knew how to play his cards, even with the royals.

"I'm wondering," Marina said as she gazed up toward the ceiling thinking, what will Rosemary Harris make of all of this? It might change her viewpoint." She looked at her watch. "We should pay her a visit, don't you think?

Face the lioness in her den? Hmm, that sounded like a good idea. "You think she'll confess to being part of the scheme?" I asked.

"I'm not sure she is." Marina's expression turned shrewd. "She may have met the Duke at some high-brow soirée, and he hit on her. She probably didn't realize he was chatting her up in expectation of wheedling some money out of her as an investment for the winery. After all, she's a Cultural Trustee with a title. He probably saw her as someone with deeper pockets than his."

Marina grew more confident. "She knows everything that's going on at the museum and saw something in the shady Duke that made her suspicious. Made her want to find out more."

Marina considered her following words before she spoke. "Remember how calm you said she appeared after Gabi ordered everyone out of the conference room? Sitting back and assessing the situation? Afterward, she ordered Gabi to apologize. Maybe the Duke had already approached her, and she was considering her options."

She shrugged. "That's one scenario. Or, she may have realized there was an opportunity to increase her own fortunes."

From what I remembered from Marina's file, she wasn't that wealthy. I still hadn't discovered what a Cultural Trustee received as a salary. Anyway, I hoped she was the one turning the screws on the Duke.

I looked at Marina and scowled. "So, who do you have in mind?"

"Soon, Nick. Soon."

Chapter Fifty

The New London Arts Museum opened for business on the dot at ten a.m. People filled the towering glass, sun-filled lobby designed to strategically highlight the art at the entrance, which couldn't have been more spectacular: one of "The Water Lilies Series" by Claude Monet.

Since we started on this case, I'd been learning more about art. Even I knew that a masterwork of this magnitude was a spectacular get for a relatively new museum.

A massive and brilliant artwork that he painted while surrounded by the beauty of his Japanese-inspired gardens, it seemed to come alive as it shimmered in the sunlight. It was hard to tear your eyes away from it.

We could hear the patrons' exclamations of delight as they queued up to pass through security to enter. The anticipation was contagious, and people were discussing which exhibits they wanted to view in this exciting place that people recently seemed to be discovering. London had many world-famous museums, all free, and people had their pick.

I was glad to see the crowds thronging the lobby. A few people inquired about when the European Masters Exhibit would be opening. The New London Arts Museum had done a massive publicity campaign about the paintings and the artists included. Expectations were high, and people were looking forward to seeing it.

Marina and I bypassed the line and walked up to the security desk. We said we were here to speak with Dame Harris. The guard didn't ask if we had an appointment, and we didn't say. By now, we were familiar to the staff. He nodded and called to inform her we were on our way to her office.

We took a detour and walked past several galleries, including Gabi's, which had an "Exhibit Opening Soon" sign on an easel in front of a curtain hanging from the entrance. If the visitors had been disappointed, I could only imagine how Gabi felt.

The guard trailed behind us until we reached the private elevator and unlocked it so we could travel to the third floor.

Dame Harris's office was a big corner space, of course, with a commanding view of the gardens in front of New London. *If she squinted,* I thought, *she could almost see the Palace.*

When we entered, she rose from behind her desk. "Ms. DiPietro, Mr. Donahue." Her tone was cold and professional. Not happy to see us vibe at all. Nope. None. "This is unexpected." She gestured for us to take a seat in front of her ornate Regency desk, then sat back, steepled her hands under her chin, and waited.

"We'd like to ask you what…" I began, anxious to get this over with, but stopped short as Marina kicked me hard in my ankle.

Okay, she could take the lead. My masculinity wasn't offended.

"Dame Harris," Marina began, "thank you for seeing us."

We hadn't given her a choice, had we?

Marina continued. "We have new information about the forged Gentileschi and were hoping you could help us." The smile never left her eyes or her voice.

"Me?" Dame Harris put a hand to her chest as if in shock. "How could I possibly help you? Me?" she repeated. "I can't imagine how." It was easy to tell she was as conversant in the art of stalling as a player fiddling with their stack of chips.

"Yes," replied Marina. "You." She waited a beat. "And Duke Harrington Peake Jones, Lady Gabriella Peake Jones' father."

Too bad Marina hadn't said 'pater'; that would have sounded classier.

This time, the shock was genuine. "I…I hardly know the Duke. How dare you come into my museum and accuse me of…of…"

Marina interrupted, holding up her hand. "Why would you think we're accusing you of anything?" Sincerity dripped from her voice. "We all would like to find the original painting and return it to New London for the upcoming exhibit, ensuring that everyone, here and at the Meade and Medina Gallery, will be satisfied. Can you tell us what you know to help us with our inquiries?"

Wow. Now, she added some *Law and Order* dialogue. Nice touch.

Dame Harris sat up straighter in her padded Regency chair, a companion piece to her desk. "I…I don't know anything and have nothing to say, and if you persist in harassing me, I'll have to take steps." She folded her arms in front of her chest for emphasis. "Now, I'd like you to leave. Be assured, the Museum's Board will hear about this…this…" She pushed a button on the side of her desk, and her assistant came in shortly.

Pasting a fake smile on her face, she said, "Please show Ms. DiPietro and Mr. Donahue out."

* * *

"Good job," I said sarcastically once we were outside in the gardens. "We didn't get much. What next?" I asked.

Marina ignored my remark. "Let's just sit and wait to see what happens."

I shot her a sideways look. "She's up there." I pointed toward the top of the building.

"And we're down here." I patted the bench we were occupying. "I don't think she'll come running out the door in a panic anytime soon. What are you up to?"

"Be quiet. Let's just listen for a while." She pulled out her cell and clicked on an app I didn't recognize.

"Did you bug her office? Surprise and admiration vied for a place in my voice.

"I did. With a tiny microphone, she'll never see." Glee gleamed in her eyes.

"Is this Nigel's doing? You know it's illegal, right?"

She made a rude sound and told me again to be quiet and listen. I did. It was very illuminating. Dame Harris hadn't wasted any time ringing the

Duke. Telling him she was being accused of misdeeds and art theft because of him. Things she had absolutely nothing to do with, she reminded him several times. Covering her butt, just in case someone was listening like we were.

"Stay away from me. Our relationship is over." I raised my eyebrows at that.

"You won't be getting another pound for your winery. You and your nasty little daughter can go screw yourselves."

Ouch. And, from the mouth of a Dame. What was London coming to?

"What do you think?" I asked Marina.

"I told you, she's not the one. She didn't steal the painting."

"No, but she helped finance the forgery. She's not an innocent bystander."

Marina continued. "But she is frightened. Maybe rightly so. She suspects who is responsible and doesn't want them to know what she's thinking. And, most assuredly, not about her relationship with the Duke. And frightened people make mistakes."

Marina fiddled with her phone and deleted the app. I was a little disappointed. Eavesdropping was not her thing, but I enjoyed it from time to time. Especially at the Blackjack table. You never knew when something juicy might come your way.

Chapter Fifty-One

Back home, Marina checked in with the operatives who were tailing the possible Hamilton Capital traitors.

I hoped they'd discover who it was by the end of today. Knowing Dad, he wouldn't rest easy until he could confront the person responsible. Unlike me, who'd boot their ass out the door, he'd just ask them to leave.

"Anyone rise to the top of the pile?" I asked Marina.

She nodded. "Not who I expected, though."

"Care to share?

"Not yet, Nick. My person put a tap on their phone and is confirming the suspect has a meeting with Windsor Smythe this afternoon. He's going to get it all on video."

"Even though he's expecting this, your dad is going to be heartbroken." Marina's voice filled with a sad note. "He's such an honorable man; it's hard for him to fathom someone close to him, and the company could sell them out. Especially someone he trusts."

I was beginning to have an inkling of who it was. "People do many bad things for money," I replied. Sometimes, it was for a misguided belief, as I'd learned recently, but more often than not, cash was the culprit.

"We'll know very soon." I could see she was contemplating how she'd tell my dad. "It's always devastating news when someone you trust breaks that bond, isn't it?"

Take Gabi and her poor excuse for a Father. He hadn't given it a second thought when he financed the forgery, never mind considering the possibility that she would suffer. Who could do that to their own child?

I must have spoken the last out loud. Marina reached over and took my hand. "You'd be surprised, Nick. Not everyone is as honorable as you."

Again, I wondered who, if anyone, had betrayed her in the past? She didn't speak much about her life before we met or her days with MI6, which was okay with me. We all had our secrets. We were together here and now, and that made me very happy.

"I've got this figured out," she said. I just need one more piece to fall into place."

Lloyd Bennings was still my preferred suspect, but I'd have to wait and see. At this point, all bets were off. It could be anyone, even the smiling security guard at the front desk who waved us through.

* * *

"Donahue," Nigel said imperiously when I answered my cell. "I have important news," he continued without even waiting for me to say hello.

"Chimini has seen the light, like an artist capturing a heavenly glow on a canvas." Now, satisfaction filled his voice. "He has confessed to forging the 'Weeping Magdalene.' I could almost see him beaming. "You notice I said forging, as in to present it as an original, not a replica. Interpol will be looking into the case immediately."

I was delighted they'd finally got him on something, but was it enough?

"Did he cop to any other forgeries for the Meade and Medina people?" I asked.

"Not yet. But we're not quite done interrogating him. Surprisingly, he volunteered some information that might be of interest to you."

Nigel made me wait for it. Of course, he did. "He explained that he's been copying masterpieces for Oxford Alliance Ltd for their new endeavor in the art market segment."

"He confessed to that? Why would he?" I asked.

"I believe he thought it might help his case if he came clean. You know, buy a little insurance." Nigel considered his following words. "To put it in plain terms, he's scared out of his mind that the gang and or Windsor

Smythe will kill him."

"He should be. If Windsor Smythe gets wind of this, Chimini will be toast." I remembered how Dad described the man's not-so-subtle threats at their meeting.

"Yes, unfortunately." Nigel couldn't disguise the snark he was projecting. "Well, it would be nothing more than he deserves. You Americans let him go even when you had him in flagrante delicto."

Why was he lumping all of us Americans together? It was the *F.B.I.* who had let Chimini escape to forestall a major crisis in the art market. It was *their fault* he was still around. *Not mine.*

Oh, your Caravaggio is a forgery. So sorry. How much did it set you back at auction?

I hadn't even met Chimini until last week. "Did he tell you what masterworks he painted for Oxford Alliance Ltd.'s grand scam?

'It was quite a list. Matisse, Picasso, a Rembrandt." Nigel paused to snort, then continued. "Let me see." He must have been reading from a list. "A Van Gogh, a Damien Hirst, a Dali. The inventory goes on."

Well, he was undoubtedly talented. My cut-up Picasso replica was a testament to that. I wondered why he hadn't just painted his own pictures. He must have realized he'd never reach the exalted heights of the artists he copied. Or attain their fame.

Nigel wasn't finished. "I have a plan to undo Windsor Smythe and his band of fraudsters. The publisher of the *Financial Times* is a good friend."

Of course, he is. Please don't tell me you golf together. I thought and rolled my eyes even though Nigel couldn't see me.

Nigel spared me the details of their kinship. "He's agreed to plant a small story that Oxford Alliance Ltd is in dire straits for fraudulent representation, and Windsor Smythe may be looking at being indicted on several counts. I left the wording up to him. It's his newspaper."

"You know he's been after my dad to bring some Hamilton Capital clients to his firm. In fact, he's been quite insistent. This is great news." I paused, thinking things through. "Nigel," I asked. "How did you know about all of this?"

Nigel tsked into the phone. "Give me some credit, Donahue." Then he was gone.

I clicked off and turned toward Marina, whose smile reached from ear to ear. I didn't have to tell her Nigel's plan. She already knew. In fact, I was sure it was her doing.

"You should call your Dad, Nick. He'll be pleased at the news."

"Thank you for interfering," I said and pulled her in for a huge hug. "What would I do without you?"

"Probably play Blackjack all day," she replied as she chucked me under my chin.

* * *

I called and let Dad know what was happening with Oxford Alliance Ltd. It raised his spirits somewhat. "I still don't trust them, Nick. He'll probably find a way to get out of this and keep his business going."

"Well, at least you won't have to deal with him again," I said. "You should uninvite him from the Hamilton Capital Gala."

"He invited himself. I'll send a note to his firm that we've canceled. I'm sure he'll find out it's still on. Show up anyway. All bluster and false charm like he's the man of the hour rather than a scheming thief.

"That might be fine, though. Then I could have our security manhandle him and his cohorts out the door." He couldn't hide the satisfaction at the prospect of that happening.

Dad got down to what was really on his mind. "Has Marina found the traitorous mole in my company?" An edge had returned to his voice, and I could feel his anger radiating through the phone.

"She's working on it," I replied. "She'll have a name for you soon." I didn't want to give him false hope that she'd have an answer by today. It would be a real coup if he could confront this person after hearing the news about Windsor Smythe's upcoming indictment. They'd be backed into a corner with nowhere to go. And knowing Dad, he would be calm while showing no mercy.

CHAPTER FIFTY-ONE

We agreed to speak again later when Marina had more information.

She was on her way to her office to meet a potential new client. "Please review the files, Nick, and see if anything stands out that we might have missed, would you?"

She knew I would. I still had my favorite suspect, but no actual proof. Maybe I could find a detail we'd overlooked. I was still carefully considering Lloyd Bennings and maybe his extra-relationship partner, Jose Bidenstock. I sat down at the kitchen table and began to read.

Chapter Fifty-Two

I was only at it for a minute when I heard the doorknob turning. "What did you forget?" I asked, thinking it was Marina.

"Donahue, you bastard!" were the harsh words that assaulted me when I turned around.

Clive Hastings Cargill was standing in the lounge. "Cargill! What the hell," I bellowed. "How did you get in?" I studied him carefully to see if he was carrying a weapon as I slowly rose to face him. He wasn't, and I walked closer. Just a red face flaming with anger. Sweat pouring off him in buckets. Hands balled into fists, like a caged animal preparing to strike. I decided weapon or not. He could be dangerous and edged closer to the knife rack on the kitchen counter.

"I waited until your girlfriend left and managed to get to your door before it closed."

This was terrible news. Cargill must have been hiding under the staircase to the front entry. Marina had been in a hurry and must have forgotten to lock our inside door. We'd have to tighten our security again. All this breaking and entering was making me nervous.

"What the hell are you doing here? You'd better tell me before I call the police and have you arrested." *Or before Marina returns and clobbers you.*

"You've put me right in the middle of everything, haven't you?" The words came out in a mash of rage. His shoulders were up around his ears, arms away from his sides, wide like an ape. His breathing was labored. His hands clenched and unclenched as if operating separately from his body. And I thought he might strike out with his fists. I stared at him until he calmed down and his hands finally hung limply by his side. Cargill's anger was spent. At least for the moment.

"My boss, Windsor Smythe, is sniffing around everyone at the firm, looking for who might have spilled the news to the *Financial Times* that the company was engaging in fraud.

Our clients are already calling and demanding their investments be returned. They want their money. Now. Today. He's going crazy and trying to reassure them." His shoulders slumped, and he hung his head. "It's not working. I'm terrified he's going to blame me."

Cargill's eyes were red-rimmed, and tears leaked out and trickled down. He swiped at his face with a sleeve to dry them.

I relaxed my stance and faced him. "You? Why?"

"He'd asked me to report on you…and find out anything I could about your father's intentions. He knows I approached you at the casino, and he's suspicious that I might have told you more about the firm than I should have."

Cargill must not have mentioned spying on us at Fortum and Mason or my talk with him at his local pub. Did the firm know I called him to set up that meeting? If they kept a record of outside calls to their associates, that was all it would take for a paranoid Windsor Smythe to become more than suspicious. We'd been all over this, but I had no idea what he'd disclosed to his boss after I threatened him. Not much, I suspected. Not if he wanted to keep his job.

Full-on panic mode took hold again. Unable to control the shaking that overtook his body, he appeared like a man coming up for air for the third time. "If he thinks I gave you, or your father, any information, I don't know what he'll do."

I thought I might. And it wasn't pretty. Windsor Smythe was a vindictive, evil bastard. He'd take his revenge in any way he wanted.

"What makes you so sure he believes it was you who caused the leak?"

He hung his head and mumbled so softly I couldn't understand his words. "What? What did you say?"

"He knows about Mia and me and everything that's going on at the museum. He thinks I've given him up to protect her."

That was ridiculous. Only Cargill didn't know that. Oxford Alliance Ltd.'s forgeries had nothing to do with Mia or The New London Arts Museum. It was a separate scam Windsor Smythe was directing. Now he was running scared that it would all blow up, and he'd lose his business at best and become a convicted felon at worst. He was trying to plug the leak with whoever would fit the hole.

"Be honest with me. It's the only way," I said. "Do you know about the fake artworks he's commissioned to be offered as originals to Oxford Alliance Ltd clients?"

He cast his eyes down to the floor. "No. No. I swear. It must be someone else in the firm. It's not me." He was desperate for me to believe him. I didn't. But I couldn't let him off the hook.

"If you don't tell me the truth right now, I'll call your boss and drop you right in the middle of this." I lifted my cell and began to punch in a number.

"Stop!" He pleaded. I don't know anything."

He obviously didn't know about Chimini, and I couldn't tell him. That would only make him give in to his panic. And maybe run back to his boss to try and save himself. The art forger had painted a clear picture framing Windsor Smythe.

"Go back to work, Cargill," I said. "Calm down. Try and act normal." Whatever that was. "Don't give Windsor Smythe any more reason to suspect you."

He took in my words, but I wasn't sure they were registering. I was almost tempted to offer him a cup of tea. Almost, but not quite. Then, I showed him to the door.

* * *

When he left and I made sure our apartment was secure, I sat down with the files again. *Who,* I thought, *had the means, the motive, and the* opportunity—the classic traits associated with committing and solving a crime?

I read over the notes on each person connected to the museum. One by one, I tried to rule them out. Or in.

I opened a notebook and decided to map out the people who had the most to gain or lose.

In the center was the Gentileschi.

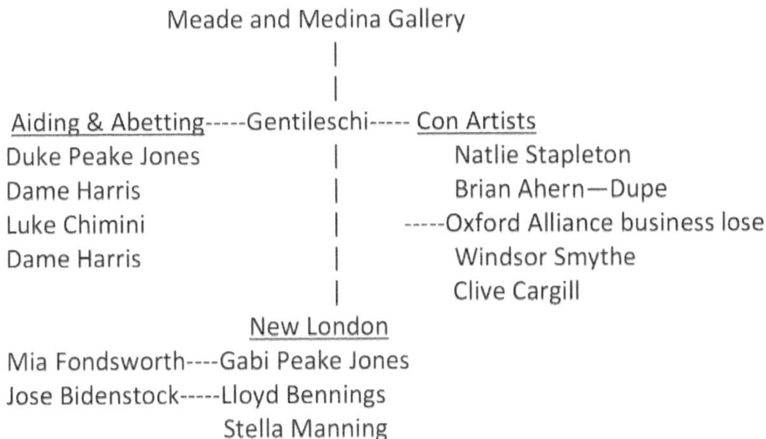

I drew lines above, below, and to the sides to connect each person to their roll in this mess.

At the top, I connected George Colabello to Maxime Meade and the Gallery, those who would collect the most money, and possibly the real painting.

Off to the right side and below that, I added Natalie Stapleton and under her, Brian Ahern, who was the Mark.

Another line on that side was for John Windsor Smythe and Clive Hastings Cargill, who would lose their business.

Below the painting I added the New London people who stood to lose not only the painting but their livelihoods. Gabi Peake Jones, Lloyd Bennings Stella Manning and the adjacent Mia Fondsworth and Jose Bidenstock, who had multiple connections.

Did it help? I'd have to ponder it a bit more.

Of course, Gabi was never a suspect, just a victim of trusting the wrong person in George Colabello. She had the most to lose. Though not as much as Jonathan Hudson, who had been killed because of the con. When we found the thief, I was confident we'd find his killer.

Mia Fondsworth was a big question mark. Was she really more concerned with protecting her relationship with Cargill than with the forgery? She said she'd been out with her friends at her local pub the night Jonathan Hudson was attacked, and the painting was presumably removed and exchanged. Also, I imagined she'd like to keep her job.

Then, there was Dame Rosemary Harris. We now knew her motive was financial. A piece of the profits from the insurance money and penalties. Did she substitute the forgery for the original? Her actions didn't support that. She appeared ice-cold on the surface, but as we'd seen in her office, she was as frightened as a fox being chased by hounds. She just signed on to partially finance the scheme with the Duke. They were reprehensible, but I couldn't see them slipping into the work room, coshing Jonathan on the head, and carting away the original Gentileschi. The Duke would most likely have been too drunk to manage it. And Harris too afraid.

Once again, I thought about how many ways the insurance money and penalties would be split. I agreed with Marina that the Dame and the Duke would be out of luck. The gang would laugh their way to the bank with their share, and there was not much those two could do about it.

Chapter Fifty-Three

I'd been at this for a while, jotting down notes on a legal pad as I went along. I was just about to tackle the two art experts from New York and London when I tossed down my pen and decided to go for a walk to clear my head.

I tossed on my prized NY Mets baseball jacket over my tee shirt, grabbed my keys—this time I checked the locks on both the inner and outer doors—and headed to Kensington High Street and a café that served a great Cappuccino. Our neighborhood was a quiet place for a walk. Well-kept houses lined the street like a row of sentinels to good taste. It was sunny, not always the case in London, but there was a chill in the air, A sign of a late spring frost. I zipped up my jacket and continued my walk.

I hadn't gotten far when something that sounded like a bee buzzed past my ear. Startled, I brushed at my ear, expecting an insect. Instead, I realized the sound was the crack of a shot that had been fired. I turned in time to see a chunk of plaster fly off a white stucco wall in front of me.

I dove for one of the broad cherry trees lining the path and scrabbled behind it, panting. It took me a few seconds to catch my breath before I could venture a quick look at the street. It was totally empty. No shooter. No sirens screaming their way closer. And not one person was interested enough to come outside and see what had happened. In the city, they'd be out in a New York minute. And the police close behind.

Someone had shot at me. *Duh, Nick, you think?* Unfortunately, I'd had this experience before. It didn't feel any better the second time around.

I was shaken up as much now as I was then. Still hiding behind the tree, I took out my cell and sent a 911 text to Marina. While I waited for her reply, I slowly slid my head out from behind my hiding spot and quickly glanced around. Whoever had pulled the trigger was long gone.

Flashes of Tommy 'B' Bonnanniano flew through my mind. He wasn't in London. At least, I didn't think so. And we were square. At least, I hoped so. If he sent a guy to kill me, he wouldn't miss. I didn't think it was the Salafi terrorists either. Their method of eliminating any opposition was more inclusive. A bomb was standard operating procedure. And the whole block would be gone, not just me.

Marina called back, and I explained what happened and where I was. "Stay put," she said. A course of action I'd already decided on.

She arrived in minutes, and we headed home together. Forget the Cappuccino. The moment we got inside, I doubled down on the Scotch.

Chapter Fifty-Four

"Are you sure it wasn't Cargill?" Marina asked.

I shook my head. "No way. He was a total wreck. If he had a gun, he'd probably shoot himself by mistake."

"Whoever the shooter was must be from the gang. We're getting close, and they're running scared. They're getting desperate. They want this deal to go through no matter what."

Or no matter who gets killed, I thought.

Marina retrieved the bullet, which had lodged in the wall. The one that had been inches away from my head. "It looks like a 9mm, which could be from a rifle or a handgun." She placed it in the palm of her hand and slowly closed her fingers around it.

"It's not legal to own a handgun in England unless you have special permission. That's not easy to obtain." She opened and closed her fingers around the bullet again. "Rifles are a different story. So many people here hunt."

I got it. I felt like one of those poor foxes chased by barking hounds and thundering horses.

Marina continued. "Most of them use rifles. Like the people we're investigating. Thank God you weren't hurt."

I suspected she was right. If someone wanted to shoot me dead, I'd be lying in a pool of blood spreading along the path, empty eyes staring at the sky I had recently admired. I shuddered. Or maybe they just wanted to warn me. Consider me warned. But thankfully, alive.

I'd been accosted twice in one day. What were the odds? None that I liked.

Marina was assessing me and my state of mind. Fearful, I'd say if she asked. I hoped she wouldn't.

"Nick," she took my tumbler and added another generous pour of Scotch. Maybe we should ask Nigel to assign someone to watch the flat again."

Our protection had left after Simone and Alex returned to New York. To watch over me, she meant. "No," It came out harsher than I meant. "It's just still scare tactics. A gambit to make us edgy so we'll make a mistake. Or give up." I pulled myself up to my full six-foot-two height. "I can handle this. We can."

"Nick," she said again, her expression growing more serious. "Just think about it, okay?"

She was right. The threats were escalating. I was sure it was all up to Natalie. Stalking Simone and Alex in Brighton. Breaking in and slicing up the replica Picasso. Now being shot at. Not to mention Cargill sneaking in earlier. Well, he'd planned that on his own. Couldn't blame Natalie for that.

"Okay." I swallowed the Scotch and turned to look at her. Relief flashed across her face. It didn't last long. "I'll think about it, and we'll see."

It was not the answer she wanted, but it was all I had to give.

* * *

The smooth, smoky Scotch had worked its magic, and I felt calmer. I was able to take in a full breath. Not jumping at every sound. Marina and I had moved to our comfort zone—our couch. And, we were both quiet for a moment. The delayed reaction finally hit me. I could feel my body becoming clammy, a cold sweat prickling my skin as if it was anticipating danger. My brain understood that the threat was past. The rest of my body still had to catch up.

I remembered what Marc had said about a con going sideways. Was being shot at an example? Again, I wondered if the gang was responsible, although it didn't make much sense since they were close to getting a deal.

I cleared my mind as best I could and tried to shake it off. "Let's have a fire," I said, and rose to build one in our fireplace. Once the wood caught and the flames danced around, casting shadows on the walls and offering a touch of warmth, I sat back down.

Marina moved closer until our bodies were touching. Shoulder to shoulder. Hip to hip.

"I have to call your dad," she tilted her head toward mine.

"You found the traitor?" My voice deepened and became gruff, making the word sound like I was describing a Nazi collaborator from the war.

"I did. It's Danielle Burkett."

"Oh, God. Dad will be devastated. He backed her bid for her appointment as chief of the London office." I could imagine his face while I was saying these words to Marina. Sad. Disappointed. Angry. "He trusted her. Respected her. Counted on her. God only knows what he's going to feel." I leaned forward and cradled my head in my hands. My temples throbbed.

Marina touched my shoulder. "I need to tell him. Now. Before anything else happens."

I nodded that I understood and rose to leave the room. "I'll be downstairs." I walked past the bar and poured one more Scotch as I headed for our bedroom, downtrodden and dejected for my father. Losing at the casino made me feel bad, but nothing came close to this.

Chapter Fifty-Five

Marina and Gabi were on their way to New London for what should be the penultimate meeting with the New York contingent. Today, they'd work out the final details. Prepare to transfer the funds tomorrow. Natalie would be preening like a player raking in a tableful of other people's chips. Snuggling close to Ahern. Smiling up at him in adoration. Unless we could find the painting. I wasn't going to stop trying. Neither was Marina.

I'd pick up where I left off before the assassination attempt to end my life—I know, I know, I was being dramatic. I was still a little shaky. Not a good look for a professional Blackjack player.

The best thing for it was to continue with my deep dive into all the people involved. So far, I hadn't found any marked cards on any New London employees other than Dame Harris. Her motive had been greed—a usual carrot—financial gain that we were sure wouldn't pay out. She'd walk away like the loser she was. The same for the Duke, who deserved to go bust. For starters.

I made myself a strong espresso and went into the lounge to retrieve my notes and continue reviewing the personnel and my newly created chart.

First, I called Dad. I wanted to check on him after his conversation with Marina. I was surprised when Mom answered his cell. No hello. "Nick, your father is devastated," she anxiously whispered into the phone. "He…" she paused. I knew she was trying to compose herself and could imagine her teary eyes and downturned expression.

She continued to whisper. "He's just about to leave for the office to confront Danielle Burkett, that…bitc…that woman, and dismiss her."

I knew those were not the words Mom wanted to use. I was sure others were crowding her mind, ready to burst out.

"Should I go with him?" *I could offer moral support*, I thought.

"No!" She blurted out. "He needs to do this on his own. He trusted her, and…"

I got it. It was his mistake to rectify. "Okay," I replied softly. "Dad will handle this the right way. You know that."

"Unfortunately, I do."

I knew what she meant. I'd want to strangle her or at least have security toss her out on her butt. Literally. With Dad, there'd be no rough manhandling. His quiet, determined tone would suffice. So would having Danielle Burkett blackballed from any financial position at any firm in London. For the rest of her life. Just like a cheater at a casino who would not ever be permitted to enter the premises again.

I didn't feel the slightest bit sorry for her. She was intelligent and savvy, yet not bright enough to stay on the right side of things. She'll get what she deserves.

I said goodbye to Mom and asked her to call if they needed me. Then I took my coffee to the table with my notes, and dived in.

I was revisiting everything we had on Stella Manning. As the Managing Director, her position allowed her to have the final word on every aspect that affected the museum. She and her husband owned a small, terraced house in Primrose Hill. They'd bought it years ago when prices were reasonable. With skyrocketing home prices, I didn't think they could afford to purchase it now.

As far as I could tell, her Managing Director salary was in the vicinity of £150,000, and his, as a senior analyst, £78,000. This was a nice amount of money, although the couple seemed to carry a lot of debt. There were no kids to support, so there were no school fees. It was just the two of them.

The more I looked. The more debt I found, mostly Arthur's. About six months ago, their second mortgage had been several months overdue. There were bank overdrafts and big credit card bills at high interest rates. All in arrears. Then, two months ago, they started paying off most of what they owed. Something was not right. Where had the sudden influx of money come from? Did they win the lottery? Or was something else going on?

I had just logged on to Lexus Nexus to dig deeper when my cell chirped. It was Marina.

"Rosemary Harris had a seizure," she blurted out. "The EMTs are working on her; once she's stable, they'll take her to The London Clinic."

Fancy, I thought. *A hospital frequented by many of the Royals. Had Lloyd Bennings asked to have her brought there?*

I brought my mind back to more practical matters. "Jeez, Marina, do they know what's wrong?"

"Give me a second," she replied. "I'm moving somewhere private." I could hear her heels clicking along the marble floors. Then she was back, her voice a mere whisper. "I think she was poisoned. She was sipping from a cup of tea and collapsed."

"Who served the tea?" I asked.

"Lloyd Bennings poured a cup for himself and one for Rosemary."

"And he's fine?"

"Yes. Upset, of course, as everyone is. Especially Meade, who is making a fuss about continuing without Dame Harris being present." She paused. "Stella Manning refused in no uncertain terms. She gave him one of those down-the-nose withering looks like only the English can do." There was a tinge of amusement in her voice as she continued. "He backed off with a half-hearted apology. We will reconvene tomorrow depending on Dame Harris's condition."

"Speaking of Stella Manning—" I began to say, but Marina cut me off.

"I need to go. I want to speak to the EMTs and find out as much as possible."

Chapter Fifty-Six

This was very suspect. Lloyd Bennings was playing Mother, pouring the tea for his partner, but not being affected, while Dame Harris was nearly dying. Was he trying to get rid of her to make room for Jose?

Stella Manning called a halt to the meeting just as a deal was being made. Was it out of concern for Rosemary, or a stalling tactic? Gabi must be beside herself. This was a never-ending saga.

I couldn't figure it out. I'd try when Marina arrived home, and we swapped information.

I returned to my laptop and the Lexus Nexus search I had started. Over the last few years, more and more red flags had popped up. The Mannings' debts had threatened to crush them. Item after item with damaging financial information portrayed a sorry story. The narrative was strongly connected to Stella's husband, Arthur Manning.

Recent transactions for stock and bond trades comprised the bulk of what they owed. These bad investments ran for rows and rows. He'd apparently tried to pay one debt by borrowing from another source. It hadn't worked. Until recently, when many had been paid and moved from red to black.

It wasn't a good look for an MI5 analyst to be so heavily in debt. I wondered if the agency knew anything about his financial woes. Or if someone else did, who might use the information?

I wasn't going to find that data on Lexus Nexus, and I didn't want to turn to Nigel again. It occurred to me that I had my own source, Roger Matthews, to tap into.

I'd met Roger at an embassy function a year ago. Nigel had invited Marina as his plus one, and he took pity on me and added me to the guest list.

When we arrived, Nigel steered Marina away from me and toward a group of diplomats, no doubt wanting to impress them with his gorgeous 'date.' I, on the other hand, headed straight for the bar. I was just lifting a flute of champagne to my lips when a tall, distinguished man who looked like a younger version of Idris Elba, with a gleaming bald head, leaned against the bar and spoke.

"Is that stunning redhead Nigel is showing off with you?" he asked, waving his flute in their direction. "I believe I saw you arrive together."

"She is, and you did," I replied. "She took pity on me and got me on the list. I'm Nick Donahue," I said, extending my hand.

"Roger Matthews. Nice to meet you, Nick," he replied as we shook.

"Do you work with Nigel?" I asked. "You seem familiar with his tactics," I added with a touch of humor as I watched him showing off Marina. I could tell she was inwardly rolling her eyes.

"Hardly," Roger replied, his eyebrows raising almost to his hairline. I'm across the river, in Thames House."

Everyone in London knew what that meant. It was where MI5 was located, the internal domestic arm of the security services. Supposed partner to the espionage agency MI6. How well they worked together was a matter of conjecture.

"So, Nick, what do you do?"

I suspected he already knew my profession. But he'd done an end run around naming his job—he was in the intelligence community, after all. "Well, it's not as exciting as being connected to the British Secret Service, but I play Blackjack for a living." He knew I'd have made the connection.

He nodded his head sagely. "I'd say that's quite exciting. Tell me more."

I did that evening and in future meetings and conversations, as we became friends.

Roger couldn't tell me much about his position at the agency. Nothing at all. He even skirted around the fact that he was employed there. He mentioned that his job was like the American equivalent of Human

Resources at a big firm.

I wasn't buying it, so I looked up the jobs that were available at MI5. My best guess was that he was a Vetting Officer. A very senior VO, someone who basically reviewed the applications and interviewed nearly everyone applying to work at the agency, from intelligence services to corporate positions. Saying he was in HR was like mentioning Mick Jagger played music. I'd bet the bank he was in charge, like First Desk at the fictional MI5 agency in "Slow Horses."

I'd invited Roger to be my guest at the St. James casino.

"I'd love to, but I don't gamble."

A caveat that goes with the job, I thought.

"Not a problem," I replied. We'd go. I'd play. Then we'd have a drink and some dinner. A good evening all around.

The first time we were at the casino, Roger watched me play for a while, then wandered off to observe the Roulette and Craps games. I kept track of him from the corner of my eye. He placed a small wager on the Craps table, won his point, and picked up his chips.

Soon, he was back at the table where I was playing, quietly observing the play and the players. Something told me he didn't miss much. I cashed in, left a tip for the dealer, and we headed for the dining room.

"You're very good at this, aren't you?" he asked after we were seated. "I noticed you waited for a spot to open up on the dealer's right so you could note how the other players were betting." His face lit up in a smile. "It's a good tactic. In any game. Very astute," he nodded, and I wondered for a nano-second if he was making an overture to recruit me.

"Stop daydreaming," Marina would say and shake her head. *"You're not even British."*

The moment passed, and I sat back in my chair and lifted my drink toward him. "You don't miss much, do you?"

"I try not to," he replied, lifting his Bourbon in a toast.

* * *

Fortunately, Roger was at home when I called him. "Are you free for a late lunch?" I asked.

He was, and we agreed to meet at The Ivy Kensington Brasserie, which was not too far from his home. It was an outpost of the original Ivy where my family had dined.

I left a note for Marina explaining that I was on the case and would get into it when we were both back at the flat.

Roger was waiting at the bar, beer in hand, when I arrived. We were seated immediately and ordered Shepherd's Pie for him and Fish and Chips for me.

While we were waiting for our food, I told Roger what was on my mind. I explained everything that had happened since the original Gentileschi was switched. I named all the people involved in the con from New York, as well as those who worked at the museum. I mentioned we were still investigating several employees and their significant others, like Arthur Manning, one of MI5's senior analysts. I laid out my theory that someone could be blackmailing him or his wife regarding the painting and paying off his debts.

Roger held up his hand and started to speak. "Nick. I…"

I shook my head. "It's okay. I get it. You can't talk about your job or anyone at MI5." It was the first time I'd verbally acknowledged that I understood he worked there.

Everyone had to sign the Official Secrets Act, which was meant to prevent the disclosure of information to an enemy. Revealing the names of any employee was part of this.

"But hypothetically," I continued, "if someone's debts were suddenly erased, wouldn't that be of interest to the agency? Raise a red flag?" I paused, gauging his reaction. Stone-faced. "If they were aware of it, I mean."

"Hypothetically, yes," he replied and tucked into his Shepherd's Pie, putting paid to that bit of our conversation.

I'd planted the seed of distrust. Knowing Roger's sterling character, he'd investigate it further. If he found that Arthur Manning, and by extension his wife Stella, was accepting money from an outside source—think Maxime Meade and the gang—it might be just the hand we needed to get back in the game, find the killer and the original Gentileschi.

Chapter Fifty-Seven

arina was in pacing mode, moving back and forth across the lounge when I arrived home.

She turned on her heel and pointed a finger at me like a casino manager accusing someone of cheating. "Who poisoned her?" Frustration dripped from every word. "The gang had nothing to gain by adding strychnine to her tea." Her red hair flew around her face as she tossed her head from side to side. "They wanted this to be over and done."

I agreed. The longer this dragged on, the more the possibility of things going sideways. There was that term again, popping up.

"Strychnine? Doesn't that kill you immediately? What exactly happened?" I asked.

"I already told you." She hadn't. "One of the café people brought pots of tea and pastries and placed them on the sideboard. Rosemary had her own mug with her and was about to go to the sideboard where everything was set up. Lloyd Bennings took the mug from her and told her that he'd be happy to get her tea. He filled her mug. Then his own. And brought both back to the conference table.

I think Meade was speaking when Rosemary clutched her throat and began making horrible gasping sounds. Everyone was stone silent for a minute. Then all hell broke loose.

She tumbled from her chair and landed on the carpet, grabbing her stomach and twitching. Lloyd and Jose jumped in to help her. Gabi called 999 and asked for an ambulance.

"At first, we all thought she'd had a seizure of some sort. But I wasn't convinced. She looked terribly out of it. Her breathing was labored. Her eyes were rolling around. She was covered in perspiration, and I thought she might die.

"Jose, who'd reacted quickly to help her, was just reaching to pick up the mug she'd dropped. Someone called to him, and he was distracted. That's when I grabbed the mug before he could and sniffed at the tea. There was no odor, but I was sure something was off. I slipped it into my bag and took it to a friend at LabSystems for analysis.

"They got back to you already?" I asked in surprise.

"They did a down-and-dirty test. And found a few crystals of strychnine on the side of the mug. My friend thought whoever had done this had added only a very small amount. Not enough to kill her. Just enough to make her ill."

"Enough to stop the meeting cold," I added.

"Exactly." Marina bit her lower lip and started pacing again.

"Sit down, please. I have something to tell you, as well."

She nodded and folded herself into one of our armchairs.

I sat opposite on the couch. I took a deep breath and began to explain what I'd learned about Stella Manning and her husband, Arthur, a senior analyst at MI5. Then I mentioned my lunch with Roger Matthews, whom Marina had met briefly at the embassy party.

"I told him what I'd discovered about Stella and Arthur Manning's finances and their supposed turnaround from being in the red to sailing off in the black. And how that might look to the agency."

"What did Roger make of this?" she asked.

"Roger has never actually discussed MI5 or his position there except mentioning something about HR." I lifted my hands in an 'as if' gesture. "I presented what I'd found hypothetically. And wondered if the agency would view this in a negative light?"

"And?"

"He didn't give anything away." *A good spy wouldn't,* I thought. "Just tucked into his Shepherd's Pie.

"My intuition's telling me he'll make inquiries. I didn't mention the gang.

Left it open-ended. As far as Roger is concerned, the sudden uplift in Manning's finances could be coming from anywhere."

Marina's face broke into a smile. "You wanted Roger to think they might be selling secrets to foreign agents, didn't you?"

"The thought had crossed my mind. Especially when I remembered the Official Secrets Act, which everyone in the Services must sign."

Marina rose from the chair and came over to hug me. "Thank you, darling. You're brilliant."

I loved when she called me that. I knew she could see the gleam in my eyes. If I played my cards right, maybe I'd get a few more "brilliants' from her.

* * *

Her cell beeped, breaking the moment. It was from Marina's source at the hospital. Dame Harris was on the mend. Thankfully, the poison, which mirrored the symptoms of a seizure, had just incapacitated her. It really must have been just a few crystals. They would keep her for observation overnight and release her sometime tomorrow.

"Does the hospital know it was strychnine in her tea?"

"Not unless they got her bloodwork back. It would probably show up then." She shrugged. "They're still working on the theory that she had some kind of minor episode or a mild stroke."

Only someone at New London could have done this, I thought. *Knew that Rosemary used her own mug and added the poison.*

"Do you think she needs protection?"

"I don't believe anyone would go after her again."

"What about Gabi and the other employees?"

"We need to let them know it was poison. They have to protect themselves and be extremely careful of what they eat and drink at work." She paused. "I think Gabi has a connection with an officer at Scotland Yard who helped with security planning and procedures. I believe they became friends, and she could speak with him."

210

Now, another branch of the government would be involved. It was beginning to feel surreal. Would New London ever get the real Gentileschi back? If I had to lay odds, I'd say it wasn't looking good. Not good at all.

Chapter Fifty-Eight

Today was frustrating in so many ways. We were at a standstill. Dame Harris was still in the hospital. She would not be released until tomorrow. She made it clear she would not be attending any future meetings about the Gentileschi, then, or ever.

"She texted all of us so there'd be no confusion over why she wouldn't be showing up. She cited the nasty and vindictive atmosphere pervading the proceedings and how unprofessional everyone was behaving."

"Of course, it's not like she had any part in it," I said sarcastically, remembering her upfront money to Chimini.

Marina got a wicked grin on her face. "I'd still like to send out a group text of my own, those very revealing porno pictures of Natalie and George."

"Play nice. Just for a few more days." I gave her what I thought of as my most winning smile and got a 'humph' in response. "Harris must be scared to death," I continued.

Who could blame her? Near-death by poisoning tends to do that to a person. Especially if they thought someone might try again. She'd probably never set foot in The New London Arts Museum for the rest of her life.

Marina continued. "Stella Manning made it clear the meeting would go forward tomorrow. No more delays. She told Gabi she wants to get this whole business over with."

"And what, just fork over the seven million insurance and the penalties the gang demanded?"

Marina nodded. I still wasn't buying it.

"Gabi has arranged to have the Scotland Yard security experts she met cover the premises. They'll be undercover in plain clothes and hopefully fit in with the patrons. One of them will be stationed in the café just in case someone tries to slip anything else into the tea."

"Did she have to confer with Stella Manning for approval?"

"Don't know. I think Gabi just made the call on her own."

"Have you heard anything more from Nigel? Has Chimini spilled his guts?"

"Actually, he's poured more fuel on the fire." She paused. "He must have decided that staying alive beat the alternative. He told Nigel he suddenly remembered part of a phone conversation he overheard while speaking with Maxime Meade. Meade asked him to hold on and put his hand over the microphone, but Chimini could hear the person in the background speaking. 'She's got this. It's done.'"

"She?" I asked. The only she's left in the game were Dame Harris, Stella Manning, Gabi, and Mia. And the only two with any real power were Harris who was out of the picture, and most likely would be permanently. That left Stella Manning.

Given what I learned about her, it was time to give Roger Matthews another call.

* * *

Roger was free for lunch, and we met at the Ivy Kensington Brasserie again. With lagers in hand from the bar, we moved to a quiet booth. Not surprisingly, Roger sat with his back to the wall. Good tradecraft, I noted.

Roger got right to it. "I know why you're here, Donahue."

"You do?" I asked, not surprised he'd guessed.

"I spoke with Nigel about you, and he seems to think you're a persistent bugger but trustworthy.

He had? I thought. *That was unexpectedly nice of him.*

Roger pinned me with his dark brown eyes and held mine for what seemed like minutes. "I hope I'm not making a mistake here, Nick."

I cleared my throat before I finally croaked out, "No. You're not." I knew he wasn't planning to extend an offer to join the service. But I'd take whatever information he could give me.

"I realized you wanted me to believe that Arthur and Stella Manning were selling secrets to our adversaries."

"No, not at all," I replied, sitting up straighter as if good posture could vouch for my veracity. But Roger's expression told me he known what I'd been up to. This guy was on top of his game.

His mouth formed a grimace, which he shook off before continuing. "Arthur Manning stole the painting. Although he swears he didn't murder Jonathan Hudson." He paused. "He made a deal with Meade to pay off their debts and keep Stella out of it. He proposed hiding the painting with a promise to return it after the insurers paid the proceeds to the gang. Obviously, since the painting is still missing, that won't happen."

I was shaking my head. "What?" Roger asked.

"You're mistaken." I was sure of that. "Arthur Manning didn't steal the painting. He was lying and running a scam of his own. He took advantage of the situation. Saw an opportunity to fleece Meade and walk away debt-free. Maybe even to keep his Stella from leaving him. It's too convenient for the painting to have disappeared from wherever he said he hid it. Someone else stole it and murdered Jonathan."

"You don't know that. We've made a deal with Arthur Manning."

"What?" I nearly shouted. "How could you? Even if he didn't steal the Gentileschi, he betrayed his position and the government."

He leaned closer to me, shaking his head. "Calm yourself." He looked around to make certain no one was paying the slightest attention to us. "It's been decided to keep him on as a senior analyst tracking art crimes. There will be a great deal of supervision involved. He will be under our thumb. It's a tidy solution.

Tidy! Was he kidding me? Didn't he see the irony in the situation?

"He's vouched for his wife. Told us that Stella knew nothing about his plan. That it was all up to him."

"Why would you believe him, a scheming conniver? Or that Stella Manning didn't know what he was up to?" Incredulity filled my voice. Roger had seen right through me but not his own analyst.

Roger gave me another pointed look. "Arthur swears it was all on him. Of course, he may be lying to protect her—"

I interrupted again, "—May be?" I shook my head. No may be about it.

"Arthur will be making up for his mistake for a long while."

"So, you're just going to let him get away with…all of this?" Something was very off here. Why would the British Secret Service allow this? Manning should be in prison for his crimes. And Stella for colluding with the gang.

I looked at Roger, and it hit me. MI5 suspected Stella Manning might somehow have the Gentileschi. Or know who did. In a way, that made a twisted kind of sense. If this is what the Service was thinking, Roger wasn't sharing.

"Stella's set to finalize the deal with Meade and Medina et al. tomorrow." I paused. "We need to get the Gentileschi back. Before then." Gabi's professional life literally depended on it.

"And what happens to Ms. Manning?" I asked.

"She will resign her position at The New London Arts Museum as soon as tomorrow's meeting is concluded. And leave without severance or references."

I scoffed inwardly. Somehow, I couldn't see how that would deter her. People would think it was her choice to disassociate herself from the museum and the scandal surrounding it. Not the other way around. Like when she divorced her first husband and managed to keep all the money. She was a shark who'd swim back and devour anyone in her way.

Chapter Fifty-Nine

e'd been talking so much we hadn't touched our food. Our waiter asked if everything was alright, and we said yes, fine. We'd take our meals to go.

I was surprised that Roger confided in me, even if he was wildly off the mark. How had MI5 screwed up so badly? I hoped they would locate the missing painting before the money changed hands tomorrow. I was skeptical that would happen.

There was nothing I could do about it right now, except go home and tell Marina what I'd learned. Maybe she'd have an idea to make things work out.

Walking back to our apartment, I mentally reviewed what Roger and I had just discussed. When it came to deciding who was worse, Stella or Arthur Manning, it was a push. They were both despicable, and I'd like to make sure both would pay.

As Marina listened to me recount my meeting with Roger Matthews, her agitation ratcheted to a boiling point. "What's wrong with these MI5 people? They should throw Manning in the cells they have in their basement and let him rot. And her? She's even worse. Allowing her husband to take the rap and get off scot free." She paused to catch her breath and exhaled deeply.

"What are our options? How can we handle this?"

By the time she formed her question, a plan had taken hold in my mind. It was not something I was ready to share with Marina. In fact, the less she knew, the better.

"All you can do right now is to be there for Gabi. Make sure she's calm at the meeting and doesn't jump across the table and tear out Natalie's throat.

Once they sign the legal papers and transfer the insurance money—"

She interrupted me. "—Seven million dollars, plus the seven-hundred-thousand-dollar penalty," she said in disgust.

"—just get Gabi out of there, and don't let her do anything crazy."

"What are you up to, Nick?" Her green eyes were turning steely and narrowing in suspicion.

"Me? Nothing. Honestly." I took her hand. "I just want this to be over for Gabi."

"And where will you be while all this is happening?" she asked.

"After you and Gabi leave for your meeting, I'll go to where I'm always welcome, at the casino. I don't want to lose my edge," I said, flexing my fingers. "After I win, I'll take you to dinner tomorrow night."

She didn't reply, and I knew she wasn't focusing on what I'd just said. That was fine with me. The less she paid attention right now, the better.

I knew where the painting was—well, I knew who knew where it was—and tomorrow, I'd make sure I was right.

Chapter Sixty

A soft knock on the door at ten-thirty the following morning let me know Gabi was in the hall waiting to leave for the fateful meeting at the New London Arts Museum. I couldn't imagine what was going through her mind. Most likely, she envisioned both her career and reputation floating away on a sea of deceit and misery.

Maybe I could change that. I gave Marina a hug and reminded her to be careful. Never mind at the door, the wolves were already inside and were more dangerous than ever.

I sprang into action as soon as she and Gabi got into the waiting Uber. First, I called Europcar and requested a dark-colored Vauxhall Corsa. I paid extra to have it delivered to my home and arrive in an hour.

Then, I called Clive Hastings Cargill. I hoped he started sweating when his cell rang at his desk, and he saw my name pop up. When he answered, I cut off his greeting, and in the most menacing voice I could muster, demanded he step outside of his office and call me back within the next two minutes.

He demurred at first, hemming and hawing, until I explained that if he did not comply with my request immediately, my next calls would be to his boss to the Financial Services watchdogs, to his wife, and to all the daily papers in that order. And his career, maybe even his life, would be over.

Not surprisingly, my cell rang exactly two minutes later.

"What do you want from me, Donahue?"

"Where is the Oxford Alliance Ltd Free Port?

"I...I can't say. Why do you need to know that?" he asked, biding for time.

"Cargill," I said, "just tell me."

"I don't know," he replied.

I hung up, waited thirty seconds, and called him back. "I just left a message for Windsor Smythe. I wouldn't go back inside if I were you. Still don't know?" I asked.

"You're ruining me!" he screamed.

"Okay, ten seconds and I call the Financial Services."

"Wait, Okay." He finally dribbled out the information.

The nervousness in his voice was vibrating like a tuning fork. His warning signals were on high alert. This was a man who knew disaster was about to smack him senseless. Good. He should be terrified. "It's at the Thames Free Port near Tilbury, in a separate building at the end of the complex, in room 211. Windsor Smythe takes his would-be clients there to impress them. Show them how valuable the art is and how much money they would make if they invested in the firm's art sector."

From what I learned about these spaces, they offered designer-appointed display rooms with all the amenities and plenty of room for viewing the merchandise. They could be very impressive, and Windsor Smythe very persuasive. Especially if the buyer believed they were getting a bargain along with a nice glass of Champagne.

Cargill hesitated.

"What?" I asked. "Your wife is next on my list."

"Don't please, "he begged. "I'll tell you.

"There's a problem, though. None of the art in the Free Port is real. Each piece is a genuine fake." He laughed at his little joke.

"So, where are the original paintings kept?"

"In a warehouse in Hackney on Wick Lane, at number 415," Cargill answered. "But you won't find the Gentileschi there. My boss is going apoplectic. His source was supposed to turn over the original last evening, but never showed."

"Who is the source?" I asked.

"I don't know. No one does. Mia...rang me...right before the meeting. She thought I might have discovered who had the original painting. I'm afraid for her. She's totally undone by what's going on and knows the outcome will be bad for New London and for her career. Even so, she was more concerned for me and how Windsor Smythe might react if he discovered our relationship. You know, considering she works there. A lot of people know he's after that painting. I have no idea where it is. And neither does he.

"He's lined up a buyer who's planning to view the 'Weeping Mary Magdalene' today."

"If you're lying to me, you'll regret it," I said. "I'm not joking about ruining you, or what Windsor Smythe will do."

Cargill continued. "I'm not. This is an unheard-of situation for him. I gather that the buyer is quite anxious to obtain the Gentileschi. If it's not available, he'll walk, and Windsor Smythe will lose out. Not something he's apt to take lightly."

People who knowingly buy stolen art don't usually give the thief a second chance to make good. It was too risky.

Cargill wasn't finished. "I suspect he's planning to split the profits with whoever turns over the painting. Of course, he'll keep the lion's share of the money." I could hear the resignation in his voice. He was aware of how Windsor Smythe operated.

"There's one more thing."

What else, I wondered?

"He thinks you have the original Gentileschi."

I snorted. "Me? If I had it, we wouldn't be having this conversation."

"Watch your back. He's looking for you."

Not after I give you up, I thought.

"He'll be very disappointed, then. Look, I need to go, but we're not done yet. I hope you understand that." I clicked off.

A slight tap on the horn signaled that my rental car had arrived. As requested, it was black, a small sedan that would blend in with the London traffic.

As Mr. Holmes might say: "The game is afoot."

* * *

The weather had been spectacular for London. Clear and crisp. Until this morning. Now, the rain was coming down sideways, fueled by the wind—a torrential downpour that nearly drenched me in the short distance I traveled from our building to the car. I tipped the delivery person, shook out my extra-large umbrella, stowed it, and slid behind the wheel.

Surprisingly, traffic was light today. Londoners may have decided to take the tube or the bus and avoid the bad weather. In any case, I arrived at my destination, The New London Arts Museum with plenty of time to spare.

I parked across the road and a way down from the Georgian building, where I could watch the entrance and exit. Even if you worked there, and used the staff entrance, you'd have to walk to the front to access the parking facility on the right.

While I was waiting for my target to emerge, I reviewed my plan. It seemed solid, but as I knew, it could change on a dime.

I took a minute to call my dad. After Danielle Burkett's deceit and departure, he was going to the Hamilton Capital office to regroup with the employees.

"I want to reassure them that the company is still on firm footing," he said. "It's a small office and we have several talented people working there. I'm going to assess each of them and see if I can't pick a new affiliate chief from their ranks."

I knew Dad would find the right person, whether from inside the firm or out.

"What's Mom up to today?"

"More shopping," he replied in a flat tone.

I suppressed a laugh. Was that a register ringing I heard in his voice?

"She met someone at tea at the hotel yesterday, and they hit it off. They're going to Harrods together to consult with a personal shopper this afternoon."

"Did you ask Marina to check out Mom's new friend?"

"Taken care of. I spoke with Marina's man here. I've gotten to know him, and he told me Annable Crouch was legit. She's from Bristol and is in London with her husband for a few days while he attends several meetings.

"It will be good for Elizabeth to have company other than mine."

"Marina and I have been so busy the last few days, and I'm sorry we didn't have more time to spend with you guys."

"Don't worry about that, Nick. We'll have some time after the gala at the firm, which, as you know, I'm relieved you'll be attending with me."

"Give Mom a kiss for me and tell her not to spend too much money."

Dad laughed. We said our goodbyes, and I went back to surveilling the building.

* * *

Marina called to give me a sit rep. The news was as bad as I expected. The museum's insurance company transferred the seven million to the Meade and Medina Gallery. And they paid the seven-hundred-thousand penalty, which wasn't covered by their policy.

Worse, if the original Gentileschi was recovered, it would now belong to the insurers, and they could sell it to whoever they wanted for whatever they could get for it. I was sure it would be more than they paid.

Of course, Gabi was inconsolable and blamed herself for ever trusting George.

I watched the entrance as people drifted out. Natalie and Ahern, exited, looking super excited. She was clinging to him and whispering in his ear. No doubt about all the fun they'd have with the insurance money he thought he'd be getting from Meade and Medina. Was he in for a big surprise?

Marina was still on her cell with me. She thought I was home getting ready to hit the casino, not snooping outside the museum. "Now that the deal is done, it might be a very good time to send Ahern those photos," I said, like it had just occurred to me. "It will be a fond remembrance of her after he throws her out."

"Oh, what a good idea."

As they were walking toward the car park, I could see Ahern reach for his cell. Must be Marina's text. He clicked on the screen, and his face twisted into a mask of shock that quickly turned to anger as I watched, imagining him scrolling through the images of Natalie and George. He spun toward her and waved the phone in her face. She knew what he was looking at. She tried to move closer to him to plead her case, and he pushed her away, nearly sending her flying. He was relentless. Red-faced. Furious. Waving his phone and yelling. Since I couldn't hear them from inside the car, I could only imagine what he was saying to her. Then he stalked off, leaving her standing on the stone steps. You had to give her props. Her posture was defiant, and she furiously poked at her cell as she walked off down the road. Probably calling George Colabello for help.

Maxime Meade and the New York contingent came out a few minutes later. They shook hands and departed. Everyone looked very pleased. Pocketing large fees tends to do that to people.

About half an hour later, Marina and Gabi emerged from the front entrance. Marina had her arm linked through Gabi's and held her close. Even this far away, I could see the young woman's distress. A minute later, they got into an Uber that had pulled up.

I sat in my rental car, trying to contain my anger. If I played my cards right, I could get the Gentileschi back. Even if the insurers now owned it, the authorities could go after Meade and Medina for wire transfer fraud. They have been a part of the con from the start, colluding to steal the original and plant a fake. All I had to do was get it back.

I'd relaxed my posture but sat up straight when my quarry emerged. Stella Manning opened her designer umbrella and looked up at the sky as if the rain was a personal affront. I was still banking on her leading me to the painting.

A few moments later, a late-model Mercedes arrived, and a driver emerged to open the door for her. She slid in easily next to a man who was already in the car, who turned toward her and kissed her on the cheek.

I had an idea who it might be, but I couldn't get a good look at his face.

I followed cautiously, hoping they wouldn't notice another nondescript car behind them on the road. It was like a slow-speed car chase in a funny cop movie.

I believed they were headed for Heathrow, where Stella had stashed the painting in a locker, but I was wrong. And not just about the destination.

Chapter Sixty-One

Soon, I found myself entering Primrose Hill, a road I recognized as Stella and Arthur's address. She exited the Mercedes and returned a few minutes later with a small suitcase.

Call me gobsmacked. Meade exited the chauffeured Merc and stowed her baggage in the trunk. What was going on here?

The two Inside Men had gotten together and were planning to do what? Run away? Flee the country?

I had my finger on my cell, intending to call Roger Matthews the moment they headed for Heathrow or the Chunnel. Instead, the car turned north toward the outskirts of London.

I continued to follow the car on the M4, having no idea where they were going. A little over an hour later, it pulled into the drive at Danesfield House, whose sign identified it as a romantic, luxury country spa hotel overlooking the Thames River. Wisteria vines trailed down the front porch columns, and sculpted topiary bordered the burbling fountain and stairs leading to the main building. It looked ideal for lovers, and I bet they'd chosen a suite with a canopied bed. I'd have to bring Marina here sometime.

Once the couple had been escorted inside, I parked and made my way to the lobby, keeping well back from the reception desk. When the lift closed on their backs, I walked over to the desk clerk and smiled. "I think a friend of mine is staying with you, Mr. Maxime Meade. Do you know if he's arrived yet?"

She was a young woman with a peaches and cream English complexion and a short blonde bob. "Let me just check for you, sir," she said as she straightened her uniform jacket. Efficient, too.

She scanned her computer and shook her head. "Not as yet," she replied. "Would you care to leave a message?"

"No," I replied. "I'll walk around the grounds instead and check back in a bit."

"Of course, sir."

The money must have been payment enough for Meade. Stella had spun her web, and I knew she'd get her share, and most likely his, as well. He apparently didn't care whether the original 'Weeping Magdalene' was returned to the gallery, Ahern, or resold. He must not have, or he wouldn't have stopped for a romantic break at this hideaway. Meade had chosen the iron maiden over money. Somehow, I was sure he'd regret it.

Something told me the rest of the gang would be extremely upset when they heard the news. More than upset at this turn of events. I was sure they were counting on double-dipping by reselling the original through Windsor Smythe and making even more money. It didn't seem like that would happen now.

Although it wasn't over yet.

* * *

I gathered my thoughts and immediately called Roger.

"Good afternoon," I said when he answered his cell.

"Nick. What's going on?"

"Well, I'm sure you know that the New London's insurance company paid out the money for the Gentileschi earlier today.

"Yes, we do. We've been observing the proceedings carefully."

Not carefully enough. I thought.

"Ah, then you know Stella Manning and Maxime Meade have run off together?"

Roger was astute enough not to show his surprise at my words. But his silence said it all.

"Yes," I continued, "they've just arrived at a lovely country inn, the

Danesfield House, outside the city, where I suspect they'll be staying for a few days." I paused. "I wonder if Mr. Manning is aware she's left him."

"Thank you, Donahue. I'll be sure to let him know," he replied sarcastically. "What about the rest of the crew?" He asked. "Have they joined them?"

"No. This appears to be a private party." I snorted, thinking of Natalie almost being dumped on her butt. "I believe they've been left twisting in the wind, as the saying goes.

"That seven point seven million had gone right into the gallery's account, and I'd bet the bank it's already been transferred to several accounts in the Caymans by now."

"The money's just part of our problem," Roger said. "Of course, we want to get it back, as impossible as that may be. However, we'd like to find the original 'Weeping Magdalene' and the person who now has it."

And Jonathan's killer, I thought.

Roger continued. "I'm sure we could work something out with the insurers.

"Have you discovered who that might be?"

"No. I thought you might have," I replied, "but I'll keep you posted if I figure it out." I didn't think it would be wise to tell him Windsor Smythe thought it was me.

* * *

I had no reason to remain at the inn. I wanted to return to London and Marina to explain all that had occurred. She would be as surprised as I was regarding Stella and Meade. They'd kept their involvement on the down-low, and no one had suspected a thing. Marina would also be delighted at how things had taken a bad turn for Natalie. I hope she was already on her way back to New York with her tail between her legs. And paying her own fare.

We'd have to watch out for her. She appeared to be the vindictive sort. I couldn't see her letting this go without trying some kind of payback.

I'd let Marc Rivers know where things stood, and maybe he could keep me posted. As far as George Colabello, Natalie, and the Meade and Medina Gallery were concerned, the con had been a colossal failure. I hoped Ahern learned his lesson and wouldn't be such an easy mark in the future. Or maybe not.

Chapter Sixty-Two

Marina listened in disbelief as I explained that I'd waited outside New London and planned to follow Stella Manning, who I thought would lead me to the Gentileschi. Instead, she'd run off with Meade for a cozy rendezvous in the country.

I wish I'd taken a photo of her face when I told her. Her beautiful eyes went wide, and her mouth opened in a perfect 'o'.

I also explained how her photos of Natalie and Colabello affected Ahern and how he stormed away. She laughed and started doing a happy dance at the scene I knew she was imagining.

"Thank you, Nick," she said. "You're amazing."

I preened a little at the compliment before asking about Gabi and how she was holding up.

"She's devastated and exhausted and believes her life is in ruins."

There was not much I could say to that. The usual platitudes, 'she's young', she'll bounce back," seemed ridiculous. She might not come back from this.

"What can we do to help?" I asked.

"Get the painting back," was her answer.

"I'm trying," I said, relaying what I'd pried out of Clive Cargill, who had grudgingly told me about the fake and real Free Ports, both minus the original 'Weeping Magdalene.'

"We're no closer to finding it, are we?"

I shook my head. "Or Jonathan Hudson's killer." I picked up my cell. "I should let Nigel know what's occurred. I don't think Manning and Meade will stay in their love nest for too long. I wouldn't be surprised if they snuck off to the Caymans." That's where I believed the money was.

I called Nigel to make sure he understood the gravity of the situation: "They could leave at any moment. You need to alert Interpol. You can't let that happen."

A world-weary sigh escaped his lips before he replied. "I spoke with Roger, and we already have people in place."

Well, well, MI5 and MI6 did cooperate with each other. That was nice to know.

Nigel continued. "They won't be going anywhere, especially Stella Manning, who was told not to leave the country as part of our deal with her. Of course, now that we know she's with Meade and the money, that changes things. If she tries to abscond, we'll nab her at the border, as you Americans might say. We're still working out how to officially detain Meade, but we'll get there."

Roger had done more than I expected by confining Manning to Britain as part of the deal. Nigel would make sure it stuck. And tack on some prison time if she tried to escape.

"There's one more thing," I said.

"Isn't there always with you, Donahue?"

I ignored his sarcasm and continued. "Natalie Stapleton was extremely distraught when Ahern rejected her." I'd put it politely. "He got a little heated when he saw the sex snaps of her and George Colabello." I took a breath. "It would be excellent if you could make sure *she* did leave Britain with a persona non grata status, forbidden to ever set foot in the kingdom again." *Or threaten Marina,* I thought.

"Yes. We can make that happen."

I clicked off. Too bad Nigel couldn't make the Gentileschi reappear with the same ease.

That was still up to Marina and me.

* * *

Marina had gone upstairs to comfort Gabi and Syd. I didn't know how much good it would do except for the women to know we were on their side.

I lit the fireplace and poured myself a Scotch. The rain had persisted into the evening, and it was cold and damp. The flames from the fire were beginning to lull me to sleep, when I remembered my conversation with the reluctant Cargill. There was a clue in there somewhere. My tired brain would have to work harder to suss it out if it could.

I woke up a few hours later. Marina had covered me with a soft throw. She was at the dining room table working on her laptop.

"Any new thoughts?" I asked.

"Only of murdering everyone involved in the con," she said in exasperation.

She smiled at me, and I continued. "How was Gabi?"

"She believes New London will close, at least until the leadership is restructured.

"Does that mean Gabi is out of a job?"

Marina nodded. "She thinks so, and she's probably correct. After this debacle, whoever takes over will want new people under them. They'll be cleaning house. I imagine the Crown will have a say."

Rosemary Harris made it abundantly clear she 'was never ever getting back together with New London' as Taylor Swift might say, and Stella Manning was lucky she wasn't in jail—yet.

"What about Lloyd Bennings? He's cozy with the King."

"Maybe he can spin it enough to keep his job. Who knows?"

"I expect Mia will be looking for a new position, as well." It didn't seem to be the type of situation where the assistant was promoted up.

I thought about my conversation with Cargill. "You know, Mia called Clive Cargill right before the meeting to ask if he knew who had the painting. When he told me, it seemed odd. She obviously knew it hadn't been found.

"He said she was sympathetic; she told him she was worried about him and to watch out for Windsor Smythe. It's like she knew he was on the warpath."

"How could she possibly know," Marina said. "Unless Clive told her about his boss getting shafted? And, that if he couldn't provide the 'Weeping Magdalene,' his customer would walk."

I was wide awake now, remembering everything Cargill and I had said to each other.

I knew my expression was skeptical. "No, I don't think he did. He was falling apart. He snuck out of the office, so Windsor Smythe wouldn't notice him on his cell. He was barely able to converse. His voice halting and shaking. I'm sure he thought he was being watched. Talking to me made it even worse. He said his boss thought *I* had the painting and that *I* should watch my back." I raised my hands to the ceiling. "He only confided in me, if you could call it that, because I threatened him. I don't believe he wanted Mia to know what was happening at Oxford Alliance Ltd or that his position was in jeopardy. Never mind his life if Windsor Smythe thought he'd betrayed him."

Marina jumped up from her seat. "I'm going upstairs to speak with Gabi again."

What did I say, I wondered? Before I could ask, she was out the door and flying up the staircase. Something had gotten into her brain. Something important.

In her haste to visit our upstairs neighbors, Marina left her cell phone behind. It pinged with a text, and I wasn't sure if I should read it, or ignore it. Looking at the message, fell squarely into the category of invading her privacy, but when I glanced over at the phone, I saw the caller ID. It was from Natalie Stapleton. I opened it knowing Marina might forgive me for co-opting her message under the circumstances. If I told her, that is. Natalie was fast. She'd barely had time to pack her bags.

The text was filled with invective and disgusting threats. Natalie's language was as foul as her description of what she'd do to Marina, no matter how close she watched her back.

Whoa! Talk about a woman scorned. Ahern had dumped her like a pile of you know what and she was steaming.

I had an idea how to make sure she stayed that way. I'd thought about calling Marc Rivers for help, and now I was certain it was a good play. I told him how the con had collapsed and how Stella Manning had turned the tables on Meade—at least I thought she had—and conned him into running off with her and the seven point seven million.

I explained my real reason for the call: to ask him to reach out to his legion of former contacts and blackball Natalie. Make her life so miserable that she'd forget about Marina.

It took him a while to stop laughing. "Okay, it's not actually funny. I feel sorry for your friend Gabi with all those vipers surrounding her, but I'm not surprised. It was a bad plan all around. I think Meade thought he could pull this off. With the right crew, he might have."

Was Marc being nostalgic for the 'old days'? I hoped not. Unlike this crew, his had been extremely adept at this. Plus, he'd never been caught.

"I'll spread the word and make sure no one hires her. She might have to work for a living," my old friend added sarcastically.

"Or find another mark," I said.

"True dat. Any idea where the original painting is?" he asked.

"Not a clue," I replied. *Well maybe the inkling of one,* I thought but didn't share. "When we find who has the painting, we'll find Jonathan Hudson's killer. That's more important."

"Absolutely," Marc replied. "And don't worry, I'll make sure Natalie Stapleton never works in this town again." He said the last in a Don Corleone 'make him an offer he can't refuse' tone. But I knew he meant it.

"I'll see you in London when you and Marina solve the case, find the killer and the painting. We'll celebrate the win."

If only I could be certain, it would be a win and not a bust.

Chapter Sixty-Three

Marina had been gone for quite a long time. I had been dozing again and woke up when she returned to the flat.

"Hey," I said, rubbing the last vestiges of sleep from my eyes and pretending to look wide-awake.

"Why were you in such a mad rush to speak with Gabi?" I asked, moving from prone to sitting.

"It was something you mentioned about Cargill and Mia." Marina's eyes narrowed. A sure sign something didn't add up and was making her suspicious. She continued. "She called him to ask if he knew who had the Gentileschi," she said in a pensive tone. "It feels like she was fishing for information."

"Trying to save her job?" I asked.

"Maybe. I'm sure Cargill would have told her if Windsor Smythe had it, which we know he doesn't. She knew we hadn't found it yet." Her arms flew up to the sky in incredulity. "So, why would she ask?"

"Do you think she's hiding something? Either about the painting or the murder?"

"Do you remember when Gabi mentioned that Mia had had a terrible childhood, that she'd been abused and had to work hard for everything she's accomplished?"

"Like Artemesia Gentileschi," I replied.

"I think she has a personal connection to her, thinks of her as a kindred spirit," Marina continued.

"Enough to make her desperate to find the original?" I asked.

"If she knew who had the original, it would have been in her best interest to mention it, don't you think?" Marina's voice had risen with each word.

"Unless," I said, "she also knew that person murdered Jonathan Hudson."

Marina's head was bobbing up and down. "Exactly."

"What did Gabi think about all this?"

"She was surprised to learn about Mia's relationship with Clive Cargill and that he was married. Mia never mentioned a word about him or their relationship. And she didn't believe her assistant could be involved with the switch. She trusts her implicitly."

That trust could use a good dusting off, if you asked me.

Marina had paused to collect her thoughts. "Gabi wanted to call Mia and speak to her about Cargill, but I convinced her not to. I told her that I would handle it. That she was probably correct in having faith in her and that her assistant's relationship was not her business."

"In other words, you deflected her from the main point, didn't you?"

"Yes, I did. Which was that Mia might have an ulterior motive, protecting her lover or the person who's hiding the painting. Something's wrong, and I want to find out what that is."

"Do you believe Mia knows more than she's letting on?"

"Yes." Her right shoulder shrugged up to her ear. Then she turned serious. "So can greed and revenge."

"How did Syd take this?"

"While we were talking, she wrapped her long fingers around Gabi's and never let go. She had the most intense look on her face the whole time, as though she was thinking through the plot for her next mystery and working out where the holes were and how to fill them in. I'd say she was skeptical of Mia. In fact, distrustful. The look she gave me when I was leaving reflected her writer's spidey sense of doubt."

Marina looked around the lounge. "Have you seen my phone? I left it here when I went upstairs.

"It's on the table," I replied. I almost added that she'd received a threatening call from Natalie Stapleton, but I couldn't bring myself to tell her about it or what I'd done.

I realized Marina would not be happy if she found out I'd read the text. Invading her privacy wouldn't be the reason. She'd be annoyed because I'd butted in, deleted the message, and blocked the number. Then, she'd tell me how she could handle Natalie and didn't need my, or anyone's, help.

This time, she'd be wrong. Blocking her number would not deter Natalie. I was counting on Marc Rivers to do that.

Chapter Sixty-Four

The next morning, I called Roger again. He answered on the first ring. "Matthews here."

"Roger," I replied. "I have some new information you and your special art crimes analyst might be interested in, you know, Arthur Manning."

"You're quite the comedian, aren't you, Donahue. What is it you want to tell me now?" The exasperation was thick in his voice. I decided not to leave him hanging.

"Oxford Alliance Ltd has a secret Free Port. The real one. Where Windsor Smythe keeps the good stuff.

"According to my source, it's where the original works of art he's stolen and plans to sell are stored until he finds a buyer on the black market. Unfortunately, the 'Weeping Magdalene' is not there.

"And, you know this how?"

I ignored his question and continued speaking. "The place is in a down-market neighborhood in Hackney at number 415 Wick Lane. Although, even without the Gentileschi, I imagine there'll be some fascinating pieces to confiscate.

"The other fancy, Free Port he uses is the Thames Free Port near Tilbury. It's in a free-standing building in room 211. That location is where he brings the marks he's hoping to con into investing.

"You should check that out, as well. You never know what you might find."

"Thanks for the advice," he replied sarcastically. Then in a more civil tone, he added, "We'll be sending investigators to both sites immediately. And confiscating any art we find. I doubt that Windsor Smythe will be present.

"Hold on for a moment." He paused and called for his assistant to come into the office. He covered the phone's mic while he issued instructions, so I couldn't hear his directives. The wheels were already in motion.

"Who's your source on this?" he asked.

"At the moment, it's better if the source remains anonymous." I paused. "I don't want to put them in danger." We both knew that Windsor Smythe was a brutal thug.

"So, you still don't know where the Gentileschi is?" he asked.

Why did everyone think *I* would have this information? Okay, I did have a hunch. Nothing I wanted to tell Roger yet.

"When I do, I'll be happy to share with you. In the meantime, watch your back and Arthur Manning's, too."

"Who was that?" Marina asked as she came into the room, wrapped in a terrycloth robe that made her look sexier than ever. It reminded me of the first night we met in Venice. This morning, she was drying her hair and getting ready for work.

"It was Roger Matthews. I shared what I'd learned about both of Windsor Smythe's Free Ports. He'll be sending his people for a search and seizure operation." I looked at my watch and smiled. "They're most likely already on their way. The private space should at least offer up a few original pieces."

"Will he be seizing Windsor Smythe, as well?"

"If only it were that simple."

"If only."

Her green eyes were affectionate as they met mine, and she saw my smile reflected in them.

"What?" she asked teasingly as she went to the kitchen counter and poured a cup of coffee for each of us.

I shook my head. "Oh, nothing. What are you up to today?" She still had hopes of finding the Gentileschi before it disappeared for good. This was a resilient woman who never gave up or never gave in.

"I'm meeting Ana and Nikki at the office to work on a few new cases," she said almost too casually as she ran her fingers through her shimmering hair, avoiding my eyes.

"Anything I can help with?" I asked.

"No. We've got it covered." She left the lounge and went to get dressed. When she emerged, she looked every inch the professional private investigator in a teal blue suit and silky white blouse, with a string of pearls draped around her slim neck. *A little too formal for a day at her office*, I thought. She was up to something.

"Well, okay, then. Have a good day." My intuition told me Marina had dressed for an important meeting, probably something related to the painting.

"I'll see you this evening," she said, "after your dad's gala. I'm heading to the Connaught after work to meet your mom for dinner and the theater. Join us at the hotel when you're done."

She grabbed up her briefcase and handbag. "What painting has Hamilton Capital chosen to add to the collection?"

"I actually don't know," I replied. "I'm sure it's something magnificent. With everything else going on, I never asked." Was I totally failing as the oldest scion of the family? No. Dad knew I was interested, just distracted right now.

"Well, try and have fun. You're going to a party, Nick, with your dad. I'm sure you'll enjoy it." She came around to the table and pecked me on the cheek. "Your mom and I will see you later. Ta," she added and left the apartment.

Fun? Sure. It would be loads of fun mingling with a bunch of boring Hamilton Capital bankers congratulating themselves on their latest art acquisition. Dad would be all smiles for the high-powered clients, working the small crowd in his quiet way, while I'd be on the lookout for Windsor Smythe, who I was sure would show up, even knowing the British Secret Service was pursuing him. Or despite it.

Dad had hired extra security, who were armed with his photo. They'd been informed he and his minions should not be allowed to enter the event, and the police should be called if they tried. By now, he'd know there was not going to be an after-party at either of Oxford Alliance Ltd.'s Free Port spaces, which should be under lock and key and guarded by the police, thanks to Roger Matthews.

I had plenty of time to get ready for the event—too much time. I needed a distraction. A positive one. Like checking up on Mia, who'd tweaked my mistrust—it was always the quiet ones you had to watch. I called The New London Arts Museum and asked to be connected. I was informed that Mia Fondsworth was no longer employed there. Was Lady Peake Jones in her office? I'd asked. She was. Thanks, I said and clicked off.

Did Marina know? Was Gabi aware that her assistant was gone? Of course, she must be. Was the young woman fired, or had she resigned? I quickly called Marina, but I only got a voice message that she wasn't available.

I decided against calling Gabi. She had her own problems to sort out, and today would be a hard one for her. It made no sense, making it worse.

Chapter Sixty-Five

I dressed all in black—jeans, a sweater, and a jacket. I checked the mirror and added dark lensed black framed sunglasses. I either looked like a Ninja or a would-be spy. I thought that it would be good to find Mia, wherever she might be. I'd start at her apartment building in Shoreditch.

After two Cappuccinos, I was still watching her building one hour later when she finally emerged. She was dressed in jeans, a red pullover, and a vest—a big departure from her blend-in-to-the-background, neutral-colored work clothes, which made it easy to keep track of her.

She didn't seem in any hurry as she sauntered along Shoreditch High Street, one hand in her jeans pocket, the other holding her cell, like she didn't have a care in the world. I stayed back and followed, hoping she wouldn't notice me. She ambled past Spitalfields Market and along Bethel Green Road until she entered Liverpool Street Station.

She'd walked out of her way to catch the tube, and I was sure she had a reason. The station, one of the deepest in London, was a hub for several lines. Mia used her metro pass to enter and took the long escalator down toward the Metropolitan Line. I hung back and pretended to study the connections map on the wall before I followed. She waited on the platform for the incoming train, but instead of stepping on when it arrived, let its doors open and close. She joined the throng of travelers who exited the train, following along toward the up escalator at the other end of the platform. As she rode up, a man in a grey hoodie, his face partially covered, was riding down. As they passed, their hands touched. It was quick. If you weren't looking for it, you wouldn't have noticed the slip of paper she passed him.

She hadn't missed a beat. Just kept going up.

I was stuck on the up escalator, several feet below the man, who had turned toward the tile wall, trying to conceal his face. He wasn't looking at me, and most likely wouldn't recognize me even if he glanced over. I pulled out my phone, pretended to scroll through my messages, and snapped a photo as I passed the guy.

It was in profile, but I recognized him. His hoodie had slipped back enough to show his dreads, which were poking out. Jose Bidenstock was more than an art handler for New London. He was in deep with whatever plan they'd cooked up.

I ran up the escalator and out onto the street, trying to catch up with Mia, but she was nowhere to be seen. I'd lost her and in doing so, had put myself in the sights of someone I now suspected might be a killer.

I called Marina's cell, and it went straight to voicemail again. I didn't want to leave a message, but she needed to know about Mia and Jose.

I rang the office, and Ana answered on the first ring. I cut her off in the middle of her greeting. "Ana, put Marina on, now!" I demanded.

I must have sounded like a madman. I'd frightened her. "Nick, what's wrong?" she asked in a shaky voice a few octaves higher than usual.

"Please, just get Marina."

"She's not here."

"When did she leave?" I asked.

"She hasn't been in the office at all today."

"What!" I shouted. "Do you know where she is?"

"Nick...I..."

I realized I was making things worse by yelling. "Sorry, Ana. It's...I really need to speak to her."

"I'm not sure, but she may be at the United States Embassy. Yesterday, she mentioned something about meeting with the Ambassador." She paused. "I'm not quite certain, though. If she rings in, I'll have her call you immediately."

I calmed down and thanked Ana. I'd already unsettled her enough. I clicked off. Marina had said she'd be at her office all day but lied, which was not like her. She was up to something. Something she wanted to handle on her own. I knew she'd met the Ambassador, Miriam Armstrong, through Nigel. It flashed through my mind to contact him, but I let it go.

The best I could do for now was to warn Gabi about my suspicions about Mia and Jose Bidenstock, who might have returned to The New London Arts Museum. I called an Uber and gave the driver the address. Then I thought about what I was going to say.

Chapter Sixty-Six

The atmosphere at The New London Arts Museum was very subdued. The staff stood around, whispering among themselves in small clusters. I wouldn't be surprised if they knew it might be closing, and they would soon be out of their jobs.

There were fewer people thronging the lobby or visiting the exhibits than there were a few days ago. It was almost like the public sensed something terrible was happening and decided to stay away.

One of the security guards recognized me and broke off from the group he'd been gossiping with. He escorted me to the private elevator, and I got off on the third floor. The corridor was quiet, and all the doors along it were closed except the one to Gabi's office. She was alone in a deserted place. My heart sank. Gabi had started packing up her personal belongings and the decorative objects she'd collected over her time as Assistant Director and Curator. She didn't see me standing in her doorway, so I knocked softly.

"Hi, can I come in?"

"Of course." She gestured to a seat in front of her nearly empty desk, then sat back in her chair and gave me a wan smile.

"Somehow, I don't think you have good news for me," she said.

"Unfortunately, you're correct." My voice sounded as serious as I looked. "It's about Mia."

"Mia? She's gone. Deserted a sinking ship. Left me floundering." Her dark eyes had lost their brilliance, and she was holding back the tears that threatened to spill out.

I reached out and took her hand in mine. "There's no easy way to say this.

Mia is the thief. I have evidence that she's the one who replaced the original Gentileschi with the fake." I didn't exactly have hard-core evidence, but I was certain I was right after today.

Gabi was shaking her head from side to side. "No. That can't be. Why would she do that? Betray the museum. And me."

I let her draw her own conclusion. "Money? Do you think it's the money she'll get for the original 'Weeping Mary Magdalene'"?

"Yes, I do." *She'd use it to escape her life and lick her wounds,* I thought.

"And what about Jonathan? Do you...do you believe Mia killed him?"

"It seems likely. But she may have had help. Jose Bidenstock," I added and watched her take in the news.

By now, Gabi was in shock. Her face had turned as pale as the winter moon, and her hands were shaking. "What are we going to do?" she asked.

"We're going to find them and put them away for a very long time. Now, why don't we go back to the house together?" I told her. "You can leave your packing for tomorrow."

She called Syd to let her know she'd be home soon. I tried Marina one more time, and once again, my call went straight to voicemail.

Once we arrived at Vicarage Gate, I turned Gabi over to the capable Syd. She mouthed 'thank you' as they walked upstairs.

I was feeling down and depressed, and not even remotely looking forward to the Hamilton Capital Gala. Of course, I would go. I could never let my dad down by sitting this one out.

Marina hadn't called. I wouldn't see her until we met at the Connaught after the party. This time, I left her a message about Mia and Bidenstock, detailing what I'd seen and believed. I said we'd discuss it together later this evening.

I showered and dressed in my new tuxedo, switching out my red bow tie for the more subdued black one. I was as ready as I'd ever be for this so-called party.

Chapter Sixty-Seven

The party planner and the caterer had done a spectacular job. They'd turned the office into an elegant space that struck just the right tone—chic, affluent, but not over the top.

The star of the show was a Degas, one of his ballerina series, an 18" x 24" oil on canvas painting valued at just under ten million dollars, or about $23,100 per square inch. Give or take. On an easel in a prominent place, this addition to the collection should make the Hamilton Capital investors secure in the knowledge that the bank was extremely solvent and planned to stay that way.

Evidently, it worked. All the guests were drinking and eating, mostly drinking, and having a very nice time. Except for me. I kept looking over my shoulder for the disinvited Windsor Smythe to show up. Of course, after today, he wouldn't. Probably in custody by now. Or, on the lam. There'd be no after-party for us to attend. No quiet chat about stolen art. Thank God.

After Dad wished the last guest a good night, we prepared to leave for the hotel. We dismissed the extra bodyguards and left the regular security staff to lock up the office. Since Mom and Marina had the Escalade and a driver for the evening, we called an Uber and decided to wait outside.

No sooner were we out the door than a black-clad, masked figure came barreling toward us. The person took me by surprise and propelled me hard toward the open door of a waiting car, shoving a needle into my neck and shouting about Windsor Smythe while their accomplice grabbed Dad. The next thing I knew, we were both semi-conscious in the back of an SUV.

When the rats finally woke me, I realized we were surrounded by blackness in an ancient warehouse on a quiet part of the river. I realized it was Mia Fondsworth who had brought us here and tied and bound us. She must have figured out I followed her this afternoon. I'd overheard nearly everything she and Bidenstock had been arguing about, but it took my fuzzy brain a while to process it. Bidenstock realized she'd double-crossed him, as well. That note she'd passed him on the tube must have said the Gentileschi would be here, at the warehouse.

Now he knew it wasn't.

She'd moved it. Told him they'd get it later. After she killed us.

He'd protested, shouting wildly at her. "Mia, you can't do that! Stop. Give me the gun! It's insane. Murdering Jonathan was bad enough…this…" That sealed his fate.

I heard a laugh, the sound of the slide on the gun being pulled back.

"Mia! No. What are you doing? Please, don't," he'd begged. "We can talk…"

A loud shot rang out, and there was a thump as Bidenstock fell to the floor, wailing in agony. Then it was quiet. Too quiet. She'd gotten rid of her partner. Now, only Dad and I were left.

I heard footsteps approaching, and I knew we'd be the next to die.

Suddenly, a voice called out to her. A voice I recognized. "Mia, don't do this. Put the gun down! Stop! You can't murder them."

"You? What are you doing here?" The contempt in her voice was palpable.

"I followed you. I knew you were planning something." It was Clive Cargill who was speaking. "We can leave. Go away together. Start a new life."

Her laugh was mocking. "Go away. With you? Bloody hell. Never. How could you think I ever cared about you?"

"Don't say that. I…I love you. We can start over. Just give me the gun."

I heard more footsteps. Louder this time, hurrying. Cargill moved closer to her and grabbed for her weapon. Sounds of a loud struggle overtook the once-silent space. Crates crashing to the ground. Splintering wood. Grunts and gasps. Then, another shot, followed by a low moan.

"Mia. Mia. Oh, no. No…"

After that, it was pandemonium. A battalion of police in full riot gear battered down the door. The clamor of cracking and splintering wood filled the night as they burst into the space, shouting and screaming over each other, their heavy boots making the old wooden floor tremble.

"Put the gun down. On the floor! Now! Do it! Don't move!" It was mayhem. Their big submachine guns were pointing everywhere, and their bright torches cast wide circles on the walls and floor until they landed on the writhing body on the filthy floor.

She looked at me and laughed mockingly. "The Artemesia belongs to me. We both had to struggle to…" She began to cough, and her voice wavered in and out. "…abused, raped, discarded." Again, she paused. This was costing her everything. "You'll never find her."

Then, Mia Fondsworth was dead, sprawled in a pool of red gore slowly spreading out around her. It was just like in the movies. Only this time, the blood was real.

* * *

Marina had rushed in right behind the wave of police that engulfed the warehouse. Cargill had made a frantic call to her and told her what he'd seen. He'd followed Mia and had waited, lurking outside the Hamilton Capital office. He'd watched as Mia and Bidenstock nabbed and drugged us. Then he'd trailed her to the crumbling and decrepit unused warehouse near St. Saviours Dock. Marina told him to wait for her and the police, who were already on the way. But thankfully, he hadn't, or Dad and I wouldn't be alive.

Chapter Sixty-Eight

The EMTs arrived and checked us out. Dad and I were both dehydrated and somewhat scraped up, but otherwise fine. I could go home, but the hospital wanted to keep Dad for observation.

Mom was leaning over his bed, touching him, and whispering encouragement. I was waiting for her to blame me for everything, just as I had imagined in my drugged confusion. She tore herself away from Dad and walked over to me. *Here it comes,* I thought. Instead, she hugged me. "Thank you, Nick. If you weren't with your father, I don't know…"

"I promised I'd help. I'm sorry I couldn't prevent what happened." I could hear the emotion in my voice. We'd had a close call.

She hugged me harder. I tried not to wince. My body was still sore from being tied up.

Her words petered out, and her eyes threatened to overflow with tears. I hugged her back and gazed at a smiling Marina over her shoulder. Dad would be remaining in the hospital overnight and would be released tomorrow.

Clive Cargill had been read his rights, placed in handcuffs, and marched away by the police. He had a lot of explaining to do, starting with his murdering Mia. Although, since he saved us, if he had a smart solicitor, he might have a shot at self-defense.

His involvement with Windsor Smythe's ongoing defrauding of the company's investors and his boss's plan to steal and resell the Gentileschi, was another story. How much did he really know? And had kept hidden?

Cargill was begging for police protection against his boss, who'd managed to escape the MI5 agents who raided all his known premises. Thinking Cargill had betrayed him, I knew he'd go after him with a vengeance. It didn't take long for Cargill to give it all up, including all the Oxford Alliance Ltd deals he knew had been crooked.

As for his relationship with Mia, he'd had no idea she'd arranged to meet him and become close, so she'd have the inside scoop on Windsor Smythe's plans. Through friends of hers, she heard about his reputation. It wasn't sterling. The police found her diary, and she'd planned this on her own right from the beginning. She believed the "Weeping Magdaline" should be hers. Greed and jealousy took hold, and murder was a mere hiccup. She'd been running her own long con with Cargill as the Mark and the Gentileschi as the prize.

* * *

Mom was staying at the hospital overnight with Dad. Marina and I returned home. We were both knackered. She kicked off her stilettos. I undid my bowtie and removed my ruined tuxedo jacket. Then we collapsed next to each other on our oversized, comfy couch. A few large Scotches were in order, and I roused myself to pour them. I swallowed mine in one gulp, then filled my tumbler with another. The ordeal was over. Or it would be as soon as I got those big fat rats and their beady red eyes out of my head. I shuddered at the memory.

"What are you thinking about?" Marina asked, snuggling closer and taking a sip of her drink.

I shook my head. "Just happy this case is over. *And that I'm alive.* I thought. "Where were you all day?" I asked.

"I paid a visit to Nine Elms Lane."

"Ana mentioned you might be going to the American Embassy."

Marina gave me a sly grin and took another sip of her drink before replying. "I had a meeting with Ambassador Miriam Armstrong. We discussed the possibility of a quick extradition of Maxime Meade and having charges filed for his crimes in New York in absentia."

"Can she do that?"

"Evidently so. Ambassador Armstrong coordinated with the British higher-ups and Roger, and they got right on it." She paused. "I'm sure the management of Danesfield House was surprised to see the American Embassy's Secret Service Security Detail pull up and escort Mr. Meade out in handcuffs. To say nothing of the shock on Stella Manning's face."

Imposing men in black. Pretty scary.

Her eyes grew wide with excitement before she continued. "They were also able to freeze all of Meade's banking activity. His personal accounts and those attached to the Meade and Medina Gallery. They have a Specialized Financial Recovery Task Force going after the money he's stashed offshore."

Good luck with that. I'd bet the bank Stella Manning had somehow finagled the codes from Meade and moved the money again.

"What about Windsor Smythe?" I asked. "Any sign of him?"

"No. He's eluded Roger's people. Roger is certain MI5 will track him down. In the meantime, the raid on the 'real' Free Port was quite a score, including a Bonnard, a Magritte, a Pissarro, and several other valuable original works. When the agents capture him, he'll go away for a long time."

Marina finished her Scotch while she was filling me in. I took the tumbler from her hand and refilled it. "Nice work," I said, handing her the drink and clinking glasses.

I leaned my head back against the couch and stared at the ceiling. "The only one who came out of this okay is Lloyd Bennings."

Marina's voice took on a teasing lilt. "He was your prime suspect all along, wasn't he?"

I held up my hands in mock surrender. "You're right. The only crime he committed was having extremely poor judgment. Indulging in an affair with Jose Bidenstock, who was a crook at the least, and most likely an accomplice to murder.

"The real killer is dead," I added.

I realized Mia was the one who'd shot at me on Kensington High Street. I don't think she'd missed on purpose; last night had been her chance to make it up.

She slipped up when she'd asked Cargill if he knew the whereabouts of the painting. He mistook her questions for concern, her fake sweetness for love. It was his undoing. And hers.

The paramedics had tried to save her. Her injuries were too severe. It was too late. Mia had died on the old, rotting boards of the warehouse floor. Before she finally passed, she turned her head and stared into my eyes. Then just for a moment, her face lit up with a shit-eating grin. It must have taken the last ounce of strength she had left. It told me we'd never find the 'Weeping Magdalene' no matter how hard we looked. She was going out with a winning hand, even if it wouldn't do her any good where she landed.

Chapter Sixty-Nine

For the next six weeks, special task forces from Interpol, MI5, and MI6 scoured every inch of the city, looking for the painting in a coordinated effort. Buildings and lockups along the docks were searched from top to bottom. Police detectives descended on The New London Arts Museum, opened every crate, and looked in every corner. Mia's apartment was tossed more than once. Ditto for Windsor Smythe and Cargill's. It was exhausting just thinking about it. Finally, it was decided the 'Weeping Mary Magdalene' was gone for good. Or until it turns up on the black market or in a private collection, which we might never discover.

"Where do you think the painting is?" Marina asked.

My face morphed into a frown. "It could be anywhere in London or in some other country by now. We should go look for it."

"You're serious, aren't you?" Marina shook her head and bit her lip to stop herself from laughing. "You like being a hero, don't you, Donahue?"

I started to speak, but Marina interrupted. "Never mind." She held up her hand. "Don't answer that."

"Will the insurers ever get their money back from Meade and Medina?" I asked.

"It's in the hands of the U.S. courts now," Marina replied. "Who knows who'll benefit. If they can find the money, that is."

So much for the Specialized Financial Recovery Task Force. My money was on Stella Manning. She was still in Britain. I was sure she'd scarper the minute she thought it was safe to leave. Roger Matthews had people watching her day and night, like an insect under glass. It was the least she deserved.

Windsor Smythe was also in the wind. He'd disappeared without a trace, deserting Oxford Alliance Ltd and its employees to fend for themselves. Nigel had made sure the press knew all about the fiasco and fraud, and the hedge fund had nothing left with which to hedge its bets. If his clients ever found him, they'd tear him from limb to limb.

Marina interrupted my musings. "So, which country should we start with?"

"To look for the painting?" I asked in surprise. "Would you do that with me? We could begin—"

She pulled me up from the couch. "No, darling, for dinner. Italy, France, Spain, China? I'm starving. You choose."

Chapter Seventy

Three Months Later

Gabi and Syd were married at the Kensington and Chelsea Registry Office, an elegant Victorian building near our flat. The ceremony, conducted by a Registrar, was held on a beautiful early summer evening. Softened sunlight streamed in through the large windows, and the wedding room was filled with the scent of lavender and roses.

The women looked radiant, beaming at each other with love and joy. Both had decided on long, sleek black dresses embellished with beading for Syd and a layer of embroidered lace for Gabi. A la Adele, one of their favorite singers, or so Marina explained to me. Gabi's dark curls were piled on top of her head, and Syd's blond hair was loose and flowing down her back. They made a perfect couple.

Sydney's parents, the Parker Glynnes, were in attendance and beaming at their beautiful daughter and her wife. Duchess Peake Jones was there, as well, minus the Duke. Gabi's mother had finally left him to his estate, winery, drinking, and debts. The money train had come to a stop. She'd said goodbye to his abuse, taken her inheritance with her, and moved to the city. Maybe the Duke could try and hit up Dame Harris, but I wasn't sure she'd be buying what he was selling this time.

The women had asked Marina and me to be their witnesses, and we were delighted to oblige. The room was filled with their closest friends and family, all the people who mattered most and who sincerely wished them the best.

We'd invited everyone to a small reception at our flat immediately afterward.

The last few months had knocked us sideways. Swindlers, con artists, forgers, and thieves. A regular conclave of miscreants. Most of them were accounted for. Stella Manning had tried to sneak out of the country with a forged passport. She was caught and tossed into jail. Luke Chimini had gotten into a squabble with another prisoner and was stabbed to death. All that talent ultimately amounted to nothing. Clive Hastings Cargill was awaiting trial for manslaughter and fraud. His wife divorced him the minute she found out what he'd done. And, according to Marc Rivers, Natalie Stapleton was one step away from living on the streets. It's too bad she wasn't already there, at least in my opinion. My parents had weathered a vacation they never imagined and were happily back in New York. Not that being home would stop Mom from worrying about me.

I was smiling to myself as Gabi brought me back to the present and pulled me aside. "Nick," I have something to ask you." She hesitated, swallowed, then spoke again. "Thanks to my mum, I'm starting my own small gallery in a lovely space in Notting Hill. Nothing too ambitious. A few paintings and drawings..." Her voice trailed off, and I gave her a questioning look. She cleared her throat and began again. "And I was...wondering...if you might help me?"

"Me?" I asked in surprise. "Help you, how? I really don't know much about art..."

Gabi was nodding vigorously. "I quite realize that," she said, "but I meant as more of someone who could assist with setting up the space and give me your opinion about where to put the pieces, and..." Again, she waited to continue. "But mostly, I'd want your help to look for Artemisia's 'Weeping Magdalene.' I truly believe it's somewhere nearby. And I'm determined to find it." Her face lit up with anticipation. "What do you think? "Crackers, right?" She gave a self-deprecating chuckle.

"Oh, so you mean be the new Jose Bidenstock, aka Art Handler, and fill in as an Art Detective? Are you sure about this?"

"Yes. I mean, no. Not like Jose at all. It's a frightful idea, isn't it?" She was flustered. "I shouldn't have asked."

"Of course, you should have." I smiled at the beautiful new bride and entrepreneur. "I accept, albeit with a few conditions." I paused. "I won't accept any money for this. I'll be the volunteer laborer. I play Blackjack professionally to earn a living, and I would never give that up." *Sorry, Mom.* "But I love the idea of helping you get started with your gallery, and searching for the Gentileschi is something I've been thinking about."

Gabi's deep brown eyes sparkled with excitement and resolve. "I have a plan. We will visit every gallery, art shop, and museum in London until we find her. It may be in a private collection or hidden away," she added with apparent scorn for people who would do this. "Someone is bound to know something, and if we dig deep enough, it could lead us to the painting."

Marina was speaking with one of the guests, and I caught her side-eyed glance at us. Somehow, I knew Gabi had cleared this with her first. Or maybe she had even suggested it. Her head tilted up, and her lips curled into a smile. She'd known I was jonesing to find the original painting. And she'd been right. I liked being a hero, and if we found the Gentileschi, maybe I could claim that status for real. All I'd have to do was get very, very lucky.

The End

A Note from the Author

I was inspired to write this story after reading an article about the TEFAF Maastricht Art Fair in the Netherlands. The article mentioned a recently rediscovered Artemisia Gentileschi "Penitent Magdalene," from about 1626, that sold for seven million dollars.

Hmm, I thought, what if another 'original Gentileschi' surfaced, but this time its provenance was suspect?

That could be interesting. So, I created my own Artemisia masterpiece, "Weeping Mary Magdalene," and told its story through the voice of my protagonist, Nick Donahue. It would be the perfect crime for Nick to investigate and solve.

But what exactly, I asked myself, did finding a 'rediscovered original' mean? Had it been hidden away for years? Stolen decades before? Or, on view in plain sight in someone's living room? How did the experts determine if a painting was genuine or a forgery? Those are questions Nick and his partner, P.I. Marina DiPietro, face in *No Good Time*.

I've always admired Artemisia, who lived from 1593 to 1656, and was the most celebrated female artist of her time. The first woman to become a member of the Accademia di Arte de Designo in Florence, she was known for her paintings of strong and heroic women from allegories, mythology, and the bible, such as "Lucretia," "Susanna and The Elders," and self-portraits such as "Self-portrait as Female Martyr."

After being raped by Agostino Tassi, who worked in her father Orazio's studio, and a trial that found him not guilty, she overcame her adversity, continued painting, and became famous. Gentileschi has become known as 'the Old Master Poster Girl of the #Metoo era'—a reputation I believe is well-deserved.

I hope the story presents Artemisia and her work as the masterpieces I believe they are. And, as for forgers and con artists, well, you'll see what happens to them.

About the Author

Cathi Stoler, a native New Yorker, drew on her travels to interesting and exotic places to write her mystery suspense novels, *Nick of Time, Out of Time,* and *No Good Time,* featuring professional Blackjack player, Nick Donahue.

Her suspense novels, *Bar None, Last Call, Straight Up,* and *With A Twist, The Murder on the Rocks Mysteries,* are set on the Lower East Side of New York City and feature The Corner Lounge owner, Jude Dillane, and have been nominated for several awards. She is also the author of the three-volume Laurel & Helen New York Mystery series, which includes *Telling Lies, Keeping Secrets,* and *The Hard Way.*

Stoler is a three-time finalist and the winner of the Derringer for Best Short Story "The Kaluki Kings of Queens." She is a board member of Sisters in Crime New York/Tri-State, and a member of Mystery Writers of America and International Thriller Writers. She lives in New York City. You can find her at www.cathistoler.com.

AUTHOR WEBSITE:

www.cathistoler.com

SOCIAL MEDIA HANDLES:

https://twitter.com/cathistoler
https://www.facebook.com/CathiStolerAuthor
https://www.instagram.com/cathistolerauthor/
https://www.goodreads.com/author/show/4807990.Cathi_Stoler
https://www.linkedin.com/in/cathi-stoler-2806803/

Also by Cathi Stoler

The Nick Donahue Adventures
  Nick of Time (#1)
  Out of Time (#2)

The Murder on The Rocks Series
  Bar None (#1)
  Last Call (#2)
  Straight Up (#3)
  With A Twist (#4)

Laurel and Helen New York Mysteries
  Telling Lies (#1)
  Keeping Secrets (#2)
  The Hard Way (#3)

www.ingramcontent.com/pod-product-compliance
Lightning Source LLC
Chambersburg PA
CBHW020719130726
47899CB00011B/463